MARVEL

The Unbeatable

Squirrel Girl

SQUIRREL MEETS WORLD

The Un

Squir

SQUIRREL

eatable

rel Girl

EETS WORLD

SHANNON HALE & DEAN HALE

LOS ANGELES   NEW YORK

© 2017 MARVEL

First Hardcover Edition, February 2017
First Paperback Edition, February 2018
10 9 8 7 6 5 4 3 2 1
FAC-020093-17356
Printed in the United States of America

This book is set in Columbus MT Pro, Picastro Bold Blade,
Picastro Bold Drop/Fontspring; Arial MT, Arial Narrow MT,
Bad Neighborhood Badhouse, ITC Zapf ChanceryPro/Monotype.
Designed by Maria Elias
Squirrel illustrations by Bruno Mangyoku

Library of Congress Control Number for Hardcover: 2016944544
ISBN 978-1-4847-8852-3

Visit www.DisneyBooks.com
www.marvel.com

SUSTAINABLE FORESTRY INITIATIVE   Certified Sourcing
www.sfiprogram.org
SFI-00993

THIS LABEL APPLIES TO TEXT STOCK

For Shelley "Lady Servo" Bush

1

DOREEN[1]

 oreen Green liked her name.

1. It rhymed.

2. "Doreen" was a combo of her parents' names: "Dor" + "Maureen."

3. Her initials, *D* and *G*, were both big, sweeping letters you could form with a squirrel tail, if, for example, you happened to have one.

Which Doreen totally did.[2]

"All I'm saying," said Doreen Green, "is this neighborhood better be chock-full of squirrels."

---

1 Hey, that's me! I'll be reading this book along with you if you don't mind. If you do mind, just pretend those adorable little numbers are word hats and ignore these footnotes.
2 It's true. I was totally born with a squirrel tail.

"It will be," said her mom, who looked similar to a lot of other moms you've probably seen around: i.e., human, with no squirrel tail.

If you ignored the tail, Doreen also looked similar to a lot of humans you've seen around. Specifically, this human was a fourteen-year-old of the female variety, with pale, freckled skin and red hair that never grew longer than her jaw. Also, her two front teeth were a little longer than their neighbors. She had to gnaw on things to keep them from getting even longer. Things like logs.[3]

"Chock. Full. Of. Squirrels," Doreen repeated.

"I researched the area before we moved, sweetie, and there isn't a neighborhood in New Jersey that isn't teeming with squirrels," said Maureen. "Or any neighborhood in almost any climate anywhere in the world, actually. Squirrels get around."

"Yeah. Squirrels are awesome."

They were unpacking boxes in their new house, which smelled a little damp, like an overturned pile of leaves, and not at all familiar. Maureen was stacking their towels and sheets in the hallway linen closet. Doreen was perched on the curtain rod above her window, taping a poster of She-Hulk onto her ceiling. One time when Doreen was little, she and her mom were walking

---

3 Mm-mm, logs: nature's crackers! Maple logs are my favorite, fresh with syrup. . . . JK, I don't eat logs. That would be weird. I just chew on them to keep my front teeth trim. Which isn't weird at all. If you're me.

down a sidewalk in Los Angeles and saw She-Hulk punch a truck full of bank robbers.[4] In New Jersey, there was little chance Doreen would happen upon She-Hulk. Her new home was closer to the Avengers, of course, since the Super Heroes were based in New York, but they were still a whole state away.

"Can you put this on your mattress?" asked Maureen, tossing her daughter a sheet. Doreen leaped off the curtain rod, caught the sheet in an airborne somersault, and landed feetfirst on her bed.

The Avengers on the sheet were washed out and threadbare in places. The red in Captain America's suit had turned pink. The Hulk's angry faces were faded to pale green blobs. Doreen refused to ever get so old and serious that she'd be embarrassed to sleep on Avengers sheets. She held it to her nose and inhaled. It still smelled like home—or their former home. A little salty, like the California air. A little salty, like the tiny tears of the squirrel friends who had gathered on her bed that final night to say their farewells.

Doreen sniffed. A small whimper escaped her throat.

"Oh, sweetie," said Maureen. "I know it's hard. Why don't you go out and prowl around, huh? Meet some new friends? You can finish unpacking later."

---

4 Also one time I saw She-Hulk walk into a smoothie shop, but the punching-a-truck-to-make-it-stop was more memorable.

Doreen nodded. Her tail swished, as if it were excited to get outside.

"Just . . . don't stay out late, okay, punkin?" said her mom. "The real estate agent warned us that Shady Oaks isn't like our old neighborhood, where it's safe to roam around after dark."

"No sweat." Doreen bounded down the hallway, jumped from the top step to the bottom, and opened the front door.

"Here I am, New Jersey!" she said. "Doreen Green, age fourteen. Over five feet tall and not an inch mean."

Inspired by her name, sometimes she liked to rhyme. It wasn't her strongest skill.

She stepped outside and felt a pleasant but alarmingly unfamiliar sensation: a breeze tickling her tail hairs.

"Doreen!" her mother called from the top of the stairs. "Your tail!"

Doreen leaped back and slammed the front door shut. She hadn't made that mistake since she'd been tiny and barely old enough to understand that girls with squirrel tails have to hide them snugly away.

Everyone who saw you would feel so sad that they don't have a tail, too, her mother always said. *Above all, we must be kind. Hide your tail; keep your secrets secret.*

Doreen had always suspected there were other reasons to keep this particular secret secret. Secret reasons, in fact. But Doreen dutifully tucked her tail into the seat of her pants. It was mostly fluffy fur, and fur compacted pretty well.

"Good girl," said Maureen.

Doreen opened the front door again, but she didn't feel like rhyming anymore. She felt half as clever, half as strong, half as interesting. Half herself.

She sniffed the air, detected the direction of tree pollen and squirrel nests, and turned left. Off to make friends and climb trees.

The neighborhood was old. The trees were so large their roots had grown under the sidewalk, cracking it from below. The houses were mostly two-stories, standing close together and at attention. A breeze rustled discarded cans and wrappers in the gutters and sent litter rolling down the sidewalk.

The tree smells led Doreen to a large neighborhood park. A soccer field there was crawling with kindergarteners kicking in the general vicinity of a ball—and occasionally at each other. Their parents pointed frantically at the ball and shouted, "Kick that! Kick *that!*"

Over a hillock on an expanse of green, Doreen spied a few people around her age. They were wearing sort-of-belted nightgowns with knee-high boots and hats, long vests, and lots of leather. Was the fashion in New Jersey so different from California? Their apparent leader was a kid with deep brown skin, his hair a short Afro under a feathered cap. He sported a terry cloth cloak and kept calling out, "Forsooth! Forsooth!"

Doreen had never met anyone in a towel-cape yelling "Forsooth" before. She was intrigued.

"And now you walk a narrow stone bridge over a lake of bubbling lava. . . ." he was saying.

The other creatively dressed teens began to step carefully through the grass. Because it *was* just grass. Not lava. Though Doreen caught herself looking to make sure.

"Out of the lava rises . . ." the forsoother said, pausing for effect, "a red dragon!"

Doreen looked around for a dragon, just in case. As far as she knew, dragons were imaginary, but after all, she *was* living in a world where a photo of Thor, the God of Thunder, buying shawarma from a street vendor currently held the Twitter record for most retweets, so YOU JUST NEVER KNEW what was possible.[5]

"Aah!" cried out a pale blond girl in a belted nightgown and knee-high leather boots. "Not a dragon!"

"I choose to fight it!" cried out another girl in a belted nightgown, her black hair full of ribboned braids. She raised a sword. "Yonder scaly fiend's hide will decorate my mead hall!"

"Hey there!" said Doreen. "You guys look and sound really interesting, and I would like to be your friend."

They all stared at Doreen, frowning. This was not the reaction Doreen had hoped for.[6]

---

5 I think that photo went viral because that shawarma looked *soooo* delish. Mom thinks it had something to do with Thor not wearing a shirt.
6 Ideal reaction: "Yes, please! We've been hoping that someone EXACTLY LIKE YOU would find us here so we could make her our BFF!" Or something. I'm not super particular.

The forsoother stepped forward. "I am the baron of this domain. You, maiden, are trespassing. Go on your way or you may summon the wrath of our guardsman, the he-giant Derek Facepunch."

The tallest of them hit his palm with his fist in what Doreen guessed was supposed to be a menacing gesture. Doreen smiled apologetically for not feeling menaced.

"So," said Doreen, "are we friends now or . . . ?"

"Begone!" said the forsoothing baron. "Now . . . back to our adventure. Lady Blightbringer de la Poisonarrow, slay the dragon!"

"YAAAAH!" screamed Lady Blightbringer. She slashed at the air with her sword.

"Okay," Doreen whispered.

As she turned to leave, one of the boys jogged over to her.

"Hey, hi, uh, sorry about that," he whispered under the noise of Lady Blightbringer attacking the imaginary dragon.[7] He held out his hand to shake. "I'm Sir Reginald Foxgood—well, to normal people like you I'm Vin Tang. We're LARPers, you know? Live Action Role Players. We like to dress up and pretend to be in a fantasy world, which is a totally reasonable thing that mature people do."[8]

7 It didn't occur to me till now that it could have been an *invisible* dragon and not an imaginary one. I should thank Lady Blightbringer for saving us, just in case.
8 I suspect Vin Tang has had to defend LARPing to judgey people before.

"Oh."

"But it's a closed group. That's what the baron was trying to say. Sorry."

"It's okay," said Doreen.

Normal people like you. If Doreen showed them her squirrel tail, would they think she was cool and invite her to be their friend? Or would they just dissolve into sticky puddles of sorrow that they didn't have tails of their own?

Doreen sighed. Maybe squirrel friends would be easier to make than human friends.

Doreen checked to make sure the LARPers weren't watching her, and then she climbed a tree. It was a huge old oak, and she scrambled up the trunk like a spider climbs a wall. Or rather, like a squirrel climbs a tree: with ease.

A little brown squirrel on a branch leaped back when it saw her.

"Hi there! Sorry, I didn't mean to startle you!" she said. "I'm—"

The squirrel ran away.

She climbed higher, discovering a pair of squirrels trembling, staring at Doreen with eyes wide.

"Don't be afraid," said Doreen. "I'm like you!" She turned and stuck out her bum. "See that big booty? It's not that big by itself. I'm hiding a squirrel tail. . . ."

The squirrels ran down the tree and away.

"Okay, then, we'll just compare tails some other time," she called after them, a bit defeated.

If they had seen her tail, Doreen wondered, would the squirrels have liked her? But she knew she couldn't show them. Ever since she was a little girl, her parents had drilled it into her: WHEN IN PUBLIC, HIDE YOUR TAIL.

Suddenly a gray squirrel was right in her face, chittering, mouth open, teeth bared.

"OH! Hey there!" said Doreen.

"*Chukichit-chit!*"[9] said the squirrel, gesturing menacingly with one tiny fist.

"I'm sorry," said Doreen. "I wasn't trying to encroach on your territory. I just wanted to introduce myself. You see, back in California I had lots of squirrel friends, like Monkey Joe, Pippy Longtail, Gamma-Phi-Pie, Roscoe and Murph—"

The gray squirrel sneezed. It was not so much a pardon-me-I-got-a-bit-of-pollen-in-my-nose-hole sneeze or even a head-colds-amirite? sneeze. Rather more like a good-day-madam-I-said-GOOD-DAY! dismissive sort of sneeze. And with that, the squirrel turned tail and leaped into the next tree.

"Sorry," Doreen said softly.

She barely had a moment to feel bad for herself when from the next tree she heard the opposite of a squirrel sneeze.

---

9 I'm not translating this because it's pretty rude. But to be fair, if she'd known that I could understand squirrel language maybe she would've been nicer. Maybe.

Yes. One of nature's rarest sounds. A squirrel gasp of fear.

Doreen forgot to check that no one was watching before jumping. That is to say, she *didn't* look before she leaped.[10] She landed in the upper branches and scrambled toward the trunk.

"Are you okay, little friend?" asked Doreen, her keen vision raking the shadows for signs of a squirrel. Instead what she found, well-hidden under the bushiest of branches, was a small metal cage.

"*Chatti-chit,*" said the gray squirrel from inside the cage, her eyes burning with rage.

"Don't be so hard on yourself," said Doreen. "Accidentally stepping into an animal trap concealed in a tree could happen to anyone, especially if—WHOA!"

One end of the cage had begun to move. It was squeezing in, like some kind of weird squirrel death trap.

"What the heck?" said Doreen. "What kind of a jerk would make this?"

The squirrel was chittering in panic. Doreen tried to open the cage. *Locked.* The metal wall had already moved halfway. The squirrel and her tail were curled up in a ball in the far corner and would be squashed like roadkill in seconds. Doreen worked on the lock. No luck. The squirrel looked up at her with wet, frightened eyes.

---

10 "Leap before you look" is kinda my motto.

"Not today!" said Doreen.

Doreen had always been a good deal stronger than her parents. Could she also save squirrels from evil death traps? Grasping the steel sides with each hand, Doreen pulled. The metal screeched. She squeezed her eyes shut and pulled harder. "I can do this," she said, her voice tight with exertion. "I am Doreen Green. I am . . ." Then she thought it, the name she only called herself in her head. The secret name she'd never said aloud because it felt like a Super Hero name, and only in her head did she dare dream herself a hero.

I am Squirrel Girl!

The metal screeched even louder and popped. The cage fell apart in her hands.

The squirrel was just a streak of gray, leaping free of the cage and running off.

"Yay, Doreen!" said Doreen, because no one else did.

And then, quietly, hopefully, she whispered to herself, "Yay, Squirrel Girl."

2

DOREEN

On Monday morning, in the middle of the fall term, Doreen Green started as Union Junior High's newest ninth grader. Union Junior was a great big brick monolith of a building, four stories high, windows black and glinty like a Super Villain's eyes.[11]

"This is gonna be great," Doreen muttered, glaring up at it. She didn't believe a word she was saying—but she said it with so much confidence she almost forgot she didn't believe it. "This is gonna be a fuzzy ball of fantasticalism!"

If the school had suddenly sprouted arms and legs, picked up a club, and splatted her on the sidewalk, she would not have been surprised. She scowled at the building, just in case it had

---

11 Off the top of my head I can't think of any glinty-black-eyed Super Villains. I'm sure there is one, though. That sort of thing is their jam.

any arm-sprouting ideas. But it just stood there, like totally normal brick buildings tend to do.

Doreen pointed two fingers at her eyes and then back at the school. If it secretly *was* an evil robot, now at least it knew she was onto it.

"What is that girl doing?" she heard someone whisper.

Doreen turned to find the speaker, a black-haired girl who was walking with a blond girl.

"I'm staring down the school," said Doreen, because it was true—even though she worried it sounded odd.

The black-haired girl started. "Are you talking to me?"

Whoops. Maybe the girl hadn't meant for Doreen to hear that whisper. Sometimes Doreen forgot to ignore her slightly-better-than-normal-human hearing, and all those little extra abnormal things about herself. Sometimes hiding all those things made her so exhausted she felt like sleeping till Cake Day.[12]

"Hi, I'm Doreen Green!" When she didn't know what to say she defaulted to extreme friendliness.

"Lucy Tang," said the dark-haired girl with a frown.

"So . . . uh, you *looked* like you might be wondering what I'm doing, even though you didn't speak aloud whatever question might've been in your brain, at least not so that any normal girl could hear. Which I am. A totally normal girl. In case you were

12 Cake Day is any day our family has cake, which includes birthdays and holidays and really any day when cake sounds like a swell idea.

wondering, I was staring down the building, like you do when you're a little nervous because you just moved from California and it's your first day."

"Freak," said Lucy Tang, this time speaking loud enough for normal-girl ears to hear. And then the girls walked off into the school, leaving Doreen alone.

If Monkey Joe had been there, Doreen would have turned to him (probably perched on her shoulder) and asked, "That was weird, right?"

"Totally weird," Monkey Joe would've said, except in Chitterspeak.[13]

But he wasn't there. So Doreen just glared one more time at the school and entered through the front doors, greeted by the smell of old milk and sweat.

Unlike her school in California, all the hallways were on the *inside* of the building! And so were the classrooms! And there was an entire lack of courtyards with palm trees! Or any trees, really. She felt like a tree squirrel trying to live underground.

Doreen Green was all for new experiences, but she was beginning to wonder if the whole Dad-gets-a-new-job-so-they-move-across-the-country thing was actually a bad idea.

And her mission to score a friend still wasn't going so hot.

---

13 In Chitterspeak, or squirrel language, *"chkucht"* means bad-kind-of-weird, as opposed to *"chkicht"* which is cool-interesting weird. E.g., girls being randomly mean is *chkucht*, and girls randomly tossing free ham sandwiches in the air would be *chkicht*.

During first and second periods there was no scheduled pause-to-chat-and-make-friends-now time. During third-period US History, the teacher shushed Doreen for whispering to a girl, "So, hey, do you like climbing trees or anything?"

Doreen scratched her scalp, hard. It was itching, she thought, because of all her unspoken thoughts. Also her tail was crammed in her pants, but that was nothing new. Life as Doreen Green involved a lot of nuts, scads of cakes, a number of nut cakes, and a great deal of aches.

At lunch hour, she walked down the hallway toward the cafeteria behind a group of five girls, who were chatting nonstop like a nest of squirrels. Doreen sighed.[14] In California she always had a friend here, a friend there. But she'd never belonged to a burrow.[15]

As awesome as that group of girls looked, they were awfully slow, so Doreen picked up the pace trying to get around them. One of the group was the girl from that morning.

"Lucy Tang! Hi!" said Doreen.

"Uh, hi," said Lucy, who then whispered to the others, "She's the one I was telling you about."

"Whoa, baby got back," said the blonde in the middle.

"Huh?" said Doreen. Did she just make a comment about Doreen's badonk? Because it was a fact that Doreen sported a

---

14 Do I really sigh that much?

15 Or a group, rather. Humans don't belong to burrows, right?

supersized badonk. It was a real challenge, frankly, to find pants that would fit her tail-enhanced badonk as well as her naturally thick thighs.[16] "Um, do you have lunch this period, too?"

"Uh, yeah," said the blonde. She pointed at Doreen's face. "Do you have your lunch stored in those rosy cheeks?"

Doreen ran her tongue on the inside of her cheeks just to make sure. She didn't *think* she had food in there, but it was a very useful place to store a few extra nuts. . . .

Or wait, was that girl implying that her wide, full cheeks were something to be ashamed of instead of a useful adaptation?

"Hey, honest help," said a brunette. "If you want my orthodontist's number I'd be happy to share. Maybe he can do something for your . . ." She gestured toward Doreen's mouth, where her front teeth stuck out below her top lip.

Fuzzmuppets, Doreen swore to herself. She stopped and let the group pass by. How in the known universe was a girl supposed to make a lifelong very best New Jersey friend if everyone was being so weird?[17]

Doreen glared up at the school ceiling, shaking a threatening fist. At moments like this, she briefly considered giving up on optimism. Expecting the worst sounded so much easier than demanding wonderfulness from life. But no! She would not be defeated! She took a deep breath and entered the cafeteria.

---

16 Seriously, jeans are impossible. I'm all about the stretchy pants. Throw a little flare skirt over 'em, top with a T-shirt that has a cool print, and that's my go-to.

17 Definitely *chkucht,* not *chkicht.*

It was teeming, like when you turn over a log and all the worms and stuff start to wiggle away.[18]

Doreen was seconds away from leaping onto a table and declaring to the room, *I am Doreen Green, age fourteen, and I'm looking for a friend. Who among you is most likely to want to hang out with me and talk for hours and eat trail mix once it's been picked clean of the abominations known as raisins?*[19]

But Lucy was staring at her. The word "freak" seemed to vibrate in the air like a rung bell. Doreen just stood there, like a squirrel frozen on a street, a car coming at her. The tail crammed in her pants ached like a bad secret.

But wait! There was a table over there, mostly empty. Just one girl. She had acorn brown skin and hair as black as black squirrels, and she was bent over reading a math textbook and nibbling dry crackers.

Doreen sat down and started pulling her lunch out of her paper bag: two almond-butter sandwiches, three apples, and a half pound of raisin-free trail mix.

The girl looked up, frowning.

"Hey, I'm Doreen Green. Just moved in. What's your name?"

"Ana Sofía?" The girl said it like a question.

"Ana Sofía is your name?"

The girl nodded, but she seemed uncertain.

---

18 I've never eaten a worm, but squirrels say they're not half bad in a pinch.
19 Harsh words, I know, but when you're eating nuts, YOU WANT NUTS, amirite? It's disturbing to bite down on a dead grape when you're expecting a pecan.

SQUIRREL GIRL

"Awesome," said Doreen. "I've never had a friend named Ana Sofía before, and I've always wanted one. See, I have a life goal of having at least one friend with every name ever."

Ana Sofía pointed at her ears and shook her head. Doreen noticed now that the girl was wearing behind-the-ear hearing aids. Ben, one of Doreen's Canadian cousins, wore hearing aids like that.[20]

"Oh, are you deaf?" said Doreen. "Or do you say 'hard of hearing'? I think some people prefer 'deaf' and some prefer—"

"I can't really understand you," Ana Sofía interrupted. "I read lips, but I need to hear some of what you're saying to make sense of it, and my hearing aids pick up too much background noise in here."

She'd clearly had to explain this to people before.

Doreen scooted closer. "Do you want to go eat outside? Does it help if I TALK LOUDER . . . or if I move my mouth big like this when I talk—wait, no, Ben told me that's super-obnoxious. Ben's my Canadian cousin. One of my Canadian cousins, I have like twenty—"

Ana Sofía sighed. "I can't understand you. Besides, I'd rather sit alone."

Doreen's heart felt as if it were curling up, a snail pulling

---

20 He also wears lumberjack shirts and runs around with a rubber ax, screaming *"Tiiiimber!"* How am I possibly related to someone whose fantasy is *cutting down* trees? He's six, though, so whatever.

18

back inside its shell. She tried to say, *That's cool, whatever,* but she couldn't seem to get her voice to work. Besides, Ana Sofía had looked back at her math textbook. Because apparently her math textbook was a vast improvement over Doreen Green.

Pressing her lips together to keep herself silent, Doreen re-bagged her lunch and slumped outside to eat on the front steps. Maybe the Doreen who was capable of having friends had been left behind in California. Maybe the nut of her was lost and she was just the discarded shell. She glared up at the school. It might as well have grown limbs, picked up a club, and splatted her from the get-go. Today had gone *that* badly.

And then . . .

"Hey," said a bald white man in a suit, leaning out the front door. "No eating outside. The cafeteria is for eating. Outside food attracts wild dogs."

Doreen gave him a you've-got-to-be-kidding-me look, which he returned with an I'm-serious-as-death look.[21] So she went inside into a bathroom stall, let her cramped tail out, and put on some headphones, blasting a song so loud it rattled the thoughts in her head and almost hacked away the heavy feelings in her chest. She stayed there the rest of the period, eating her lunch next to a toilet.

Doreen's mom had homeschooled her for most of elementary

---

21 I thought he was joking at first because "wild dogs"? Really? Who in this century worries about attracting wild dogs?

school, which had been okay and all, but Doreen had started to get really, really, really, really, really, really lonely.

But maybe being lonely would be better than this?

She turned the music up even louder. She needed something good today. One good thing could undo so much bad. Doreen believed that like she believed in salted caramel nut clusters. And she believed in salted caramel nut clusters a whole, whole lot.

3

TIPPY-TOE

"Sorry," she'd said.

Humans never apologized to squirrels. They barely said sorry to each other.

But this red-furred human girl with inexplicably strong haunches had apologized to *me.*

And then there was that business with the delicious cashew in the metal box that I should have known was a trap. Inexcusable. When are there ever delicious cashews just lying around in metal boxes? Never, that's when. I'd been careless, distracted by the human-girl business.

And yet . . . she saved my life. Tore open that cage with her bare hands. Plus she smelled a little like my dear, departed mother.

Mom always said folks were scared of things they didn't understand. And being scared of things is not something I do. I most certainly did not understand that girl, but I couldn't pretend it hadn't happened.

I tailed her all the way to one of those large cages humans call homes before I came to my senses. I went back to the park, killed a few acorn weevils, found a perfectly good half-a-sandwich inside a discarded plastic bag. Turkey. On rye. Whenever I get bird meat, I like to eat it in the open, let the falcons and hawks see who the boss is.

Me. I'm the boss.

And yet . . . despite sandwiches and weevils I couldn't distract myself.

One night later I was back in the tree beside her house. Perched there in the branches, peering through the glass that separated her world from mine.

Much quicker than I was expecting, she spotted me. As fast as a squirrel, the window slid open.

"Hey, friend," the girl called from the window. No human should have been able to see me, hidden as I was in the shadows of the tree.

"Is that you from the park?" she asked. "You okay?"

I took a few steps into the light. I was definitely *not* afraid. I'm never afraid. Cautious? Certainly. Startled? Alarmed? From time to time. On rare occasions panicked, intimidated, or even horrified. But never, ever afraid.

"What's your name? I'm Doreen. We just moved here."

Something large and furry swooshed behind the girl, and I froze. If this girl had a dog, we were done. No matter that she saved my life, no matter that she smelled like Mom.

Doreen leaned out the window, and I gasped.

"Is that a tail?" I whispered.

She laughed, and the tail twitched back and forth in just the way any squirrel's would when she was laughing.

"It is," Doreen said. "What did you think it was?"

Had she understood me?

"A dog," I said cautiously. But definitely not afraid.

She snorted another laugh, and the sound made me smile.

"C'mere," she said, beckoning me forward with a claw. Or a finger, rather. "I shouldn't be flaunting my tail near a window where people might see. I want to give you something."

She backed away, and I scampered to the sill, no farther. Humans don't go in our trees, we don't go in their houses. This is how squirrels and humans keep our uneasy peace. Because believe me, we could find ways in. We could strip their cupboards bare while they sleep. But squirrels are creatures of honor and respect.

Doreen returned with a pale pink ribbon. It wasn't one of those shiny fake human colors. It was the color of new strawberries or the paws of an infant squirrel.

"You are my first friend in this place," she said. "Thanks for coming to see me. I really needed today to not be all horrible."

Doreen tied the ribbon into a bow around my neck, and never once was I afraid. When she'd finished, she stepped back, smiling.

"You look fantastic, um . . . what was your name?"

"Tippy-Toe," I said.

"Great name. You look fantastic, Tippy-Toe," she said.

Human noise sounded from somewhere deeper in the house. Doreen sighed. "I gotta go. Talk tomorrow?"

"Yes, actually," I said, leaping back onto the branch. My heart was beating fast. I felt like a newborn pup, excited by every new thing: a fresh acorn, a fallen leaf. A new friend.

Doreen shut the window and turned off the light. My own reflection looked back at me from the darkened glass, and I saw the ribbon expertly tied around my neck.

She was right.

I did look fantastic.

4

DOREEN

*A*t lunch the next day, Doreen returned to the cafeteria and stood in front of Ana Sofía until she looked up from her math textbook.

"Hey, do you speak American Sign Language?" Doreen asked.

"What?" said Ana Sofía.

Doreen spoke aloud and signed at the same time. "I spent a few hours last night brushing up on my sign language, just in case you speak it."

Ana Sofía's expression was frozen halfway between What-the-heck and Imma-gonna-just-run-away-now.

"One of my Canadian cousins speaks sign language," said Doreen, signing the words she knew, "and when I lived near them I used to sign all the time with his family. But it's true what they say: 'use it or lose it.' They also say, 'when life gives you lemons, make lemonade,' which I never understood, because what's wrong with lemons to begin with?"[22]

Ana Sofía's eyes widened even wider.

"You honestly spent hours practicing Sign last night?" she asked.

Doreen nodded.

Ana Sofía frowned. She looked down at her textbook. "I've always hated that lemons saying, too. My mom cross-stitches platitudes on throw pillows. Makes me want to punch them."

She looked up. She was still frowning, but her eyes weren't into it.

"Sometimes I want to punch things, too!"[23] said Doreen, happy to have found something in common with Ana Sofía. Doreen smiled. She shifted her weight from one foot to the other. "Can I sit down?" she signed.

Ana Sofía pushed a chair away from the table with her foot and gestured grandly to it. Doreen sat.

"You're okay with Sign," Ana Sofía said aloud. "Well, you're not terrible. But I'm not fluent in it either. My family is hearing and they don't sign, and my friend who I used to sign with moved away, so whatever."

---

22 Seriously. It's like saying "if life gives you people, grind up their organs for a beverage!" Or maybe not. Gross. I can't believe I even said that. It's not like that at all.

23 Not people or animals, though. Or couches that should have been able to stand up to a friendly punch. Who knew couches were so fragile?

"Moving away stinks," said Doreen, doing her best to sign the sentiment.

Ana Sofía wrinkled her nose, not understanding. So they exchanged phone numbers and started texting instead.

DOREEN

Moving away stinks

ANA SOFÍA

The worst

DOREEN

I don't get it. You're bilingual and bionic

She looked up from her phone to gesture to Ana Sofía's hearing aids.

DOREEN

And yet you're sitting by yourself it makes no sense.

ANA SOFÍA

Actually I'm trilingual hablo español

DOREEN

SEE? Also you smell really good not to be weird but I've got a good nose

ANA SOFÍA

My mom makes homemade soap

Ana Sofía rolled her eyes as if she thought this was another obnoxious maternal habit.

Doreen leaned back with exasperated joy.

DOREEN

Are you kidding? I've never met anyone who made homemade soap u just get more interesting. Clearly we're best friends now that's a relief cause I was wasting so much time looking for you

Ana Sofía frowned at her phone. "Um . . . I don't do best friends."

"No?" Doreen frowned, too. "But . . . we're definitely friends, right?"

"Let's not be hasty."

"Okay." Doreen was certain they'd officially be friends by the end of lunch. End of day, tops. She took a big bite of her almond-butter sandwich. With her mouth full, she tried to speak, but Ana Sofía shook her head.

DOREEN

What else is interesting in town

ANA SOFÍA

Nothing. Shady oaks is a disaster

DOREEN

Impossible there's that big park

ANA SOFÍA

Yeah but u try to hang out there u risk wrath of larpers or soccer moms or crazy dogs

DOREEN

???

ANA SOFÍA

A pack of crazy feral dogs wander around growling and biting

DOREEN

What do they eat

ANA SOFÍA

Garbage I guess cause it's everywhere. FYI if someone paints graffiti on your house just leave it. If you paint over it they'll do more the next night

DOREEN

Who will?

"I've heard it's mostly a group of guys from the high school," Ana Sofía said aloud. "They call themselves the Skunk Club—I know that sounds made-up, but I kid you not. Shady Oaks is an unincorporated township. Which, as far as I can tell, means that we don't have police of our own. Any time there's a problem, we have to wait for county police to come, so I guess that makes criminals bolder or whatever. It wasn't always this bad. I've been keeping track, and it's definitely gotten worse." Ana Sofía took out a notebook and paged through hundreds of notes and observations. "About two years ago, there was a spike in thefts of electronics, bicycles, that sort of thing. I'm beginning to suspect that the increased overall crime is in reaction to the initial spike in thefts. If I could only figure out who the original source is . . ."

DOREEN

Wow you've like srsly gone to town on this

ANA SOFÍA

I kinda like mysteries do you think that's stupid?

DOREEN

No I think that's awesome

Doreen didn't care much for mysteries. She preferred nuts. But if Ana Sofía liked mysteries, she was interested for her newly declared BFF's sake.

> Hey there was a bizarro squirrel trap in the park that was straight off the death star with a squishing wall and everything

"I haven't heard about anything like that." Ana Sofía jotted that new info down in the notebook.

"There was a marking on it, looked like two *M*s."

"Interesting," Ana Sofía said, adding that note. "FYI, don't even bother riding a bike to school."

"Or it'll get stolen?" Doreen signed and said.

"Yeah, and say good-bye to the stereo in your parents' car."

Doreen signed something to show disgust at the situation.

Ana Sofía pressed her lips together, as if surprised by an unfamiliar desire to smile. "That's a swearword."

"Are you serious? But Ben says it all the time! Maybe it's not a swearword in Canada."

"Or maybe Ben is just naughty," she said with a short laugh.

A boy took a seat across the table from them. He had very light skin and light brown hair. In Los Angeles he'd probably be tanned and blond, but here he looked pale and sallow, like maybe he spent most of his time in basements.[24]

"Who's your friend?" Doreen asked.

---

24 Nothing wrong with basements! Some of my best friends prefer living underground. They're squirrels TBH, but still.

"That's Mike," said Ana Sofía.

Doreen tried not to be disappointed by his name, but she'd made her first friend named Mike when she'd been, like, three years old, and was hoping for a more unique name. If only Mike were short for Michaelmas or Microphone or Mikearooni or something.

Mike said, " 'Friend' is a loaded term. *Acquaintance.* I sit here because it's usually free from self-important babbling."

With all the background noise, Doreen wasn't sure Ana Sofía caught everything he had said, but she shook her head and rolled her eyes, apparently familiar enough with Mike to catch the gist.

"You seem a little down," said Doreen.

"You seem to have a balloon for a head," said Mike.

Was that another crack at her full cheeks? "Fuzzmuppets and Beanie Babies," Doreen cursed again under her breath.

"When you're blindly and stupidly floating about," said Mike, "someone like me, with two feet firmly on the ground, might seem 'down.' The correct term is 'well-grounded.' Try it sometime."

"Sheesh, is everybody in Shady Oaks pessimistic?" she asked Ana Sofía.

"Again . . . *well-grounded*," said Mike. "But don't lump me in with the riffraff. This whole neighborhood is a nightmare of unpredictability and inconvenience. No one follows rules. No one does what they're told." He shuddered. "I *hate* it."

"Alert the news," said Ana Sofía. "Mike Romanger hates something."

"Aw, don't be so glum, Mikearooni—can I call you Mikearooni?" said Doreen.

He said, "No way in—"

"Life is just a great big fat nut hanging on a tree," Doreen went on, "and all you have to do is leap up and grab it and eat it up! Nomnomnom . . ."

Mike looked hard at Doreen and then pointedly picked up his tablet and held it in front of his face, blocking her out of his view.

ANA SOFÍA

Don't pay attention to him

DOREEN

Is he mad

ANA SOFÍA

Grumpy like always. Anyway he's nobody. The only people you need to worry about at union are the somebodies

She gestured toward a group of guys and girls over by the frozen-yogurt machine. Lucy Tang was among them, and the blonde who'd commented on Doreen's badonk. They sat around and on top of three tables they'd pushed together, eating frozen yogurt and talking and laughing, as if they were posing for a *Cool Kids Magazine* photo shoot.[25]

ANA SOFÍA

> Heidi's mom donated the froyo machine so she and her friends think they own it. Basically unless they acknowledge u ur nobody

DOREEN

> But that doesn't make sense

ANA SOFÍA

> That's just the way it is

Doreen adjusted in her seat. Her tail ached. Her back itched. Even more, her optimistic heart was screaming,[26] *Nothing is just the way it is! You don't have to accept bad stuff, Doreen. Change it!*

DOREEN

> In LA we had bunches of heroes like she-hulk and hellcat they're always fighting crime and making things better. do the avengers ever come around here?

25 I don't think there's actually a *Cool Kids Magazine*. There definitely isn't a *Cool Squirrels Magazine*. Or *Squirrel's Digest* or *Squirrels Weekly* or *Squirrel World* even. There's a shocking lack of squirrel-related media generally. Believe me, I've looked.
26 My heart wasn't *literally* screaming. In case you were confused. That would be *sooo* creepy. Anyway, could you even hear it, or would the screams be all muffled by skin and ribs and stuff?

ANA SOFÍA

> LA and NYC are big. Nobody cares about tiny
> shady oaks why would they?

Doreen stuffed another sandwich into her mouth. She wasn't sure why anyone would care about Shady Oaks either. Except that she lived here. And so did her mom and dad. And Ana Sofía. And Tippy-Toe. Wasn't that enough?

5

DOREEN

"Oh yes, Doreen is very responsible," her mother was saying on the phone.

"You're talking about me," said Doreen, trying to do her math homework at the kitchen table.

"Kids love her. And animals. Plus she is extra-strong"—Maureen's eyes went wide; she made eye contact with Doreen and mouthed *whoops*—"strong-willed. So she won't eat all your snacks. Which makes her an excellent sitter."[27]

"Ack, I almost said it!" said Maureen the moment she had hung up the phone. "I want to brag about you to all the other parents, but can you imagine how bad they'd feel about their own children by comparison? I mean, who wouldn't want their

---

27 I probably will eat all your snacks, TBH.

child to be superstrong with a squirrel tail and mad leapin' skillz? That's what cool kids say today, right? *Skillz*? With a *z*?"

Doreen shrugged. She couldn't confirm something like that until she was officially invited to be a "cool kid."

Apparently even without the extra-strength info, Maureen's recommendation of Doreen had been sufficiently impressive, because the Santinos on Guttersnipe Street hired her to watch their one-year-old boy, Dante. Or maybe the Santinos were just desperate.

Either way, a week and a half after moving to Shady Oaks, Doreen had her first sitting job. She fell in love with Dante Santino immediately. She was particularly enchanted by his preference for climbing up on tables, grabbing stuff, and throwing it on the ground. Also he made a kind of gobbling sound, like a turkey.

"Your parents are going to pay me for hanging out with you," Doreen said. She was lying on her back, one leg up, balancing Dante on her foot. He squealed with delight. "Suckers! I'd do it for free!"

By the time the Santinos got home, the autumn sky was as black as an underground burrow.

Doreen started to walk home. It was Tuesday, the night before garbage pickup, and the curb was lined with trash cans. Every single one was tipped on its side and barfing its contents all over the street.

Doreen's phone buzzed. A text message.

ANA SOFÍA

U do ur math homework yet

DOREEN

Yes

Sort of

Started it

ANA SOFÍA

Come on u like interesting stuff. What's more interesting than equalizing equations[28]

DOREEN

Ur worried about my schoolwork so def I'm ur bff now yeah?

ANA SOFÍA

I told you yes we're prob friends but no bff pls. Math homework?

DOREEN

I'll tackle it when I get home. I just finished sitting at the Santinos

---

28 If you weren't sure, Ana Sofía was being dead serious. She's so awesome.

ANA SOFÍA

You're walking home alone?

Scattered chills ran down Doreen's back. Why shouldn't she walk home alone? "With someone" was always better than "alone," sure, but Ana Sofía's question reminded her of the real estate agent's warning. What did Doreen have to be afraid of? Nothing, that's what. But just yesterday, she and Ana Sofía had spent the afternoon in the tree house in Doreen's backyard researching Shady Oaks' local history, trying to solve the mystery of why crime had been increasing. They'd struck out on that, but had randomly discovered something called the Jersey Ghost, which was a totally not real and very silly legend, unless you happened to be walking home alone in the dark, at which point ghosts started to feel kinda possible.[29]

Doreen heard a *bang* and some distant laughter. *What was that?* She hopped up into a tree and was suddenly face-to-face with a gray squirrel sporting a fetching pink ribbon around her neck.

"Oh, hey Tippy-Toe," she whispered. "Have you been here long?"

"*Chikkt,*" said the squirrel.

---

29 Info about the Jersey Ghost we found online: "It is said to lurk in forgotten spaces, preying on the unwary and unwanted." Creepy, right? It also said that it steals eggs and makes mooing noises at midnight. So maybe it was a real thing or maybe it was just a hungry weasel-cow?

"Well, you could have come in," she said. "The Santinos were out. It was just me hanging with the baby."

"Kikichet?"

"Yeah, so cute! I love it how babies get so excited and happy that they start punching and kicking things!"

The breeze shifted, and a bunch of greasy napkins and sticky wrappers blew up into Doreen's face.

"What the—*ugh!*" she said, batting away the garbage.

"Chukkichkiikiikkki," said Tippy-Toe, which basically meant, "Gross. What's the matter with humans and their garbage? Squirrels do not care for garbage. We're not common raccoons, thank you very much. Plus all the garbage is feeding that mob of wild dogs, who are harassing my squirrels.[30] I'm so frustrated I could bite an acorn in two! 'Course, I can do that even when I'm not frustrated, but STILL!!!"

Doreen nodded thoughtfully. Inside, her optimistic heart was pounding again.[31] Was this a way that she could help? Something she could do?

She set the first garbage can back upright and started scurrying around, gathering up spilled trash and dumping it back into the can.

"Chuk?" asked Tippy-Toe.

"Sometimes you gotta get your paws dirty, Tip," said Doreen,

---

30 Tippy-Toe was pretty much the leader of the tree squirrels in the neighborhood, as much as tree squirrels have a leader.
31 Not screaming, though. That was probably a good sign.

frowning at the greasy whatever smeared on her palm. She shrugged and kept working. She was quick and strong, and had excellent aim. She tossed an empty juice box from twenty feet away. Nothing but net! Or can, at any rate.

Behind her she heard a tiny squirrel sigh. And then Tippy-Toe was fetching garbage, running up Doreen's back, and tossing the bits into cans from her shoulder.

In a few minutes they'd cleaned up most of one block and had been joined by a half dozen members of Tippy-Toe's family.[32] They made a game of it, seeing who could bag the most trash.

Doreen's phone buzzed.

ANA SOFÍA

Text me when you're home I'm worried bout u.
It's trash night the skunk club might be out

DOREEN

???

ANA SOFÍA

The high schoolers I told u bout

DOREEN

U were serious theres a skunk club for real?

---

32 I wasn't sure if they were like cousin-uncle-sister family or like "family," mafia-style. Tree squirrel family trees are crazy complicated. Way more complicated than actual trees.

ANA SOFÍA

Yes they like to knock over trash cans and stick anyone smaller than them in trash cans and that's if ur lucky srsly this town is so weird u don't even know

DOREEN

You're worried about me totes something a bff wld do

ANA SOFÍA

Stop

DOREEN

But you don't have to worry I'm fine just cleaning up some trash

ANA SOFÍA

No u don't understand those are mean kids u r too trusting. I need u to believe how bad this place is so you're more careful. Don't be a hero. Hurry home

Don't be a hero? Don't be silly. Cleaning up trash wasn't what heroes did. Was it?

"Which Avenger do you think would be the best at cleaning up trash?" asked Doreen.

"*Chkkt,*" said Tippy-Toe.

"Garbage-Can Man?" said Doreen, tossing a bag of dirty diapers over her shoulder. "You're making that up."

"*Chk chuk chikka.*"

"*Ooooh.* You mean Iron Man. I don't think that's actually a garbage can he flies around in."

"*Chika chuk.*"

"Ha! No, no. That's mean! I'm sure Tony Stark is a very nice man who is just confused about facial-hair trends."

"*Chk chikka cht?*"

"Oh, I don't know, maybe Captain America. He'd be real efficient, I bet, and wouldn't complain about it being dirty work."

"*Chk chika?*"

"Horn-headed guy? Daredevil? Good idea. There's all those articles about him cleaning up the streets of Hell's Kitchen."

"*Chk chu-chaik.*"

"No way. In a fight She-Hulk would totally whoop Daredevil. We've been over this."

In no time Doreen and her furry pals had circled their way around the entire block. As they approached the corner of the Santinos' street, she spotted a group of teenage boys. They were dressed in black and gray and carrying baseball bats and sticks, as if posing in a photo shoot for *Hooligan Magazine*.[33]

"Didn't we already do this block?" said the one in the lead, a white guy in a black cap.

"Yeah, we did, Antonio. I'd swear it on a skunk."

Doreen gasped. The Skunk Club! For really real!

At the sound of her gasp, the boys turned to look. At her.

---

33 If there really was a *Hooligan Magazine* I bet Daredevil would be a loyal subscriber.

Doreen Green, age fourteen, out at night and surrounded by squirrels. She somehow felt more exposed than she'd ever been. And even . . . yes, a little . . . afraid. So startled in fact that, completely without her permission, her tail sprang free from her stretchy pants and stuck straight out like a scared cat's.

Her tail was out! That made her even more alarmed, and she jumped without thinking about it.

Up. Straight up. There was a tree there, and she clonked her head on a branch.

"Ooo," she moaned, falling back to the ground.

"Whoa!" said the Skunk Club boys, startled again.

"Eeee," said Doreen, startled again-er. She scrambled to her feet and leaped back up into the tree, managing to grab a branch with her hands this time instead of with the top of her head, which had proven ineffective.

"What the fudge, man?" one whispered.

"What . . . what *was* that?" whispered the lead one, who was apparently called Antonio.

They were gripping their bats, shifting weight on their feet as if readying for a fight. Fight her? Doreen had never fought anything except pillows, gingivitis, and the invisible monsters her kickboxing video instructed her to imagine.[34] But something inside her was tense and trembling, like a spring ready to spring

---

34 *Commander Quiff's Kicking for Confidence.* A few years ago Mom bought me some work-out videos so I could "get my energy out." I have yet to reach the bottom of my energy, but the videos are fun.

or a kernel just about to pop, and she thought she wouldn't mind punching actual *bad things*, not just throw pillows stitched with uplifting messages.

The boys started toward her tree. All the hair on her tail stood up. What was she thinking? She couldn't punch *people*. She wasn't a Super Hero or anything. And they probably weren't *legit* bad, not Super Villain bad. Just naughty kids. She had to get out of there!

"They, uh, they call me the Jersey *Ghooooost*," said Doreen in a high-pitched moan.

That seemed to work. The boys stopped in their tracks.

"The Jersey Ghost?" whispered Antonio. "No way. No. Friggin'. Way."

"The Jersey Ghost isn't real, man."

"I saw a documentary about it on the History Channel, no lie. Documentaries be fact."

"No way. No friggin' way . . ."

Antonio gripped his aluminum baseball bat and started toward her tree again, so Doreen blurted out, "I haunt these *treeeees*, ill at *eaaase*, when I see litterers I . . ." She couldn't think of another word that rhymed, so she just added, *"Ooooooo!"*

The group shifted, unsure, but the lead one kept moving toward her. And then the rest followed.

Crud! Doreen couldn't let them see her with her tail out. She pulled the hood of her sweatshirt over her head. They were close. Almost right beneath her. And she panicked.

She leaped down nearly on top of them, landing with a *thud* on the pavement. She hissed in what she hoped was an ominous manner, and just as quickly leaped back up into the next tree.

The Skunk Club screamed.

Every one of them opened their mouths as wide as they could and screamed as if they'd just been splashed with hot cheese sauce and weevils.[35]

Behind Doreen, Tippy-Toe and five other squirrels—all making screeching noises—leaped from the first tree into Doreen's, right over the boys' heads.

And that did it. The Skunk Club ran away.

Doreen and five squirrels leaned back in the tree's branches and laughed so hard they squeaked.

"That synchronized leap-and-scream was honest-to-nuts fantastic, guys. Seriously, high fours," Doreen said, lifting her hand with thumb tucked in. Tippy-Toe slapped her little four-toed paw onto Doreen's palm. Timidly, the other squirrels did the same.

Suddenly Doreen smelled something familiar—crackers and homemade soap. "Ana Sofía?" Doreen said aloud.

"Doreen?" said Ana Sofía, walking closer and peering up into the tree. "Doreen, was that *you*?"

Doreen put her hand over her mouth, but it was too late. Ana Sofía was ten feet below her and looking straight up.

---

35 I've never observed anyone get splashed with hot cheese sauce and weevils, but I'm pretty sure they would scream exactly like those guys did.

"But . . . but I saw someone jump way higher than anyone should be able to jump," said Ana Sofía. "How did you—?"

She stopped. She'd spotted the tail. In nervous panic, Doreen's tail twitched. Ana Sofía gasped.

Doreen sighed. It was useless to try to hide. She'd been spotted. She dropped out of the tree.

"It's a squirrel tail," Doreen signed as well as spoke in case the light was too low for Ana Sofía to read her lips. "I was born with it. Nobody else knows. It's a huge secret, and please don't hate me?"

But by the look on Ana Sofía's face as she gazed at Doreen, she might have been posing in a photo shoot for *I Think My Friend Is Awesome Magazine.*[36]

"Please don't tell anyone."

Ana Sofía shook her head solemnly.

"So we're friends, right? Like, officially?" asked Doreen.

Ana Sofía nodded. "Yeah, that'd be nice."

"Best friends?" said Doreen.

Ana Sofía shrugged. "My last best friend moved away and hasn't Skyped in months."

"Yeah, my last best friend called it quits on me when her other friends told her to. Last best friends stink. Good thing you and I are best friends forever and ever and ever!" Doreen said, because if you're not all in, why even bother?

---

36 Dang it! Now I really want this magazine for real!

Ana Sofía rolled her eyes, but she didn't say no. And she was still not frowning, which on Ana Sofía's face was practically a smile.

Doreen blushed. And swooshed her tail. Standing before her new BFFAEAE[37] with her tail out and proud, she felt more than a little awesome. And like maybe she could probably kinda do just about anything.

---

37 Best Friend Forever and Ever and Ever, not Big Fat Feathered Aardvark Eating an Empanada, in case you were confused.

6

ANA SOFÍA[38]

*H*earing people often assumed that Ana Sofía could use lipreading to eavesdrop on conversations from a distance. Hardly. For one thing, only 30 percent of speech sounds are visible on the lips. Then she had to be fairly close to the person speaking, both so her hearing aid could amplify the words and so she could see their mouth. She had to see the person's whole face, really. Much of lipreading depended on facial expressions and body language. Not to mention how tricky it was figuring out what someone was saying unless you kinda knew the person, their speaking style, *and* the context of the conversation.

But the next Monday at school, two girls standing by her locker were having an animated conversation about the "Jersey

---

38 This is so cool! I get to find out what Ana Sofía was thinking! Wait, how am I doing this? *Hmm*, maybe it's better not to wonder.

Ghost." After that, Ana Sofía kept catching sight of people talking in urgent, whispery ways, sometimes excited, sometimes fearful. She watched their lips and, though she was too far away to hear, she would have bet her top five pairs of socks that they, too, were talking about the Jersey Ghost.[39]

Annoyingly, she and Doreen didn't have any of the same classes, so she had to wait till lunch to tell her. She stood by the cafeteria doors, adjusting her socks (rainbow stripes today), tapping her toes, and feeling generally hippity-hoppity excited, which was a new and alarming sensation for her and made her anxious about her own mental health.

When Doreen finally arrived, Ana Sofía experienced a second unfamiliar emotion. A weird, foreign, slightly uncomfortable sensation in her heart. She grimaced when she figured out what to call it: "gladness." She wanted to roll her eyes at herself. "Glad" people tended to be shiny and annoying and too dull to realize that "looking forward to things" or "enjoying the moment" was supremely pointless. And yet, here she was, Ana Sofía Arcos Romero, too glad to even roll her eyes. In fact, she practically smiled. This whole BFFAEAE business was seriously messing with her head.[40]

---

39 It's true that Ana Sofía ranks her socks and organizes them accordingly in her sock drawers (note the plural). Not sure what to get Ana Sofía for her birthday? Pro tip: How about socks?

40 Aha! So in her mind, Ana Sofía was thinking of me as her BFFAEAE! Awesome. Unless she meant the other kind of BFFAEAE. But I'm pretty sure she didn't. Because I haven't eaten an empanada in months. Also, totally not an aardvark.

Doreen's whole face lit up when she saw her. "Hi, Ana Sofía!"

Ana Sofía signed, "Everyone's talking about the Jersey Ghost."

"Seriously?"

Ana Sofía nodded. "I'm almost sure they think it's real. I'm absolutely sure they don't know it's you."

"Come on," said Doreen, hooking her arm in Ana Sofía's. She headed straight for the Somebodies' table.

"No, no, danger, warning, turn around," Ana Sofía said, tugging backward, but Doreen was like a freight train headed downhill.[41]

"What are you guys talking about?" Doreen spoke, signing for Ana Sofía to see.

"Nope," said Heidi, one of the Somebodies. Ana Sofía knew her name, of course. She knew all the Somebodies' names. But she would have bet her top five socks that Heidi didn't know hers.

Lanessa and Janessa (no relation) both made shooing motions with their hands, and Jackson pointedly turned his back to Doreen.

Ana Sofía finally managed to pull Doreen away. "I told you, they have to acknowledge you first."

Doreen made a sign that Ana Sofía had learned meant "weird, but not the good kind of weird." But she simply headed to the next table over, where a few people from Doreen's computer class were hanging out.

---

41 In just this moment or all the time? 'Cause I feel like that a lot.

"What are you guys talking about?" Doreen asked.

Ana Sofía couldn't follow everything they said, even with Doreen attempting to sign it as they spoke, but Doreen filled her in on what she missed after.

"The Jersey Ghost," said one. "Everyone says it's real, but I don't think so."

"I'm telling you, man, my brother saw it," said another. "He had just tagged the bridge when suddenly *it* was there. It leaped up onto the side of the bridge and cleaned off the fresh paint with its massive tail!"

"It has a tail?"

"Yeah, he said the tail was huge, luxurious, and . . . and beautiful."[42] He bowed his head, blushing.

One guy said that he knew a member of the Skunk Club who had claimed the Jersey Ghost's tail was, in fact, "fat, packed, and wicked," while another asserted the tail had been "battle-ready and straight-up colossal."

Doreen and Ana Sofía left them arguing over adjectives and exited the cafeteria, ducking into a quiet, empty classroom.

"So you've been out since garbage day?" Ana Sofía asked after Doreen had rehashed the conversation.

"Yeah, just one other time. I didn't mean to. I saw some people spraying graffiti on the bridge, and I remembered how you

---

42 Check, check, and check. Clearly he's talking about my tail.

didn't like the graffiti so much, so I tried to clean it off. I didn't know anyone saw me."

"They don't know it's you. How can they not tell?"

Doreen shook her head but didn't appear to be listening. "I just meant to make the neighborhood nicer for the squirrels and for you and stuff. But it turns out I'm actually entertaining the masses! I love being a phantasmal spook of legend."

"It's the tail," said Ana Sofía. "All they see is the tail. Doreen Green doesn't appear to have a tail, so clearly you couldn't be the Jersey Ghost."

"I'm not the Jersey Ghost," said Doreen. "I mean, I shouldn't be. It's fun, but I'm not supposed to show my tail in public. I never, ever have."

"It's your disguise! They don't recognize you with your tail. You're totally safe!"

Just a week into their friendship, and already Ana Sofía could read Doreen's face like a comic book.[43]

"Will you . . . will you come out with me?" Doreen asked, looking uncharacteristically timid.

Ana Sofía nodded her fist. *Yes, yes, yes.*

---

43 Comic books are Ana Sofía's favorite books that aren't about math. As far as she is concerned, if the book is supposed to entertain rather than instruct, it'd better have pictures and Super Heroes or getitawayfromme. Her comics of choice aren't about real Super Heroes but the made-up ones, like angsty grown men who wear tights and brood between battles.

7

DOREEN

After school, Ana Sofía went to Doreen's house. Ana Sofía helped Doreen with her math homework, and Doreen helped Ana Sofía with her history homework.[44] They ate dinner—nut loaf with potatoes and gravy. Dinner at the Green home was lively. Doreen's dad, Dor, a shiny-cheeked, bald-headed, red-bearded version of Doreen (sans tail) performed magic tricks with a fork and napkin. Her mother sang Italian songs in an embroidered cat apron. Doreen broke a plate.

"It's okay," said Maureen, facing Ana Sofía as she spoke to make it easier for her to read her lips. "We buy the ten-cent plates at the secondhand store. We learned our lesson when Doreen

---

44 I'd already studied the westward migration at my old school, and Ana Sofía missed the lecture because apparently Mr. Timmons can't be bothered to wear the around-the-neck mic that helps Ana Sofía hear him better. Kinda jerky, if you ask me.

was a toddler. She's . . . special. It's really important that no one else knows that, okay? I know Doreen trusts you, but I need your promise you won't reveal her secret to anyone."

Maureen smiled, but her lip trembled a little with worry.

"Mom!" said Doreen, mortified.

But Ana Sofía nodded. "I promise," she said.

As the evening light mellowed from yellow to gold, Ana Sofía caught Doreen's eye and nodded toward the door.

"Whatcha got there? BTE aids, huh?"[45] Dor asked Ana Sofía. "Which model is that? How's it work in the wind for ya?"

"We're going now, Dad. I'm going to walk Ana Sofía home before it gets dark, okay?"

"Sure, sure. Be careful, don't talk to strangers, back before bedtime, remember who you are, look before crossing the street, don't jump on rooftops—"

"I got it, Dad. Bye!" said Doreen.

They took a shortcut through the park. The fall sunset was all peach and gold, the air a mix of cool and warm, like a cup of tea with cream not yet stirred. Doreen sniffed the air and peered into the developing shadows.

"It's like we're Super Heroes out on patrol, looking for bad guys," said Ana Sofía. "I mean, I know you can't *really* be a Super Hero unless you're super-amazing at things and are part of the

---

45 BTE stands for behind-the-ear hearing aid. Dad is sort of a hearing-aid nerd. Also a blender nerd. If you have a blender, he has an opinion.

Avengers or another equally auspicious Super Hero collective. It's like with the Somebodies. The real Super Heroes have to acknowledge you and say you can be one of them. No one just wakes up one morning all like, 'I'm a Super Hero now,' and then they just are."

"Are you sure?" asked Doreen.

"Yes," said Ana Sofía. "That's just how things work."

"Huh." Doreen figured that must be true. The hero-watch websites and news shows screamed about grown-ups who tore up skyscrapers by their foundations or flew spaceships and stopped intergalactic wars. There was nothing super-heroey about walking through the park with a squirrel tail stuffed in the seat of your pants. "But you're right, it does feel a *little* like being heroes on patrol. We're totally pards."

"What was that?" asked Ana Sofía.

"We're pards," said Doreen, finger-spelling the word.

"Pards? Is that a thing?"

"Totally. Like partners, but cooler."

"Best friends was a big leap for me. I don't think I can commit to being a *pard.*"

Doreen just nodded, but she felt certain Ana Sofía would warm up to the idea. Who wouldn't want to be pards?

"So, I brought this," said Ana Sofía, pulling a white bedsheet from her backpack. "In case you wanted to, I don't know, drop it over your head and look more Jersey Ghost-y?"

A chittering sounded from a tree, and then Tippy-Toe was on Doreen's shoulder.

"You don't say!" said Doreen. "Well, of course, Tippy, I'll be right there."

Tippy-Toe sneezed, the kind of sneeze that meant "Very well then," but in a completely adorable way that would probably make you go *awwww*. Tippy-Toe would disagree that she sounded adorable. She felt completely professional, thank you very much.

"The squirrels have found another of those weirdo traps in the trees," Doreen told Ana Sofía. "A chance to save the day! BRB, 'kay?"

"'Kay. Do you want the sheet?"

"No thanks, it'd probably get in my way." Doreen and Tippy-Toe loped off like lopsided twins, leaving Ana Sofía standing there. Alone. In the LARPer-infested park.

Doreen looked back. Ana Sofía had wrapped the sheet around her shoulders and head as if for warmth. Doreen almost went back to her, but she was certain she'd only be gone for a few seconds. She followed Tippy-Toe to a tree, found the trap, and with a bit of effort managed to dismantle it. But just then a new squirrel chirped an alarm. Another trap! By the time Doreen had climbed that tree and destroyed the second one, news of the traps had spread. The trees came alive with squirrels on the hunt, sniffing out and calling alerts on more "danger cages." Doreen followed their calls. She was traveling farther and farther away from Ana Sofía.

There was a click, a squeal, and a dozen squirrels at once cried out, "Help!"

Tippy-Toe came running, screeching about the horrific situation. Little Candy Creeper, a squirrel no more than six months old, had discovered a trap, but in her excitement had bumbled her way inside it. Now the door was locked shut. The wall was crushing inward. She had only moments before her last breath would be squished right out of her.

"I'm coming!" said Doreen, running along the thickest branches, bounding from tree to tree. She was off-balance running that fast, so mid-stride she lifted her tail free. But what if someone saw her out in the open, flying her freaky tail? She pulled up her hood.

With tail out and hood up, Doreen leaped from a tree.

"Chkkt!" replied five squirrels, carrying the trap down the tree and rushing it toward her.

Using their tails, the squirrel posse catapulted the cage in the air. It whooshed across an empty soccer field. Doreen was coming from the other side. She leaped, caught it at the apex of its arc, and in midair, gripped the sides of the cage. "AAAARRRH!" she yelled as she ripped it apart.[46]

---

46 Turns out you don't really need to yell "AAAARRRH" when you rip things apart, but it sure feels good.

When she landed, tail-first, and rolled to a stop, Little Candy Creeper lay nestled in her hands with no more than a bruised backside.

"You okay?" asked Doreen.

"*Chkkt,*" said Little Candy Creeper, pointing to her tiny bum, which was, as mentioned, bruised, but still in one piece.

"Yeah," Doreen agreed and collapsed on the grass, damp with sweat, breathing hard. A dozen squirrels were celebrating by running up and down her limbs, burrowing behind her neck and around her shoulders, bouncing on her tail, and generally squeaking with excitement. This had been a big day for the squirrels.

Tippy-Toe chittered at her.

"I don't look like Doreen anymore?" said Doreen.

Her huge tail was free and twitching in the breeze. She was wearing the hoodie her Canadian grandma had given her on her last birthday. It was nut brown, and the hood had little bear ears attached.[47]

"*Chktt-kit,*" said Tippy-Toe.

"No way!" Doreen sat up, holding out her hands, and Tippy-Toe leaped onto them. "Actually, you know what? That's the name I call myself in my head. Just when I'm feeling sad or

---

47 Bears aren't really my thing. But Gramma *is* my thing. We like to go to rock concerts together and stand close to the stage.

worried." She whispered, still shy to say it aloud, "Like, *'Come on, Squirrel Girl, you got this.'*"

All around her, the squirrels began to repeat the nickname. *"Chktt-kit, Chktt-kit."* In Chitterspeak it didn't mean "female squirrel." It combined the words for squirrel with human girl. A creature who was two things at the same time.

One squirrel on her shoulder put its bitty paw on her forehead, looked into her eye and declared, *"Chktt-kit."*

"Wow," Doreen breathed out. Her skin prickled with goose bumps from the top of her head to the tip of her tail. The parts that had been curled up tight inside were starting to stretch, fill up the empty spaces. Never had she felt so fully herself.

In the distance, Doreen's keen ears became aware of voices speaking.

"I'm not the Jersey Ghost! I swear!"

Was that Ana Sofía? And then other voices.

"Thou speakest truly, and yet clearly thou art pretending to be the Ghost of Jersey in thy spectral white shroud in order to frighten the peasants and cause unpleasantness! Thou wilst pay for thy crimes of deception and buffoonery—"

"Not to mention subterfuge and tomfoolery."

"You are correct, Lady Genevieve von Orkhead-Schlinger, this one most definitely hath committed the grievous twin crimes of subterfuge and tomfoolery."

"My lord, what sayest thou? What be her fit punishment?"

"The royal we declareth her punishment fitteth the named crimes of deception, buffoonery, subterfuge, and tomfoolery. She shall be clamped in the pillory."

"I don't know what you're saying, but it's probably not true. Somebody, help!"

Definitely Ana Sofía, Doreen thought as she jumped to her feet. A dozen squirrels went flying off her in various directions, like kernels of popcorn out of a pot.[48]

"Ana Sofía?" Doreen said even though Ana Sofía surely couldn't hear her. "I don't know what in the heck a pillory is, but I'm coming!"

Moments later, she cleverly deduced what a pillory was. Most likely, it was that wooden stand in the middle of the green with three holes in it: two that snapped shut around Ana Sofía's wrists and a third larger one around her neck. Doreen had seen pictures of things like that in history textbooks, clearly some kind of medieval device for punishment. That the LARPers had randomly built in the park. A reasonable thing to use against her BFFAEAE Ana Sofía Arcos Romero?

Uh, no way, nohow, nowhere, no duh.

Doreen leaped into the green, higher than she'd ever done before. Excited from having just saved a freakin' adorable baby

---

48 Don't worry, they were fine. Squirrels had been landing on their feet millions of years before cats showed up and tried to claim that as their thing. But dang it, now I'm craving popcorn!

squirrel, pumped up with the freedom and confidence of having her tail out, and most of all vibrating with the joy of hearing her secret name spoken aloud by a clan of squirrels, she screeched a squirrel-ish shriek. She landed by the pillory.

"Let her go!" she said.

"Kill it!" said the baron. "It's a monster! It's a demon! It's a dragon! Thing! A dragon thing!"

The baron came at her, sword swinging. Doreen ducked and dodged, leaped up, and landed on her attacker's shoulders.[49]

"Oof," he said, crumpling to the grass under her weight.

"What in the cheese was that?" said Doreen. "Seriously, attacking people with swords in the park? Time to rethink your leisure activities."

A second LARPer came at her, sword overhead, yelling *"AAAAAAA—"*

But she stopped short when Doreen swished her tail, knocking the girl aside like she was swatting a fly.[50]

Ana Sofía's head observed all this from her wooden neck lock, her eyes wide.

"Wow," she said. "Whoa," she said. Also, "Holy cannoli."

Doreen tried to release Ana Sofía, but the pillory's clamping bar was locked shut. So she gripped the boards and pulled

---

49 This was totally instinct after months of working out to *Commander Quiff's Hip Hop Leap Squats* every Thursday morning.

50 This move probably came from *Commander Quiff's Zydeco Zumba*. Also from watching squirrels. They do this all the time.

till they cracked and broke apart. Ana Sofía stood up straight, shrugging off the bedsheet and massaging her wrists.

"Thanks," said Ana Sofía. "I thought you'd left me."

"Duh, of course not."

"Ana Sofía?" Vin Tang took a step closer. "I'm so sorry, I didn't know that was you!"

Doreen felt movement behind her and she swirled around, claws out.[51] But instead of attacking, the dozen LARPers had begun to drop to one knee. The baron she'd knocked down with a shoulder-strike was kneeling in front, eyes wide and wet as if he were about to weep.

"Your speed and combat prowess is a mighty thing to behold." He bowed his head and lifted up his sword in both hands, offering it to her. "My great-tailed liege."[52]

"What? You guys are silly. Honestly I'm dead confused by whatever game you're playing, but if you like it, that's cool. Just don't, like, kidnap people and lock them up in weirdo wooden head traps, 'kay?"

Ana Sofía was still looking a little shaky, and despite the kneeling and the *my-leige*-ing, all those sword-wielding LARPers

---

51 Yeah, I have superstrong, retractable claws. They slide out from under my fingernails. My parents put mitts over my hands till I was four years old to keep me from scratching myself or accidentally cutting through glass or something.

52 What's a liege? Maybe the yoga pose he was doing kneeling with one knee? Lemme google it. . . . Oh. It's like a king or queen or someone you swear to serve. I think I knew that already, LOL.

seemed a bit unstable and possibly dangerous, so Doreen picked up Ana Sofía, slung her over her shoulder, and leaped away.

They'd nearly bounded right out of the park when she heard Ana Sofía's strained, hiccupy breathing. Was she crying? Doreen stopped and put her down.

Nope. She was full-on laughing.

"What? What's funny?" Doreen said.

"I. Don't. Know," said Ana Sofía between laughs. "I think I'm freaking out a little. You tore apart that wood with your bare hands!"

"Well, yeah, it was super-easy actually. Maybe it was half broken already?"

Ana Sofía shook her head. She was searching on her phone. "Squirrel facts, squirrel facts . . . Aha! Listen," she said, reading from her phone. " 'Squirrels can lift several times their own body weight.' "

"Yeah, squirrels are awesome."

Ana Sofía continued to scroll through her phone. "They can run up to twenty miles an hour. Gnaw through solid metal. Jump five feet in the air. They regularly leap ten feet horizontally. What if . . . what if you don't just have a squirrel tail and front teeth, and are pretty strong? What if you actually have the *proportional* strength, speed, and agility of a squirrel? So if a squirrel can leap five times the length of its own body, let's say, then you should be able to leap five times the length of *your* body, which would be . . . thirty feet. *Thirty feet*, Doreen."

"Nah, I can't jump that far."

"What if it's more?"

"I mean, I have some skills," signed Doreen. "But it's not like I'm Spider-Man."

"No, you're not Spider-Man," said Ana Sofía. She looked her dead in the eyes and said with great solemnity, "You're Squirrel Girl."

"Whoa." Now not just her skin had goose bumps but her bones, too. Electric thrills zipped through her veins. "That's so amazing. I was just telling Tippy-Toe that that's . . . that's . . ."

She cleared her throat. Why was it so hard to speak aloud the secret?[53]

"Squirrel Girl," she whispered. "That's what I call myself in my head."

"*And* you can talk to squirrels! Doreen, I think . . . I think you could maybe be a Super Hero."

"Nah," said Doreen. Adults were Super Heroes. Adults like Captain Marvel, Captain America, Captain Britain, Captain Universe, and all the other captains, plus gods of thunder eating shawarma with or without shirts.

"But what if you kept doing hero stuff? And the Avengers noticed you? And asked you to join? Then you'd be a *real* Super

---

53 Have you ever had something super-precious? Not diamonds or gold or whatever but precious to you, like your favorite stuffed bunny so worn down from hugs it had one ear left and all the pink fuzz on its nose was worn right off? And you kept it safe but also hidden because if your friends or brother or anyone made fun of it, that would have crushed you? That's sort of what my secret name was like for me.

Hero. And you'd probably get to hang out with Thor. . . ." Ana Sofía blushed and looked at her feet. "I guess that'd be cool or something, not that I've thought about Thor much ever."

Doreen *had* been able to destroy those traps. And dodging the LARPers' swords had been easy as nut cake. And people didn't usually leap as high as she did. . . . But no. No way was she a Super Hero.

Not yet.

8

TEXT MESSAGES

On my way back. Walking ana sofia home took
longer than I thought

Are you dressed warm enough?

Wearing gramma's hoodie

With the little bear ears? Adorbs!

Can I say adorbs or is that too hip for a mom?

I can't keep track of all the hip things so yes maybe

SQUIRREL GIRL

MOM

How's your strength? Have you been eating enough protein to keep it up?

DOREEN

I need a fanny pack or something to carry spare nuts. I hate purses they bounce around when I leap

MOM

You're leaping? In public? Is your tail tucked out of sight?

DOREEN

Yes

Prbly

I'm such a terrible liar!

MOM

Doreen what's going on?

DOREEN

I had to save ana sofia from some teens dressed up medieval who put her in a pillory which is a thing and also destroy squirrel traps designed by a wannabe James bond villain and people think I'm the Jersey ghost but the tail is so distracting no one looks at my face

MOM

Well yes I can see that all makes perfect sense but still you can't expose yourself

DOREEN

Ok

MOM

No more going out with your tail out

DOREEN

I know I know

MOM

And we'll need to talk about some kind of

What do parents do when their kids disobey and make dangerous choices?

DOREEN

I dunno I've read about groundings

MOM

Yes you should probably be grounded. Or something

DOREEN

Ok

SQUIRREL GIRL

MOM

Stay warm! Come home soon! I love you! You're grounded!

DOREEN

Love you too

9

TIPPY-TOE

*T*ree squirrels and ground squirrels, we're like cats and rats: their names might sound similar, but if you stick them in the same burrow, you're going to have a ruckus.

We tree squirrels stay in our parts of the neighborhood and keep messes to a minimum. But after that first unfortunate incident with the trap and my falling into it (which we aren't talking about), I took it upon myself to hunt down every wretched trap I could find and send them to the big scrap-yard in the sky.

I found a lot. And not just in trees. Whoever made them wasn't just a problem for my tree squirrels. They were a problem for all squirrels. It was time we worked together and got rid of them all.

A month ago I might have laughed at the idea of working with the groundies on anything. But I would have said that about humans, too.

It was dusk, and my nose twitched with the scents of humans cooking their evening meals. I scampered away from houses to the cracked foundation of an abandoned building where I knew ground squirrels sometimes burrowed. Immediately three groundies surrounded me, those stumpy things they called tails twitching behind them.

"Ay-yo, Tippy-Toe," said Miranda Creepsforth.

Miranda was one of Big Daddy Spud's enforcers. Big Daddy pretty much ran the ground squirrel clans around here, and like his name suggested, he was a big one. But Miranda was no petite peanut herself. Or any kind of peanut. Peanuts are delicious. Miranda did not look like a tasty treat for anything but an owl with gut bugs.

"Shuck and scratch, Miss Mandy," I said, speaking in traditional Jersey squirrel dialect. "Just the squeak I wanted to see."

The group of ground squirrels arranged themselves around me. I had nothing but good intentions, but I wasn't sure the same was true of them.

"You got no reason to chitter with me," she said, her short tail vibrating.

"Truth," I said. "I got chitter-plans settled on Big Daddy Spud. But as you're on the chew for Spud, I figured you could squeak the meet."

"What chit you got with Spud? Delivering a message from your owner?"

"*Ooooh,* burn," said one of the other two groundies.

"Excuse me?" I asked. Miranda was purposefully trying to irritate me. Squirrels were not *owned*, and to suggest otherwise was an insult I was just about impatient enough to repay.

"Everybody knows you're some skin monkey's pet, Tippy-Toe," Miranda said.

My teeth ground together. *Skin monkey.* Hearing that mound rat apply the slur to Doreen made my blood boil. And *pet*?

I put my face in front of hers. "Is this cracked chitter from Big Daddy Spud himself? Or are you being a cat-addled branch dropping on your own time?"[54]

Miranda smirked. "Nice leash," she said, flicking the bow around my neck with a claw. "Your skin monkey owner give you that, little pet?"

Fast as a snake, my paws were around Miranda's throat, lifting her off the ground. Her companions twitched to move, but I rattled my tail at them.

"Stay where you are, or Miranda loses an ear."

Their eyes darted from me to Miranda and back again, but they kept position.

Miranda's hind paws raked the air, and her front paws tried to pry mine away. "Yeah . . . right," she said with a wheeze. "My ear. What are you going to do, chew it off?"

I smiled, showing my sharpest teeth.

"Lookit, Todd! Lookit," said a human voice. We'd been too

---

54 Jersey squirrel dialect is a tough nut to crack, isn't it? I think this part means, "Did Big Daddy Spud give you the order to disrespect me, or are you acting on your own?"

occupied with our own quarrel to notice the approach. An adult female human, older than Doreen, stared down at us. Her feet were blocking my escape. I dropped Miranda.

Another human joined her. Todd, apparently.

"Geez, Tammy," he said. "It's a whole . . . gopher . . . village."

The lot of us squirrels groaned, almost at once. For all our differences, many of our struggles were the same. Humans. Calling us gophers would be like us mistaking them for gorillas.

"Naw, naw, Todd," said Tammy. She pointed at Miranda. "That there's a groundhog, and them little ones are chipmunks."

Todd pointed at me. "What's that one then? Some kinda cat?"

Miranda laughed. Cats are not particularly respected in our community.

Tammy furrowed her brow. "Naw, that there's a rat. One of them pretty rats they sell at the pet store."

Miranda laughed harder.

"Them pretty rats are called *ferrets*," Todd said.

"Well la-de-da, Mister Doctor Professor Todd," Tammy said.

Miranda made a break for it, attempting to dart between Tammy's legs, but Todd kicked her back. Miranda tumbled, coming to a stop with a groan at my feet. *Things just got real.*

"Should we eat 'em, T-Dog?"

"GROSS, NO! Let's just stomp 'em," Todd said, and began to stomp.

Usually humans aren't fast enough to actually get us, but Miranda wasn't moving, and she was slow to begin with.

Quickly, before he could stomp Miranda, I scampered straight to Todd's foot, up his leg, across his chest, and onto his face. He screamed.

"Getitoff, getitoff!"

"I got it!" Tammy yelled, and hammered her fist toward the spot on Todd's face where I was clinging. But when her fist landed, I was somewhere else. I was on Tammy's face.

Todd groaned, pressing his hands to where Tammy had punched him. I stared into Tammy's wide, terrified eyes. I grabbed her cheeks with my paws.

"WE ARE SQUIRRELS," I yelled. "NOT GROUNDHOGS. NOT CATS. NOT RATS. NOT! FERRETS! SQUIRRELS!"

She didn't understand. No human ever understands. Except Doreen. Even so, when I leaped to the ground, she ran away. Todd followed quickly after, whimpering into his hands.

One of Miranda's companions was laughing. I'd seen him around before: a slim, quick fella by the name of Puffin Furslide.

"Shut it, Puffin," said Miranda, rolling to her feet. She ambled in my direction. "You grabbed me. Nobody grabs me."

"She saved you, Miranda," Puffin said. "That human was gonna straight-down paw-stomp you."

Miranda cast a dark glare at her companion, and an even darker one at me.

"Big Daddy Spud is going to hear about this," she said. "And then you'll be in sticky sap."

"I hope he does," I said. "That's all I was twitching for. Tell him I'd like a meeting. We have nuts to sort of mutual interest."

Miranda snarled and scampered away. Her two companions moved to do the same, but I grabbed them both by the tails. "And you two squeaks . . . when she cracks open the story, make sure the fruit of it is the truth."

They nodded. Puffin even said "Yes, ma'am," which I took to be a good sign.

I let them go, and scampered back to the trees. I had work to do. Big Daddy would be in touch, and that meant I had a family meeting to plan.

10

ANA SOFÍA

*W*hen Ana Sofía walked to Union Junior High the next day, a couple of girls were waiting out front.

"Ana Sofía!" shouted Lucy Tang—the petite seventh grader with short black hair. She looked annoyed, so Ana Sofía guessed Lucy had probably been shouting her name for a while and getting more and more irritated that Ana Sofía hadn't answered. As if she'd been ignoring her on purpose. Ana Sofía rolled her eyes and briefly considered the on-purpose ignoring after all.

Lucy said something else Ana Sofía didn't catch, and she gave up and walked closer.

"What?" asked Ana Sofía.

Lucy glared.[55] "My brother, Vin. Do you know him? He's a

---

55 Don't even try it, Lucy. You will not win a glaring contest against Ana Sofía.

LARPer, and he said you know the Jersey Ghost. He said it saved you. Is that true?"

"Well . . . kinda . . ."

The girls stood there, hugging their textbooks to their chests, mascaraed eyes blinking. Usually people didn't stare at Ana Sofía. Usually people pretended she wasn't there at all. In her better moods, when she was up for some benefit-of-the-doubting, she supposed most people weren't trying to be mean. They probably thought it was more polite to ignore the deaf girl than to engage in a conversation that might turn awkward if she couldn't understand them.

Ana Sofía glared. "What?"

"The Somebodies want the details," said Lucy's redheaded friend. "Tell us about it."

Ana Sofía glared harder. They didn't budge. Usually two glares did it.[56] People, she'd learned, hate awkwardness more than hatred itself. But today these girls cared more about the Jersey Ghost than an awkward run-in with the deaf girl.

So she gave in and told them about how Squirrel Girl had saved her last night. As briefly as possible. And she thought that would be the end of it.

By the time she left second-period Pre-Calculus, a slightly larger group of students was waiting outside her classroom door.

---

56 Glares are kinda her super power.

"Can you tell us about it?" they asked.

Ana Sofía glared. They didn't budge. She sighed and gave in quicker this time, telling the story and expanding it just a bit more.

After third-period US History, there wasn't just *a* larger group waiting. *The* group was waiting. The Somebodies themselves.

"So . . . what happened?" asked Heidi, twirling a lock of blond hair around her index finger.

Ana Sofía swallowed, only her throat was too dry. She *definitely* didn't care what the Somebodies thought of her. Or anybodies for that matter. And yet, all their expectant eyes on her, their gum-chewing mouths closed, their attention like a spotlight . . .

"Well . . . I was in the park last night, just walking home. . . ."

And she told the story. The whole story this time, excluding Doreen, of course. Doreen hadn't been there, after all. It'd been a stranger with a tail and heroic intentions.

As Ana Sofía spoke, she felt the tightness in her chest loosen; her spine seemed to lengthen. A crowd was gathered in the hallway, eyes on her. Usually her hearing aids turned the constant background noise of school into a fretful buzzing inside her brain. But now, silence. Total rapt attention.

"And then she picked me up as if I weighed nothing, placed me on her shoulders, and leaped. So fast, so high, for a moment, I thought we were flying. The ground was a blur far below. The stars seemed close enough to grab. There in midair I asked her, 'Who are you?' And she smiled and said, 'Who, me? Why, I'm Squirrel Girl.'"

Squirrel Girl . . . Squirrel Girl . . . She could see lips repeating the name with wonder and excitement.

Except for the Somebodies. They looked at one another and shrugged.

Ike, a boy with brown hair sweeping across his forehead, was talking for a bit before Ana Sofía looked at him, so she didn't catch it all, but at the end he maybe said, "A girl who looks like a squirrel?"

Jude, a boy with even sweepier hair, said something else to the group, but by the time she'd looked at him, she'd missed too much of it to guess the rest.

Yanni, the boy with sweepiest hair, was looking right at her when he said, "She sounds kinda lame."

"'Lame' is an ableist term," Ana Sofía muttered.

"What?" asked Heidi.

"Nothing," said Ana Sofía. She could feel a powerful glare coming on like some people felt the approach of a migraine.

"Okay, you can go now," said Heidi.

The crowd dispersed. Ana Sofía exhaled. But someone remained. Straight dark hair almost to his shoulders.

Vin Tang. His desk had been next to hers in fifth grade. Or was it sixth? They'd been on the same Math Heroes team. And he used to fold origami horses and leave them on her chair. She'd been certain he'd forgotten about her, until last night when he'd called her by name. For sure he'd forgotten about those little paper horses, but she still used one as a bookmark.

He waved to get her attention. "Hey. Hi." He smiled, then looked at his feet, then back at her again.

"Hey, Vin."

"Would you come with me? I want to show you something."

He led her away from the cafeteria to the quiet back hallway by the music room. Suddenly there before her were the dozen characters who'd stuck her in a pillory just last night.

Her stomach turned cold. She started to back away.

"Wait," said Vin.

Two others unrolled a ten-foot parchment and held it up like a banner. In fancy, inky calligraphy were the huge words:

We Begeth Your Forgiveness

"Um . . . you're sorry?" asked Ana Sofía.

Vin shrugged. "Yes, but we're sorry . . ."

Ana Sofía couldn't make out the last part. She shook her head. "You're sorry what?"

"We're sorry," Vin said, then finger-spelled the word *medievally.*

Ana Sofía couldn't help smiling. Vin smiled back, and she

understood both that he was aware that the LARPer stuff could get a little silly and that he still loved it. She could respect that.

"You, fair Ana Sofía, are her pard, and we honor you," said the baron, bowing. He looked much skinnier without his cape and all.

"I'm her pard?" Ana Sofía asked, wrinkling her nose. "How did that even become a thing?"[57]

"No, *bard*," said the baron. "You tell her story. What power you hold!" He lifted a fist to the ceiling and shook it as if consumed with the idea of fabulous bardish power. "She is fierce and cunning, and we swear we will follow no other liege but . . ." He raised an eyebrow, waiting for Ana Sofía's permission to name her.

"Squirrel Girl?" said Ana Sofía.

They all nodded, mumbling things to one another that she didn't catch, but their faces seemed pleased.

"Please, Lady Ana Sofía, gift her this from us." Vin handed Ana Sofía a leather belt. It looked handcrafted and resembled the ones in their LARPer costumes, but this had several utility pouches attached all the way around. And he'd worked images of acorns into the leather.

"You know what, she's gonna love this." Ana Sofía had an idea. "I wish you had your swords."

---

57 Ana Sofía may have finally agreed that we're best friends, but she won't budge on "pards." That's cool, I'll just say it in my head.

In an instant, one pulled a sword out of her duffel bag and handed it to her. Ana Sofía could see now that the blade was dull, though it was heavy. A prop more than a weapon, but a prop that could definitely clunk someone pretty hard on the head.

"Kneel," Ana Sofía said grandly.

All dozen dropped gratefully to a knee. One by one she tapped their shoulders with the sword tip.

"I dub you, each of you, a . . . uh . . . a *Squirrel Scout*, the very first Squirrel Scouts! Sworn to uphold justice, defend the weak, inspire the strong, and be valiant servants to our hero: Squirrel Girl!"

They lifted their fists into the air and repeated, "Squirrel Girl!"

Ana Sofía tried very hard not to laugh out loud. And yet at the same time she almost felt like crying. Like, happy crying. Was that a thing? 'Cause Ana Sofía was starting to believe that might be a thing. This thing—all things, frankly—had been easier before Doreen, when Shady Oaks was a hopeless mess and there was nothing ever to look forward to.

Hope was as confusing as $[T_{recon} = \sqrt[5]{T_A^2(L/12)^3}]$.[58]

"And this is for you, or whatever," said Vin. He placed something in her hand, then hurried away. It was an origami unicorn pressed into superthin leather.

---

58 Yep, definitely confusing.

Ana Sofía left the LARPers in rapture over their new callings as Squirrel Scouts and hurried to the cafeteria. She checked her pocket three times to make sure the leather unicorn hadn't fallen out.

"There you are!" said Doreen, waiting by the doors.

"Everyone's talking about—" Ana Sofía made a sign Doreen hadn't seen before. Her left hand formed the sign for an *S*, a fist with thumb across the fingers. Her right hand made a *G*, the index finger pointing. She swept the *G* hand away from the *S* hand almost as if it were a long, beautiful tail flowing behind a very specific girl.

"Wait, what was that?" said Doreen. "That last sign?"

Ana Sofía finger-spelled *S-Q-U-I-R-R-E-L G-I-R-L*.

"This?" Doreen swept the *G* away from the *S*. "This means *me*?"

Her mouth hung open; her eyes were wide and glinty. She did the sign again. And then she laughed.

"What's funny?" Ana Sofía asked, tensing for Doreen to say something ignorant about her signing or her deafness.

"You made up a name sign for me," Doreen signed. "You made up a sign for Squirrel Girl, as if she were a real person."

Doreen picked Ana Sofía up in a super-powered hug and spun around. Ana Sofía's stomach seemed to follow a second later, and she almost feared Doreen was lifting her to the ceiling. Ana Sofía glanced into the cafeteria to see if anyone had noticed how easily Doreen had picked her up. But everyone was busy stuffing their faces with sandwiches—and jabbering about Squirrel Girl, probably. Ana Sofía couldn't help but smile. Her cheeks protested, they were so out of practice, but she insisted. *Smile enacted.*

"So, what are we going to do tonight?" Ana Sofía signed when Doreen had put her down. "Walk the neighborhood? Catch bad guys? Audition for the Avengers? Save the world?"

"Um . . . well . . ." Doreen grimaced. "Actually I'm grounded. I told my mom what I did, and I guess I can't be Squirrel Girl anymore."

Doreen tried to smile like it was no big deal, but her chin betrayed her, quivering.

And just like that, Ana Sofía's weird, uncomfortable but somehow sparkly and alluring new bubble of hope popped.

"You can't?" she said.

"Tail tucked away forever," said Doreen.[59] "But thanks for making me feel like her, for a few days anyway. I really felt like her. That was unbelievably cool."

They sat at their usual table and ate in silence. Doreen picked through her trail mix, only eating the macadamia nuts and not even bothering with her second and third sandwiches. Sometimes she adjusted in her seat as if her tail were aching.[60]

---

59 Oh, man, I was feeling *soooo* bummed.
60 It was, but not as much as my heart. :(

Mike joined them, glowering over his home lunch—a bag of chips, a sleeve of cookies, and a candy bar. Without even looking at Doreen and Ana Sofía he began grumbling. Ana Sofía was able to catch some of what he said, and knowing Mike, was able to fill in the rest.

"Everybody's talking about that idiotic Jersey Ghost thing," he said. "Clearly not a ghost. Stupid to even call it that. Probably it's just some freak who was born with a tail. What kind of a freak has a tail, anyway? Some attention-hungry loner messing with other people's lives. This is the most annoying day ever. If I have to hear one more person gush about whatever thing that freak really is I'm going to explode. The freak better not show up again."

Doreen sighed, as if to say, *No need to worry about that now.*

Mike had been sitting at Ana Sofía's table since last year. He rarely spoke except to complain about how awful everything was. And honestly, she'd never really disagreed with him. Then entered Doreen, bursting like a fireball of optimism. Only now that fireball seemed extinguished. Maybe Mike had things right after all. Maybe there really was no point. To anything.

Ana Sofía pulled her notebook out of her bag. The purple cover was fading and bent from overuse, the edges of the paper soft as tissues. She flipped through the notes she'd been taking for the past two years, again scanning for a pattern.

Maybe she would postpone giving up. Maybe it was time to go hard-core detective.

11

DOREEN

*D*oreen was jamming to some dance tunes, so at first she didn't hear the light tapping of squirrel claws on her bedroom window.

Music was a kind of emotional food to Doreen. She was always hungry for literal food. There didn't seem to be enough in the world to quiet her demanding belly. Her crazy-high metabolism and thick, powerful muscles needed constant nourishment. And sometimes her emotions were like that—yipping and yapping and desperate for *something*. Dancing hard to good music was like an all-you-can-eat buffet for her feelings.

"*'It ain't fair!'*" she sang, holding her hairbrush like a microphone. "*'It ain't right! How you make me feel like my ribs are too tight! My heart just might burst, my head's all a'swim, but there's just no way I'll let you in!'*"

The tapping stopped. Doreen spotted Tippy-Toe, who was staring at her with round, wet eyes. She threw open the window.

"Not you, Tip! I'll always let you in. I'm just trying to jam away some feelings."

"*Chet-chik,*" said Tippy-Toe.

"The dogs? Well, you kind of have to expect crazy from *wild dogs*, right?" said Doreen.

"*Chkka-chtl cht,*" Tippy-Toe said.

"That's terrible, but . . . Ugh! I'm not supposed to go out. . . ."

"*Chuck-chuck.*"

"Well, if you've got a big meeting of squirrel families tonight, I can certainly understand why you'd want to make sure the dogs wouldn't be a problem. And it's just not Doreen Green style to let down her BSFFAEAE.[61] But I can't go anywhere but my babysitting job tonight. I'm grounded. Like a tree squirrel whose parents make her live in a burrow while she thinks very hard about her life choices."

Tippy-Toe sneezed a disappointed sneeze. The sound struck Doreen like a tiny arrow in her loyal heart. She was, in no uncertain terms, totally bummed to be letting down her friend.

After Tippy left, Doreen packed her babysitting bag with all of baby Dante Santino's favorites—cow puppet, board book

---

61 Not Boy-Band Songs for Festivals, Art Events and Entertaining, of course. That's BBSFAEAE. I meant Best Squirrel Friend Forever and Ever and Ever. Don't tell Monkey Joe, 'kay?

about frogs, horse-head mask, and squeaky toy shaped like a banana—adding her bear-eared hoodie and the utility belt the LARPers had made for her. Then she removed the hoodie and belt. Then she put them back on again. What could it hurt, just to check that a friend was okay?

She leaped down the stairs first before tucking in her tail. Leaping was always easier with a five-foot tail out for balance.

"Mom, I'm going to the Santinos'," she called from the front door.

Doreen expected her mom to say, *Already? Aren't you early?* But instead she just said, "Okay, have fun!"

Doreen stopped in the threshold and sighed. Then she went back. Her mom was in her studio in the front room, painting tiny faces onto tiny sculptures of elves.[62]

"I know I'm grounded, but I'm going to go to the park on the way because Tippy-Toe needs my help, okay?"

Maureen Green frowned. The grumpy cat face embroidered on her sweatshirt seemed to mirror her own expression. She pointed at Doreen with a paintbrush, size 000.

"No tail?" she asked.

"No tail," said Doreen. "I promise."

A tiny voice inside Doreen's head whispered, *Maybe she's*

---

62 Then she sells them online. Some people don't want to paint their own Paint-Your-Own Elves™ but still want to own painted Paint-Your-Own Elves™, so she does decent business.

ashamed of you. Maybe she wants you to hide your tail because she thinks you're a freak.

Nuh-uh, Doreen thought at it.

Uh-huh, the tiny voice argued back, sounding a bit like Mike. *Why else the obsession with hiding your tail? Maybe the other kids wouldn't really be jealous, like she's always said. Mike certainly wouldn't be.*

Doreen couldn't argue with that.

Maureen was still considering the situation. Finally she said, "Okay, then. A Green never lets down a friend."

It was still daylight out. The air coming from the park was so thick with tree pollen Doreen thought she could eat it. Birds were chirping at the sinking sun, bees still hummed over autumn blossoms.

There sure were a lot of bees out that afternoon. So much buzzing! Not to mention barking.

Three dogs were in the park, yipping and galloping and chasing squirrels. And one another. Anything really. One was barking at a leaf as it twitched in the wind.

"Easy, doggies!" said Doreen. "Calm the freak down!"

Yelling "calm the freak down" didn't seem to make any difference whatsoever. Since that had been plan A, now Doreen tried to think up a plan B.

Doreen could sense scores of squirrels high in the trees, trembling. Tippy-Toe came leaping from a tree onto her shoulder.

"Chkucht. Chitter-chit," she said.

"No problem, I couldn't leave you hanging like that. You're

right, this is weird, and not the good kind. What's their deal? Plus are you hearing that buzzing? I don't see any bees."

Tippy-Toe sniffed. Doreen cocked her head. Tippy-Toe pointed with one tiny claw. Doreen followed, climbed a tree, and zeroed in on something so tiny she almost didn't notice it embedded in the bark. Her retractable claws came out and she used them to cut it loose. It was the size of a ladybug, made of metal and plastic, and emitted a high-pitched buzz. A small circle of clear glass or plastic in its center looked a little like a creepy doll eye.

Doreen crushed it between her thumb and finger. Its buzzing stopped.

And yet the air was still vibrating with the squeaky hum.

"Chekk," said Tippy-Toe.

"Yeah, I bet normal humans can't hear the buzzing at all. But to dogs, maybe hearing that sound feels like someone stabbing a carrot in your ear."

"Chuk-chuk."

"You're right, a needle would hurt worse than a carrot, but I was trying not to be too gruesome. No wonder those dogs are going crazy. And look at this, Tip," said Doreen, examining the tiny crushed machine. "On the bottom? 'MM.' Those letters were on the squirrel traps. The same jerky-jerk who made those traps is now making dogs go so crazy they're terrorizing squirrels even more than normal. MM sure has it out for squirrels."

Doreen and Tippy tracked down several more of the strange little shrieking robot bugs, but oodles of them must have been hidden all over the park, because the air still buzzed with the noise of invisible bees.

"I'm sorry, I have to go, Tip," said Doreen. "The Santinos are waiting for me. Can I at least transport you past the dogs?"

Tippy-Toe and a couple dozen of her clan leaped onto Doreen's head and arms, hooking onto her shirt and pants, and Doreen ran them out of the park beyond the crazed canines.

The squirrels leaped to a front-yard tree to continue on their way. But one gray squirrel with a fetching pink bow looked back. Her small black eyes seemed to brim with disappointment at leaving Doreen behind.

Doreen sighed. Obviously she could never be a hero, no matter what Ana Sofía said. Doreen would bet her entire glass squirrel collection that none of the Avengers had homework or babysitting jobs. Or lived with their parents who sometimes grounded them for not tucking their tail into their stretchy pants.

Then again, a number of Avengers did wear stretchy pants. Maybe Captain America or the Hulk had a tail in there, rodent or otherwise. . . .

Nah.

12

TIPPY-TOE

*F*or the time being, I had to drop the dog problem. We were used to avoiding the curs anyway, but until I could manage to get rid of those buzz-machines that were making them crazy, we would just have to be more careful.

Word had come through the squirrel network that Big Daddy Spud of the ground squirrels would meet with me behind the abandoned Burger-N-Bean Bowl. Humans used the old lot to toss their heaps of trash. No self-respecting squirrel would nest there. Neutral territory.

You usually brought two or three escort squeaks to these kinds of meets. I brought Fuzz Fountain Cortez because she could race a falling raindrop and beat it to the ground, and Bear Bodkin because he could crack a nut with nothing but his paws.

When we arrived, a half dozen ground squirrels stopped us, squat tails up. In front crouched Pug Muffintop. She used to be famous, that one. When I was a tot, she came to town with the circus but stayed behind when the circus left. Now she was just an old groundie who used to wrestle cats for peanuts.

"Just you," said Pug.

Cortez's and Bear's tails twitched, agitated. My stomach felt tight as an acorn in its shell. If Miranda's account of events was slanted, Big Daddy Spud might well be setting up a trap. Could he do me in and then seize leadership of the tree squirrels?

I spotted Puffin Furslide, the groundie who'd called me *ma'am*.

"Hey, Puffin, did Miranda chitter true to Spud about our little husking earlier?"

"Total peaches," he said. "Or half a peach, anyway. I thatched the spots that she left out."

"Cortez, Bear, I trust this squeak. Nest here for a bit. I'm going in."

"This is some sour bark, Tips," Cortez said. "You on top?"

"Solid like ironwood, cousin." I walked into the lot alongside Puffin knowing I hadn't really answered Cortez's question.

Big Daddy Spud was perched on a mound in the center of the dump. He was way bigger than a ground squirrel should be. There were rumors that his mother was a marmot.

"Tippy-Toe! Leaves above, it's good to see you!" he shouted. "So nice of you to scamper by."

The dump mounds were alive with chitters and the flickering glints of ground squirrel eyes. The territory was not so neutral after all.

"This your burrow now, Spud?" I asked. I looked to the open sky above. "Seems like you could get caught with your tails out. You opening a hawk buffet?"

Spud giggled. It was a strange sound to hear coming from such a large rodent. "No eater-birds pass these mounds anymore, not ones that we can't beak-shuck and send back to Eggtown. But to answer your question," he said, gesturing around the lot-turned-garbage-dump, "this is an off-track burrow. Used for special occasions."

"Honored to be special," I said.

"You should be," he said. "But chew before spit, cousin. Let me apologize for the cat-wrangling done to you by Miranda Creepsforth. She was not acting under orders. Not 'root to branch,' as you tree squeaks say."

"Nuts under the hoard," I said, willing to let it go.

"Nuts indeed," Spud said. "And peaches in the end, as you wanted to chitter straight."

"Yes," I said. "You've seen the traps? The ones made to catch squeaks?"

"Made to *kill* squeaks, you mean," he said.

"That's them," I said.

"Seen them eye-and-tooth myself," he said. "And we've lost two of our family to them in our very own burrows."

"Underground?" I asked. "I've only ever seen them in trees and parks."

"The traps nest where squirrels nest. Which, as you know, is everywhere."

"Ground and tree mean nothing to these bad weevils, whoever they may be. To them we are the same. I think the season has come to unite."

"But who is root and who is branch, Tippy-Toe?" he asked. "Do you lead *my* people? Puffin Furslide seems to trust you, but I suspect most of us think you don't give a nuthusk about 'groundies.' Would you allow me to govern your people?"

"Naw," I said. "I wouldn't. But the need for unity stands."

"I have a suggestion. . . ." But he trailed off, his expression distant. Then the big squirrel stood up on hind legs and called out: "POTTY BREAK!"

About fifty ground squirrels, nosing out of the heaps of trash, fell in line behind Big Daddy Spud as he lumbered to a dark mound in the corner of the lot.

Puffin Furslide was at the back of the line, and I called him over.

"Do you guys always do this?" I whispered. "Go potty at the same time?"

"As long as I can remember, yeah," he said. "Unified waste management is very important to the boss."

Squirrels began exiting the potty mound. Big Daddy Spud climbed back onto his perch.

"Now," he chittered, "where were we?"

"You had a suggestion," I squeaked, trying not to laugh at the whole potty thing. The situation was tense enough as it was.

"I did," Spud said. "It is this: I offer you military command of our mighty squirrels, but only to husk the nut of our mysterious enemy."

There were gasps from the burrows. Big Daddy Spud raised a silencing paw. "This I will do *if*," he added, "you are able to prove yourself a worthy warrior by defeating a superior opponent."

He slapped the ground three times, and out of that distant dark heap, the one they had all gone potty in, thundered an honest-to-nuts true-blood marmot. If I thought Spud was big, this thing was clearly here to teach me what big really was. The creature stomped to Spud's side, its fur glistening with what I hoped was sweat.

"Gross," I whispered, unable to stop myself.

"This is Cletus Scampersaw, my brother from another mother," said Big Daddy Spud.

I wanted to ask him if he was really sure about the "*another mother*" part, but now probably wasn't the time. I also wanted to confirm the moisture on Cletus's fur was sweat. But again, not a good time.

"Cletus is my top warrior," Spud said. "If you can best him in battle, I will know you have the right combination of strength and smarts to guide my people to victory."

I fight to survive. Or to right wrongs. Or for revenge. Or, at least on one occasion, for an orange gumdrop. But I don't fight for sport. And fighting my own kind, even cousins like marmots, felt like shelling a nut twice.

"Isn't there some way—?" I started to say.

But Spud shouted, "Cletus! Fight!" And the marmot charged.

I leaped, sailing over Cletus, but he bucked his head as I did, knocking one of my legs mid-flight. My landing was not as graceful as I would have liked, and as soon as I was on my feet again, Cletus had turned and was charging again. We moved like this, charging and leaping, charging and leaping. I couldn't think of a way to win without seriously hurting him, and I certainly didn't want to hurt him. We might need this warrior's help in our fight against the trap-maker.

He charged again, and I leaped again—only this time he stopped short, rearing up on his hind legs. He caught my tail and threw me to the ground. I managed to roll away before he pounced, and then twisted back to grab hold of his moist back fur. He reared, but I leaped fully atop his back, clinging to his fur with all four paws. It was a wild ride, and everyone was shouting. But the tone of the shouts started to change from excitement to panic. Then I heard it, too.

Big paws slapping the earth. Rapid breathing. The screams of squirrel guards, and then, above it all, Cortez's panicked shouting.

"DOG!" she yelled, a split second before the beast was upon us.

13

DOREEN

*T*hat night, Dante Santino was voted Cutest Baby in the World by the National Organization of Awesomest Babysitters. The NOAB had a single member: Doreen Green. After casting the winning vote for Dante, Doreen made a paper crown and placed it on his head.

"*Gaba!*" said Dante by way of his acceptance speech. He was sitting up on the floor and gnawing on an Iron Man action figure.

"You know his facial hair is compensating for a lack of tail," said Doreen.

"*Bap!*"

"Totally," said Doreen.[63]

---

63 I don't know what "bap" meant, but I'm sure it was something like "tails are awesome." It is what a squirrel would say, and Dante is as close to a squirrel as you can get without actually being one. Or being me. I'm probably a little closer. Because of the tail.

The awards ceremony was interrupted by the distinctive sound of squirrel claws tapping at the window. Doreen lifted Dante onto her hip and went to open the window to Tippy-Toe. Only it wasn't Tippy-Toe.

"Oh! Hi!" said Doreen. "You're one of Tippy's friends, right? Fuzz Fountain Cortez? What can I—?"

The squirrel was spasming with excitement, pointing and chittering, tail wagging.[64] She hopped down onto the carpet and tried pushing Doreen's legs toward the door.

"Hang on, what's up?"

"Chkktchkktchkkt . . ."

Doreen gasped. "Is Tippy-Toe in trouble? But . . . but . . ."

She looked at Dante. Dante grabbed her nose and said, "Buh! Buh!"

A minute later, Doreen was running. And Dante was strapped to her chest in a baby carrier. He faced forward, his arms and legs kicking wildly with excitement, his mouth open in a huge grin.

Doreen ran so fast, Cortez gave up and rode on her shoulder. Doreen ran so fast, she had to release her tail just to keep her balance. She ran so fast maybe she could have raced raindrops with Cortez and won.

She pulled up short in the impromptu garbage dump behind the decaying Burger-N-Bean-Bowl.

---

64 "Tail wagging" sounds like a dog, and squirrels do not like being compared to dogs, thank you very much. Probably "tail waving around" would be a better description and prevent an angry squirrel uprising.

There were squirrels everywhere. They were all speaking at once, creating a unified chittering noise, impossible to understand. The squirrels gathered around Doreen and pushed her forward. She couldn't tell what the furry wall wanted her to see till she found herself standing before a sudden and very deep pit.[65] And in the pit were three creatures: Tippy-Toe, a second squirrel of considerable girth the others referred to as Big Daddy Spud, and a large black dog. The dog was going cuckoo, barking and growling, both trying to jump out *and* nip the squirrels. And the squirrels were both trying to jump out *and* keep from being nipped by the dog. Sooner or later, someone was going to get nipped.

Easy-peasy! Doreen would just jump in, grab the dog, hold it still while Tippy and Big Daddy Spud escaped, and then climb out with the dog in her arms. . . . Oh. She had a baby on her chest.

Dante shook his tiny fists and declared, "BAH! BAH! BAH!"

"Chkkt!" all the squirrels said, noticing the baby for the first time. They lifted their heads to smell the infant. There was a kind of reverence in their eyes.

"Squirrels like babies, right?" said Doreen. "You'll take care of him?"

She unstrapped Dante and set him down, looking for the cleanest spot. But she needn't have bothered. The baby's bum never touched the earth, cushioned instead on the backs of

---

65 Yeah, so I found out later that this "MM" had digger robots make pit traps since I'd been destroying some of his other animal traps. Jerk.

dozens of squirrels who threw themselves beneath him. Dante giggled on his squirmy, tilty fur rug.

That left Doreen free. She jumped down. Tippy-Toe leaped onto Doreen's head and from there out of the hole; Big Daddy Spud followed her. The dog leaped, too, teeth bared, straight at Spud's tail, but Doreen caught him first. She hugged him while he struggled.

"Easy, boy, easy," she said. With the dog in her arms, she jumped straight up out of the hole and landed on the garbage heap. She pulled some rope out of her utility belt, tied it around his neck, and secured him to a post. Embedded in the post was one of those creepy buzzing doll-eyed bug-machine things. Doreen yanked it out and smashed it.

"We gotta do something about the dogs around here," she said. "They aren't happy, and they sure as heck aren't making squirrel lives any easier."

But no squirrels were listening to her. They were all gathered under and around Dante, sniffing him, tickling him with their tails, leaping over his head in joyful acrobatics that made him squeal with pleasure.

"Squirrels sure like babies," said Doreen.

Tippy-Toe sneezed, the kind of sneeze that meant, *We don't just like babies, we* adore *babies.*

Then Tippy-Toe sneezed a can-I-get-your-attention sneeze. The squirrels' gleeful chirps hushed and they looked to Tippy-Toe, who stood high on a discarded lamp. From that stage,

Tippy-Toe recounted many tales from squirrel folklore. It was humans who first stole squirrels from the forests and brought them into the park. The squirrels didn't trust the humans and wouldn't stay. And just try keeping squirrels somewhere they don't want to be.

But then one day the park added a playground and sandbox. And the playground and sandbox attracted babies.

"*Chkkt,*" said Tippy-Toe.

The other squirrels nodded. "*Chkkt,*" they said in unison.

Babies. Babies smelled interesting. They spoke a language more full of *coo* than *chuk*, but it clearly had developed from the same morphological root as Chitterspeak.[66] And most importantly, babies were always dropping food. Squirrels were certain that the food-dropping thing was on purpose: babies recognized squirrels as significant beings and so made them offerings in the form of delicious sidewalk food. Squirrel folklore was full of stories about babies dropping treasures like peanut butter sandwiches, peeled bananas, half-full packets of gummy bears, and on one legendary occasion, an *entire* hazelnut layer cake (frosted).

Not to mention that babies were closer to squirrel size than to human size. Plus the "cute" thing.

All this made babies and squirrels natural allies. Once babies had entered the parks, squirrels decided it must be safe for them as well. Wherever squirrels roamed, they watched out for babies.

---

66 Fun fact: I first learned the meaning of "morphological root" from a squirrel. Squirrels are crazy into linguistics. They appreciate the roots and branches of things.

And in turn, babies honored squirrels with coos, drool, and the occasional upended baggie of honey nut cereal.

"*Chkkt-chuky chook,*" said Tippy-Toe.

And the squirrels nodded solemnly.

Dante made a wet raspberry sound. The nearby squirrels who were splashed with his saliva smeared it across their foreheads like war paint.

Big Daddy Spud cleared his throat, making a tiny squeak. The other squirrels paused their adoration of the baby. Spud then spoke many things in Chitterspeak that basically amounted to this:

> *This Squirrel Girl is good.*
>
> *1. She smells like nuts. This means she is wise.*
>
> *2. She has a tail. This means she is mighty.*
>
> *3. She speaks the blessed tongue. This means she is big-brained.*
>
> *4. She fights the dogs for us. This means she is fearless.*
>
> *5. She is a friend to babies. This means she is not evil.*

Then Big Daddy Spud climbed up Squirrel Girl as if she were the trunk of a tree, put his paw on her cheek, and tickled her ear with his tail.

"*Chktt-kit,*" he said.

Doreen's throat closed off, her eyes got wet. She'd only just met him, but he too accepted her by her treasured secret name: Squirrel Girl.

"Thank you," she managed to say.

Dozens of squirrels did the same, one after another, telling her their names and welcoming her into the clan. *Chktt-kit.* And when they spoke her name, they called her Squirrel Girl.

Doreen was so happy she sniffled, and her vision went fishbowl with the wetness of happy tears. It is a truly magical feeling to be hugged by a hundred squirrels at the same time.[67]

"Thanks, amigos," said Doreen. "I've never really belonged to a clan—"

She got too sniffly to say anything more. But squirrels get it. They get emotion. They twitched their tails. And Dante spoke for everyone as he declared, "Gaga-booga!"

"Anyhoo," said Doreen after a minute, wiping her eyes, "the dogs have been a problem. Tippy and I figured out they're super-bugged by these buzzing things that look like . . ." Doreen cocked her head, listening. She followed a faint buzz to another tiny metal bug clamped to the side of the old restaurant. "Like this! Let's find and destroy all the bugs in this lot so it can be a safe zone for the dogs. They'll want to stay here where they won't go cuckoo from the high-pitched bug sounds, and then squirrels will be safe from roaming dogs everywhere else. A plan?"

Doreen strapped Dante back into her carrier, this time with his belly facing hers. And she began to run. He laid his head

---

67 If you're ever, like, on a cruise or something and you have the choice of shore excursions between swimming with dolphins, riding an elephant, or being hugged by a hundred squirrels, I highly recommend choosing the last one.

on her chest and soon fell asleep, while she located, grabbed, leashed, and hauled the wild dogs back to the empty lot, where the squirrels had cleared out all the strange buzzing metal bugs. Relieved of that awful high-pitched noise, the exhausted dogs curled up and fell asleep.

Sleeping dogs, sleeping baby—the strange evening ended on such a restful note. And yet Doreen couldn't relax. Who was MM? And what was their plan?

14

DOREEN

*D*oreen really did mean to tell her parents that she'd broken the no-tail rule again. She'd planned on confessing over their traditional Saturday-morning banana pancakes party and cartoon-a-thon. But she was so pooped from debugging the dog lot and racing back to the Santinos' before they got home, not to mention worrying about MM till past midnight, she slept in. *Oh well.* She could confess it that night over their traditional Saturday-night calzone fest and Scrabble tournament.

After her noon breakfast, she grabbed her twenty-six dollars of babysitting money and headed toward the corner market to see how much dog food she could buy. She worried there wasn't enough garbage for them to forage at the dump. It was a shame Shady Oaks didn't have an animal shelter.

Just as she opened the door to enter the market, a frizzy-haired woman was exiting, a six-pack of powdered doughnuts under her arm. Looking toward the parking lot, the woman stopped short and dropped the plastic container. It cracked open on the sidewalk.

"My car . . ." The woman began to breathe hard. "Someone took my car."

A blond woman coming out of the store heard her. "That's terrible! Was it stolen? You should call nine-one-one."

Doreen made a pivot and walked away from the store. She ducked behind a tree and checked her backpack for her hoodie. The sight of it gave her heart a thrill, and her tail twitched in her pants. *No. No!* She couldn't chase down a car, and in broad daylight no less.

"Chikka chik chuck?" chirped Tippy-Toe, hanging out on a branch above Doreen's head.

"Yes, I think those doughnuts *are* fair game," Doreen replied. "Adult humans believe sidewalks ruin doughnuts."

"Chikka chek."

"I know, T-Toe, humans are weird," said Doreen. "Knock yourself out."

Tippy-Toe leaped out of the tree and scurried around the frizzy-haired woman's feet. Then the squirrel deftly extracted a doughnut the size of her head, before scurrying away. The woman didn't notice. She was just standing there hyperventilating, staring at the empty parking spot.

"Honey, you want me to call nine-one-one for you?" the blond woman was asking. "What color is your car?"

"Maroon. It's maroon," said the hyperventilating woman. "I left the keys in the ignition. I was just going in the store for a second, and Rodney was asleep, and I didn't want to wake him up, the day is warm so I wanted the air conditioning on for him. . . ."

"Wait, who's Rodney?"

"Rodney is my baby," croaked the woman. "My baby was in the car." She snapped out of her daze, shook the other woman by the lapels, and yelled, "MY BABY IS IN THAT CAR!"

"That tears it," Doreen said. She pulled her hood over her head and freed her tail. "It's Squirrel Time!" Doreen said. She didn't love that she said it, but it just felt like a catchphrase moment.[68]

Doreen scrambled up the trunk of the tree to the highest branch and leaped, searching for a landing spot in midair. A roof! That would do. She leaned toward the roof and landed softly feetfirst into a run and *kept* running, *kept* leaping, from roof to roof till she found a three-story house with a wide view.

Yes, it was daytime. Yes, she was still grounded. Yes, she'd never run across strangers' rooftops before like this. But . . . a baby!

Plus, never, ever in her fourteen years had she ever felt so perfectly awesome.

Tippy-Toe caught up and hopped onto her shoulder. The fur around the squirrel's mouth was dusted white with powdered sugar.

---

68 I hadn't had much practice in catchphraseology. Yet.

"We're looking for a maroon car, Tip," said Doreen.

"Chuk chuk?"

"You're right, maroon *is* a weird word. I think it means brownish-red? The car was stolen, Tip."

Tippy-Toe shrugged and casually licked her fur clean of sugar.

"And there was a *baby* inside."

Tippy-Toe sat boldly upright. Never had a squirrel's eyes been filled with such righteous anger.

"Chikay?" Tippy-Toe whispered.

"No," Doreen said. "Not Dante. But still a baby. Named Rodney, I think."

Tippy nodded. She opened wide her toothy mouth and screeched. From all over the neighborhood, squirrels screeched with anger and readiness in response.

Squirrels really, really like babies.

"Chikky chuk," came a distant squirrel call.

Tippy-Toe began to dance and point.

"I heard it!" said Doreen. "One of our furry-tailed friends has spotted a maroon car driving past the deli that smells like cheese! Let's go, battle squirrel."

Together, girl and squirrel leaped off the roof and onto the next and the next.

They were crossing the last house on the row. In front of them ran a street.

"That road looks too wide," said Doreen. "I've never jumped that far."

Ana Sofía said Doreen could leap thirty feet. Was that thirty feet?

She didn't have time to measure, and she didn't slow. She leaped—across the sidewalk, above two lanes of street, over rushing cars, and onto the far sidewalk.

"Whoa," said Doreen, once her breath had caught up with her.

"Chik," said Tippy-Toe.

"Aw, thanks, T. I *am* awesome sometimes."

Up a tree, onto the next roof, and down another row, and Doreen spotted the maroon car driving erratically.

"Huh, it looks more brownish-purple to me, Tip."

Tippy-Toe squeaked in agreement.

"Stay back, T, let me take the car, okay? Squirrels and cars don't mix."

She was running at the same speed as the car along rooftops parallel to the street. She wished she knew how fast it was going so she could tell Ana Sofía later. The light turned red. Would it stop? Not a chance. When it sped through the red light, Doreen leaped from a roof onto a streetlight and then down hard onto the roof of the car.[69]

---

69 I was singing the Spider-Man theme song the whole time. You know the one I mean? It just felt like a Spider-Man moment. Also I was changing "spider" to "squirrel" and "man" to "girl." I mean, I knew I wasn't a hero or anything, I was just playing around.

She lowered her head upside down to peer in through the windshield. She saw an upside-down white man with a beard in an orange jacket. Though probably he wasn't actually upside down. She was the upside-down one. In the backseat, snuggled tight in his car seat, was a six-month-old baby, fast asleep.

"Aah!" said the driver, startled by upside-down Doreen.

"Excuse me, I think you should stop the car now," she said.

His widened eyes narrowed. He turned the steering wheel fast, as if to throw her off the car. Which was just rude. She had to dig her claws into the metal roof to keep from falling off.

"Stop that!" she said, peeking down again once he'd stopped swerving. "And don't be such a jerk. Just pull over, okay?"

He swerved again. She clung on.

"Jerk," she muttered.

But when she poked her head down again, she saw that the swerving and the screaming[70] had awakened the adorable little baby, and he was looking around with round, startled eyes.

"Oh no, don't cry!" said Doreen.

"What are you talking about?" asked the man. "I'm not crying! I'm perfectly at peace with my career choices!"

"Boo!" said Doreen to the baby, popping her head down against the windshield and up again, down and up. "Boo! Boo!"

"Wha . . . what are you doing, you freak?" he shouted.

---

70 His, not mine.

"Boo!"

The baby smiled.

The man swerved, just like a jerk would do.

Clearly he wasn't going to pull over. Doreen had seen a show once where someone cut a gas line to make a car stop. So Doreen slid down the windshield and perched on the front of the car. The car was going fast, and the ride was bumpy. Her tail shot out, helping her keep her balance on the narrow front bumper. The hood wouldn't unlatch, so she had to force it open with a shuddering screech of bending metal.

"Which one is the gas line?" she asked, just in case the driver decided to quit being a jerk and help her out.

"You're the one who's crying, probably!" he said. "'Cause you're the one with a freaky huge tail!"

Doreen shook her head. It was so sad, the way jealousy over their lack of tails made people say rude things.

She sliced a tube with her claw. Blue liquid oozed out. Not the gas line.

"Oops, um, FYI, better not try to use any windshield-wiping fluid."

The car careened through another red light and sideswiped a minivan. It tilted onto two tires and then came back down hard on all four. Doreen's claws cut holes into the hood. She pulled it down to check on the baby. Rodney's eyes were freaked-out round again, his little dimpled chin quivering.

"Oh no, don't be sad!" she said to the baby.

"You don't know me!" said the man. "And I'm not sad—I'm just a troubled soul!"

Doreen lifted the hood and lowered it fast. "Boo!" Lift and lower, lift and lower. "Boo! Boo!"

The man gaped. "WHAT IS THE MATTER WITH YOU?"

"Boo!" said Doreen. "Uh, buh-buh . . . boo!"

The man looked ready to yell at her again—which she really didn't appreciate, to be honest—but then the baby cooed from the backseat. He looked behind him.

"What the freak? There's a baby in here!"

The man swerved again, this time extra-swerve-y. And Doreen could feel that the car was about to tip.

Adrenaline pumping, rodent-instincts fired up, everything seemed to go slow-mo. She scrambled up the hood and, as the car tilted, ran along the high side of the car, past the driver, who was saying "Hooooooly—" *something*. He didn't finish. The car was almost completely sideways now. Doreen reached the back door and yanked it open, pulling as hard as she could. The hinges squealed and snapped. She dropped the door onto the street. She reached inside, slicing through the safety belt with her claws to free the car seat. Hugging the seat to her chest with both arms, she leaped free.

As she landed on the sidewalk, metal screeched, sparks flew, and glass shattered behind her. The car was upside-down sliding along the street, finally slamming into a parked car.

Doreen put down the car seat and crouched over the baby. "How's the little boy?" she asked in a high voice. "How's the baby Rodney? Izz-he a good baby? Yezz-he-izz! Yezz-he-izz!" Rodney smiled so hard at least half the real estate of his face was taken up with the wet grin, his eyes squinting to make room.

"Yezz-he-izz a good boy, a good, good boy!"

"Coooo, cooo," Rodney said, his mouth now tiny, his wee fists and bootied feet flailing with joy.

A small crowd had gathered on the sidewalk, staring at the crash, and a few people were looking Doreen's way. She realized she should leave before the police came and made things awkward. Adults were sure to have opinions about teenage girls jumping onto the roofs of speeding cars, even if they did have the proportional strength, speed, and agility of a squirrel.

But what to do with Rodney? One of the adults nearby might help, but then again, what if they were also a crazed carjacker or even a baby-napper?

"Chikky chuk," said Tippy-Toe, just catching up.

"It's like you can read my thoughts, Tip," said Doreen. "You're right—things *are* always safer in trees."

With the car seat in one arm, Doreen clambered up a nice robust oak. Then she carefully wedged the car seat between two branches. Several squirrel friends gathered around, sniffing Rodney and tickling his neck with their tails.

"Keep an eye on him till his mom comes, will you, friends?"

The squirrels chirped in affirmation, and Doreen leaped away.

She paused, crouching beside the overturned car. Now the man was the upside-down one and she was right side up.

"You okay?" she asked.

"I guess," came his voice. "I mean, I was wearing a seat belt."

"Even when stealing a car, seat belts present the safest option," said Doreen.

"True," he said.

"You really shouldn't be stealing cars, you know."

"Yeah, I know," he said. "I got mad when I discovered that someone stole my bike, so I just . . . I just took someone else's car."

"I'm sorry about your bike," said Doreen. "And sorry that you're a troubled soul. But I recommend therapy over carjacking, okay?"

"Okay."

"Do you need any recommendations? I could maybe find a good therapist for you in the neighborhood."

"No, I'm good."

"Okay," she said.

"Wait . . . who are you?"

"Just the person who talked you out of being a career criminal and changed your life for the better."

"Thanks? But what's your name?"

"I'm . . . I'm . . ." She took a deep breath. "I'm Squirrel Girl."

Squirrel Girl stood up, ready to flee before the police arrived. Only she was surrounded. A crowd had formed on the sidewalk and was spilling into the street, staring at her, muttering to one another.

"Some kind of freak . . ."

"Look at her tail, man."

"You mean that thing is real? That's not a costume?"

"No, she's real, and she, like, lifted a car or something."

"You think *that's* the Jersey Ghost?"

"It's real. Holy cannoli, the Jersey Ghost is real."

Through the crowd, the frizzy-haired mother came running. She screamed when she saw the car.

"No! He's hurt! He's killed!!"

"I'm okay, actually," came the carjacker's voice from inside the car. "I put on a seat belt, so—"

"My Rodney! My baby, is he hurt?"

"Oh, I thought you meant me," said the carjacker. "Never mind!"

"Rodney is great! Tippy!" Squirrel Girl called out.

A horde of squirrels carried the car seat down from the tree, setting it on the sidewalk. The mother pulled out Rodney and hugged him. Everyone could hear the baby coo with delight.

"She saved my baby!" said the mother. "SHE SAVED MY BABY!"

"Who are you?" a man shouted.

"Just your friendly neighborhood Squirrel Girl."[71]

The crowd was still staring. Squirrel Girl felt as though they wanted more from her. What would a hero do now? Captain

---

71 I couldn't help it. The Spider-Man song was still in my head.

America would probably give an inspirational speech. She cleared her throat. The crowd quieted. Some rubbed their hands together eagerly. Who doesn't love a good inspirational speech?

"Um . . . some people might say you've gotta be nuts to chase down a speeding carjacker." Squirrel Girl leaped onto the top of the overturned car, thrust her fist into the air, and said, "Well . . . I *love* nuts!"

At first the crowd was quiet, as if expecting more to the speech. When no more came, a murmuring arose.

"Hey, I like nuts, too."

"Me too."

"I never really considered nuts before, but now that I think about it . . ."

"You know what? I do love nuts."

"Pecans are my favorite!"

"I'm allergic to tree nuts, but I can appreciate them in principle!"

In the distance, Squirrel Girl could hear sirens.

"Um . . . 'kay, bye!" she said. She leaped from the car to the treetop and from there onto a roof. Tippy-Toe was a streak of gray and pink beside her. As they jumped to another roof and out of sight, Squirrel Girl could hear cheering behind her. And a low chant that began to rise: *Squirrel Girl, Squirrel Girl, Squirrel Girl . . .*

That's me, she thought. *I'm Squirrel Girl. I'm really, really real.*

There was no turning back now.

15

THE MICRO-MANAGER

The Micro-Manager sat in a dark room lit by a dozen computer screens. He had not always called himself The Micro-Manager. As a child he had mostly just called himself by his first name, except during his seventh Halloween season when he was "the Doom Bat." He had toyed with using the name "King Bee," but that alias was already in use on Baddit, the online Super Villain forum he frequented. So he had gone with *micromanager* online, *Micro-Manager* in in-line text, and simply *MM* when branding his creations.

He was staring at his largest screen, currently showing a grainy video of a girl with a giant fuzzy tail. She scampered across a speeding, tilting car, plucked a baby from inside, and then leaped to safety with the baby in her arms. A crowd gathered, cheering for the deformed girl.

"I love nuts!" the girl shouted, the sound distant and tinny through the display's internal speaker.

"I hate nuts," muttered the Micro-Manager. The video jittered to a halt and COMMAND NOT UNDERSTOOD appeared over the paused video.

"IsaidIhatenuts!" the Micro-Manager shouted. The phrase remained in place.

"I also hate surprises," the Micro-Manager said, addressing the screen as if the tailed figure on it could hear his words.

Exactly two inches from the front and right edges of his desk was a perfect stack of six Oreo cookies.

The Micro-Manager plucked a cookie off the stack and ate it in a single bite.

"Prmn," he said, chewing as he gestured to something behind him. *"Grplnch."*

Servos whirred, and the sound of robotic feet descending a staircase echoed through the dark room.

"Command not understood," said the robot in a pleasant female voice. "Please repeat."

"GRPLNCH," the Micro-Manager repeated more loudly, anger creeping into the tone.

The robot, dressed primly in a yellow sundress, entered the room and paused.

"Command not understood," the robot said again. "Please repeat."

"Gah!" The Micro-Manager chewed twice, swallowed, and said, "REPLENISH! Unit P-One, replenish! Another cookie, you idiot!"

"Yes. Dear." The robot paced away.

"As if this creature wasn't enough," the Micro-Manager muttered. "Now I need to tweak the voice-recognition algorithms. Again."

The robot returned. Carefully it placed a single Oreo on top of the stack of five with its remarkably human-looking hand.

"Good," he said. "Now milk, ten ounces."

"Yes. Dear."

"Screen two," said the Micro-Manager. "Take dictation."

On one of the smaller monitors, a text box appeared.

"Wednesday," he said. "Frustration." The waveform on the bottom of the screen jumped at the words, with a transcription appearing in the text box shortly after.

"Animals are bad enough. They chew wires, scratch lenses, disrupt my carefully placed spy-bots. I've taken great pains to trap and eliminate the animal vermin in the neighborhood. People are even worse, of course, so they'll have to go eventually. And now . . . animal-people? It is as if the universe is conspiring to destroy order. Or simply conspiring to irritate me. It has succeeded. DO YOU HEAR, UNIVERSE? YOU ARE ON THE LIST! As soon as I figure out how to live somewhere besides inside of you, you're out! Out! Extinguished! Eliminated!"

A glass of milk lowered onto the table, propelled by human-looking robotic fingers.

"Milk. Dear." The robot had returned.

The Micro-Manager gave the machine an irritated wave of dismissal, and continued to speak.

"It is clear this animal-person is behind all of the trap destruction. And between the state of those traps and this recent video evidence, it is also clear the creature has superhuman abilities. Strength and speed, certainly, but what else?"

"I am not programmed for deduction and extrapolation," the robot said, still standing beside the Micro-Manager. "Please upgrade my systems for further discussion."

The Micro-Manager whirled on the robot. "UGH! I AM NOT TALKING TO YOU! GO. AWAY."

"Yes. Dear." The robot walked backward, and then began backing up the stairs, its eyes still pointed at its creator.

"And turn around," the Micro-Manager shouted. "Walk normal. That's just creepy."

"Yes. Dear." It swiveled its body around and continued to ascend the stairs.

"Okay. Where was I?" The Micro-Manager turned back to the screen. "Right. A super-powered thing getting into my business is exactly the opposite of what I need right now. Ordinary people are bad enough, but extraordinary ones? Extra-bad! My three-year plan of the inevitable recognition of my greatness and ultimate partnership with Hydra was foolproof.[72] Not so fool-proof, as it turns out. FOOLS have been my downfall! AGAIN!"

He glanced at the milk, angrily took a sip, and replaced the glass.

"Computer, stop dictation. Play *Heights of Villainy Motivational Lecture Series*, disk two, track four."

Chapter Seven: FOOLS!

Am I right, fellas? FOOLS! We're surrounded by them! Fools at the bakery! Fools at the bank! Fools on the streets! And, increasingly, fools in the air! It is NOT a party being better than everyone. How do we ensure we are not crippled by the abject idiocy of others?

The first option, of course, is murder. Alas, this is not as easy as it sounds, at least not on the scale you need to make any kind of noticeable dent in the fool population. And believe me, even if you can get those kinds of numbers, the cleanup is a BEAST. Unless you're the type of guy who enjoys the smell of decomposing meat (I'm looking at you, Mangog!); then having—

"Skip forward," said the Micro-Manager.

. . . frankly the dead make for poor servants. Loki may tell you different, but trust me, zombie butlers are a big P in the A—

---

72 If you don't already know, Hydra is a supersecret evil organization dedicated to worldwide domination. I bet they have supersecret boring barbecues.

"Forward."

... not like Thanos, who gets people to honestly believe he'll incinerate them where they stand despite his ridiculous purple head and chin of a thousand butts—

"Forward."

A note on the worst kind of fool. The Super-Fool. These butter-brained cretins that fly, shoot lasers out of various body parts, and generally cause us trouble. If you've got one of these on your tail, congratulations! You've just been legitimized by the system. People are much more likely to run away from you screaming if you've been seen fighting Thor.

Side-tip: Don't fight Thor. It's a bad idea.

My point is, if you don't have a nemesis, get one. But make sure it is one that people love and respect. I know a guy who spent years fighting the hero Star-Lord, and all he ever did was make Star-Lord look like a joke. Which, frankly, in the court of public opinion, was not that great a feat. And so now this guy is known as Star-Lord's archenemy, which is mostly funny to everyone. Except him. And Star-Lord, too, probably.

Don't make that mistake. OWN your Super-Fool. If they aren't worthy of you, make them worthy of you. Make sure the public knows it. Then defeat them in front of everyone. It'll make your rep for years.

"Pause."

The Micro-Manager turned to the monitor still showing Squirrel Girl, fist held high in a pose of triumph.

"Very well," he said to the screen. "Let's make you worthy enough for me to defeat you, you ridiculous thing."

"COMMAND NOT UNDERSTOOD."

"Argh!"

16

DOREEN

Doreen's mother turned off the television. Moments ago, it had been tuned to the local news, where reporters were laughingly recounting the story of a baby saved by a giant-tailed Squirrel Girl.

"Doreen . . ." said her mother.

Doreen stood at the bottom of the stairs, half in shadow. She twitched her tail and shifted her weight from one foot to the other.

"It's just that—" said her father.

"Don't say you want me to hide my tail because you're worried everybody will be jealous," said Doreen. "Because it's *not* that, is it?"

Maureen looked at Dor. Dor looked at Maureen. Then they both looked at Doreen.

"I knew it," said Doreen. She sat down on the couch beside them. The cushion springs squeaked.

"We want you safe," said her father. "And someone like you attracts attention—good and bad. And the bad can be *really* bad."

"I thought . . . that maybe . . . I thought I could maybe be a hero—"

"Well, of course you could," said her father. "We've always known that."

"Wait, what?" said Doreen.

"You climbed out of your crib when you were four months old," said Maureen.

"We had a special crib cage made for you so you couldn't get out and go tumbling down the stairs at night and hurt yourself," said Dor.

"But you were still a toddler when you could pull apart the bars and wiggle free."

"You clawed your way out of the sliding glass door when you were three."

"That same year you climbed a tree and fell out, breaking your leg. The doctor put it in a temporary brace, but when we went back to get the cast, the bone was already healing on its own, faster than expected."

"A year later when you fell out of another tree—remember, hon? The redwood? Mickey almighty, that was a fall—you didn't break any bones."

"And after that, you just stopped falling out of trees. Or falling altogether."

"You are fast, strong, agile, proficient in Chitterspeak, and have such a beautiful tail—"

"It is a real beauty," Maureen agreed.

"And on top of all that, you have an impenetrable sense of justice and a heart of pure gold. Well, tell me, why wouldn't 'cha be a Super Hero?"

"Really?" said Doreen.

Her father nodded. His eyes were wet with emotion, and as shiny as his bald head. "Our job as parents was to keep you safe till you were ready. And if you ask me, fourteen is still *preeeet-ty* young to be saving the day—"

"Now Dor—"

"Well, I'm just sayin', Maureen, and I have a right to say, don't I?"

"Don't go losing the rest of your hair now, Dor, no one said you couldn't say—"

"So *you* say. But when I was a kid, well, you had to be twenty-one before you could do any day-saving. Cousin Steelgrip was twenty-six. And even he gave it up by age twenty-eight to pursue a career in forensic accounting."

"For all that it's a different world now, I have to agree with your father."

"And that's not to say we're not so proud of our little girl that I'm about to pop some shirt buttons." He wiped his eyes and beamed at her.

"But running around with your tail out and face uncovered?" said her mother. "Doreen, you could be recognized, and I believe in secret identities like I believe in butterscotch pudding."

Dor and Doreen nodded. Maureen believed in butterscotch pudding a great deal.[73]

"So, you got your basic keep-your-real-name-a-secret-so-bad-guys-can't-attack-your-weaker-loved-ones rationale," said Maureen.

Dor waved, identifying himself as a weaker loved one. "Also so they can't track *you* down at home, when you're asleep and vulnerable," said Dor. "You don't want Loki sifting through your garbage."

"I'm pretty sure Loki doesn't do garbage," said Doreen.[74]

"You never know. I just can't trust a man in a horned helmet. There, I said it, call me prejudiced if you want to. But besides the safety reasons," Maureen said, touching her third finger, "most Super Heroes need a life beyond heroing, some downtime, for Pete's sake, without people after them to save this or that or take a selfie. I mean, poor Thor can't even get shawarma without the paparazzi knowing about it."

---

73 One Thanksgiving, Cousin Jenny suggested that there was no such thing as butterscotch pudding and really it was just burned toffee. Mom is normally very patient, but believe me, it got ugly.
74 I think we already established that Daredevil would be the best at waste management.

"All I'm saying is, would it kill the man to wear a shirt?" said Dor.

"But the real issue is that you were grounded and you promised—"

"I saved a *baby*, Mom," Doreen said.

Her father looked at her with sad eyes. "Chasing down a car-jacker? I don't want you to get hurt."

"Pshaw! Hurt?" Doreen smiled. "Clearly the issue here is that you hate babies and want them NOT to be saved."[75]

Her father's expression melted into a smile. "Disgusting little creatures," he said in a terrible attempt at an English accent. "Do away with the lot of them, I say!"

"We can make an exception for baby-saving, right, Dor?" her mother said. "In the neighborhood, anyway. No going to New York to save babies. They already have the Avengers."

"How about toddler-saving?" Doreen asked.

"I guess toddlers are okay, too," her mother said.

"How about grown-ups who act like toddlers?"

"Nope," her father said. "Too many of those. You'd be out all the time. No risking yourself as Squirrel Girl unless it's to save a real human baby, promise?"

Doreen nodded just as her phone buzzed with a text message.

---

75 Not *really*, of course. I just can't stand it when Dad gets sad eyes, and saying something ridiculous is usually the best way to cheer him up.

ANA SOFÍA

Alert alert is this line secure

DOREEN

What does that even mean? Wait does your phone have spy scrambler mode I want one of those

ANA SOFÍA

I meant r u in a place where people can read this

DOREEN

Just parentals

ANA SOFÍA

Good I know ur grounded but a balloon got loose

DOREEN

You really need to tie those things to your wrist

ANA SOFÍA

No srsly I was sleuthing[76] near the burger frog grand opening. A hot air balloon got untethered and is floating away. A man and woman are screaming that their baby is on the balloon

---

76 "Sleuthing" is what Ana Sofía calls her detective-ing, or her investigating of the Shady Oaks weirdnesses. Isn't that a great word? I also like "rambunctious," "elbow," and "poinsettia."

WOOHOO! My parents made an exception for
baby saving

Really u can? Yes she's back!

Doreen looked at her parents in as significant a way as she could manage.

"What?" her father asked.

Her mother blinked. "No way. Another baby?"

"Another baby," Doreen said. "In a runaway hot-air balloon."

"No way, indeed," her father said. "What is it with this town?"

"But . . . but I thought that if . . ." Doreen said. The excitement building in her chest started to curdle.

"Go, sweetie," her mother said.

Her father nodded. "Go. But keep your hood on, okay?"

Doreen smiled, pulled on her hood, and leaped out the window.

17

SQUIRREL GIRL

Squirrel Girl scampered onto the Greens' roof and scanned the horizon. Just cresting the roof of Ralph's Supermarket in Shady Oaks' town center was the curved edge of a rising balloon. Squirrel Girl leaped from the top of her roof to the neighbor's, and mid-leap was joined by Tippy-Toe, who clawed up her legs and onto her shoulder.

"*Chk?*" asked Tippy-Toe.

Squirrel Girl leaped from the neighbor's roof to a tree, to another roof, and then onto the pole of a streetlight.

"See that?" Squirrel Girl said, pointing to the rising balloon several blocks away. "It got loose."

"*Chk tchika,*" Tippy-Toe said.

"I know," Squirrel Girl said, jumping from pole to pole. "But there's a *baby* on this one. By itself."

"Chikki chuk!" Tippy-Toe said.

Squirrel Girl leaped to a nearby oak, a sycamore, a maple, and then another oak.[77]

"Usually we *do* take better care of our babies," Squirrel Girl said. "This is not normal."

With each tree-stop Squirrel Girl made, Tippy chittered to the local inhabitants, and soon a crowd of squirrels was following them. The leaping, the chittering, tail out under the sun—Squirrel Girl was feeling about as awesome as awesomely possible.

Her phone buzzed.

ANA SOFÍA

Don't head to balloon. Wind is pushing it west

Squirrel Girl veered west. She scampered to the top of an air-conditioning unit on the roof and leaped against the wall of a neighboring building, propelling herself up and to the edge of an even taller building. She flung herself onto the roof and scanned the horizon. She was only about five blocks away, but the balloon was still rising. If she didn't get to it soon, it would be too high to reach unless she had an Iron Man suit.[78]

Squirrel Girl pointed to the largest building in the town, an eight-story bland brick rectangle.

---

77 I prefer oaks generally, because ACORNS.
78 I just feel that Iron Man should give me a spare suit. I'm sure he has extra ones, and I would only use it if I really, really needed it, I swear.

"What building is that?"

"Chk chikka chit," Tippy-Toe said.

"It's called the *Throat Rope Nest*? Really? That sounds horrible!"

"Chuk chk," Tippy-Toe added.

"Oh, right," Squirrel Girl said, leaping to a flagpole, swinging around it, and flinging herself to the next building. "Throat ropes are neckties. People who wear ties go there. Business building or something."

Squirrel Girl leaped onto the roof of a building covered with a rocky gravel that scattered violently at her landing. Pigeons flapped away, cooing in a not-nice manner.

"Sorry, but you don't have to be jerks about it!" Squirrel Girl shouted after them.[79]

The balloon was rising, too high now to reach from any building except the Throat Rope one.

"If I don't catch it when it goes by that building," Squirrel Girl said, "I think it will be too far up."

"Chk," Tippy said, leaping off her shoulder. The squirrel scampered over to the edge of the building they were on and began chittering loudly toward the trees across the street. A second later Squirrel Girl saw little fuzzy heads bubbling up from the tops of distant trees.

"Wait, did you just call them to a *fling party*?" asked Squirrel Girl.

---

79 I don't speak Pigeon, but birds broadcast their anger pretty well.

"Cht-chkka," Tippy-Toe said, climbing back onto Squirrel Girl's shoulder as she ran.

"Really? You think that will work?"

"Chkkuk," Tippy-Toe said, with the tail-twitch equivalent of a shrug.

With two more leaps and a swing, Squirrel Girl hit the side of the Throat Rope Nest at about floor six. She dug her claws into the masonry and began to climb.

She heard a scream as she climbed, looked around to see if someone needed help, and spotted a young man in a throat rope[80] just inside the window she was climbing. His face was pale and horrified, and he was pointing out the window with such fear that Squirrel Girl had to turn around to see if there was a zombie or a dragon or a zombie dragon behind her. There wasn't, so she waved at the man and continued to climb.

From the building's roof, she could see the balloon. It seemed much farther away than thirty feet. And the balloon was still rising.

"Chk-chkka," Tippy-Toe said. Squirrels were streaming up the side of the building and gathering near the edge of the roof with their paws out.

"Right," Squirrel Girl said. "Fling party. Let's do this." She backed up to the opposite side of the building, and then ran, fast. She hurled herself into the crowd of squirrels and jumped

---

80 A necktie. It was a nice blue-and-gold one.

toward the balloon. As she did, she felt two hundred tiny paws and furry tails push against her, giving her lift like a little furry springboard.[81]

As she flew through the air, she grinned.

Look, Ma, I'm flying!

She wished she could enjoy it more, but there was a baby at risk. She could hear it crying now as she neared the basket. Closer, closer . . . but the wind was shifting, and gravity was tugging her down. She reached out, and her hand just brushed the basket.

"No!" she shouted, dropping. She spun in midair, her tail catching a rope that dangled over the edge of the basket. She clenched, coiling her tail around the rope and using the leverage to pull herself up and inside.

"Yes!" she said, breathing hard.

She picked up the crying bundle wrapped in a blanket and held it to her chest.

"Oh, you poor thing," she said, peering in at a little green face. "Wait." She unwrapped the bundle. "Are you a Hulk baby?"[82]

The blanket dropped to the floor of the basket to reveal a large ripe zucchini with a flat square speaker mounted to it.

---

81 It felt a little like those moving walkways at the airport, except, you know, heading into the sky. And fuzzier.

02 Which would have been AWESOME, and not just for the fact that a Hulk baby could fall out of a hot-air balloon and be just fine.

With a crackling noise, the crying coming from the speaker stopped, replaced by a repeated slapping noise.

"That is me doing a slow clap," said a voice from the speaker. It was low, electronic, as if altered with a voice disguise filter. "A sarcastic clap for your 'heroic' deed in saving a zucchini plant. *BRA-VO.*"

"Wow. I guess zucchinis can be jerks," Squirrel Girl said.

"Congratulations on completing your first test," the speaker announced.

Squirrel Girl held the speaker up to her face. "This isn't my first test," she said to the squash. "Can you hear me? I've had like a hundred at school. I think my first test was in kindergarten—"

The speaker crackled. "Your second test I call 'gaseous vengeance.' It will come NOT when you least expect it, but at high noon on Saturday. That is when you should expect it. At high noon. On Saturday."

"Yeah, I don't think you can hear me," Squirrel Girl said. "Otherwise you would have said *next test*, not *second test*. Because we've established—"

The speaker interrupted her with a high-pitched whine. "Warn the police if you wish. I don't care. Tell them you are 'Squirrel Girl' while you're at it. They're sure to take a squirrel-tailed girl freak seriously. HA-HA-HA-HA! You are a joke. Everyone knows you are a joke. But I am graciously giving you the opportunity to prove me and everyone else wrong. GASEOUS! VENGEANCE! HIGH! NOON!"

The black square emitting the sound sparked, and Squirrel Girl dropped the zucchini. She watched as the gadget caught fire and burned up. She stomped out the fire before it could set flame to the basket and rescued the zucchini, which was a perfectly good vegetable and still deserved to be saved even if it wasn't a baby. She discovered an MM logo had been burned into its green skin.

"Huh," Squirrel Girl said. "That proves it, I guess. Shady Oaks definitely has a Super Villain. And his name is . . . Muffin Master! Probably. Hopefully. It could be Murder Monkey, I guess. Or Masked Moth.[83] But I really hope it's Muffin Master."

---

83 Or Mr. Menace, Mystery Muppet, Multitudinous Matilda, Mega-Margot, Man Muzzler, Minotaur Marvin, Missile Monk, the Malibu Meteor, Mushroom Maniac . . .

18

DOREEN

*B*ack at the Squirrel Cave, aka Doreen's tree house in the backyard, Doreen and Ana Sofía were having a highly secret and private conversation.[84]

"First: here." Ana Sofía handed Doreen a small box. Inside was a black cell phone.

"What—?"

"It's nothing fancy, only good for making calls and texting," she said. "It's a burner. Prepaid, untraceable. I thought you should have a private phone for just when you're *her*."

"Wow, this is the most amazing gift I've ever gotten. Thank you!"

---

84 In case you were wondering how that last part ended, I tore a hole in the balloon to make it go down again. Which, it turns out, is not the most effective way to land a balloon.

Ana Sofía opened up her laptop and began searching for something as if the gift were no big deal at all, but the corners of her mouth were twitching against a smile.

"Now, you have to see this." Ana Sofía connected to Doreen's Wi-Fi[85] and loaded up a video. "I found it on the dark net.[86] It's a video of—wait. Double-check no one's near enough to eavesdrop."

Doreen peeked out the window of the tree house. She climbed on its roof, listened for the subtle hum of any of those weird doll-eyed bug machines, searched with her keen eyes for sight of friend or foe. She slid back into the window.

"Nope. Nobody but us."

In this case, "us" was Ana Sofía Arcos Romero, Doreen Green, and approximately two hundred squirrels. Ana Sofía glanced uneasily at the teetering tower of curious squirrels that had piled up behind her, looking over her shoulder at her computer.

"They want to see the video, too?" Ana Sofía asked.

"Oh yeah. Tippy-Toe's and Big Daddy Spud's clans have agreed to join together and help us stop the Muffin Master, or whoever is hunting squirrels. Well, those two black squirrels there, Bubo Nic and M. Scummerset Maugham, are hoping you're going to play funny cat videos, but the rest are focused and battle-ready."

---

85 Our Wi-Fi password is "SQUIRRELS," so she pretty much guessed it first try. Well, it *was* "SQUIRRELS." Ana Sofía made me change it to something more secure so I chose "SQUIRRELSrocksohard123." Crap, now I'm going to have to change it again.

86 Which is a thing, apparently. Like Evil Internet. Who knew?

"Do you know *all* their names?" asked Ana Sofía.

"Sure, the one there next to Nic and Scummerset is Pippin Sparrowfork. The little red one behind her is Sal Adtongs. Then there's Bumble Bow," she said, pointing, "and Peksi Co, Pizza Dough. There is Frizzle Foe, Muffin Glow, Ivan Hoe, Sting Lo, Sheet Chariot, Cheney Mow, Varr-Noh, Epiphany Oh, Dipsy Allen Poe, Stratus Quo, Botulism Ro, Needling Sew, Howling Woe, Holdup Whoa, Quiensoy Yo,[87] Lazy Susan, Daisy Susan and Dazy Susan,[88] Crazy Susan,[89] Suzie Skunkkiller, Fraidyskulk, Squamous Ned, Geraldine Ferraro, Campbell the Unsoup, Undertaker Tiff, Quip Natureboy, Puffin Furslide, Jerry Gnomesbane, Mister Meester, Tuppence Baldwin Squee, Sausage the Sand Witch, Alexander Hamsandwich, Penelope Underpants, Peeper Parkour (the Spectacular Spider-Squirrel), Meep the Misunderstood, Friday Gallonsaweek, Speedo Strutfuzz, Slick Undertow, Gallows Giggler, Hermione R. Giger, Hannah Scare-share, Boo Stairscare, Sparkle Starstare, Brady Spareswear, Lady Sportswear, Tom the Third, Kitty Sloughwalker, Fez Clubwiggins, Tantamount, Bea Carrotspaw, Shrimpy Scrimshaw, Spark Mector, Locke Jakely, Grievant Stan, the Night Loon, Will Wadeson, Maximus the Sane, Haircut

---

87 Sometimes squirrels like to gather in groups by rhyming names. I think Frizzle Foe is Tippy-Toe's first cousin.
88 They're twins. Daisy and Dazy, I mean. Lazy is just a friend.
89 No relation.

Medusa, Little Sissy Hotlegs, Big Sissy Hotlegs, Spockeye, Splint
Carton, Syndey Carton, Lucie Manette, Churlish Betty, Tiff
Image, Zip Archive, Her Highness Spud Willoughby (Queen of
the Upper Canopies), Indistinguishable Ben, Distinguishable
Ben, Disease Vector, Hairless Cameron, Davey Porkpun, Platypus
Kate, Cletus Scampersaw, FreelyPeas, Tammany Paul, Pallid
Paul, Regular Paul, Paul, The One that Came from the Future,
Shameless Ed, Calendar Earl, Pug-William (Lord of Chimneys),
Citizen Squee, Maz Zissimos, Palace Tom, Miranda Creepsforth,
Amanda Manylegs, Henry Hexapod, Alias the Gasbag, Leet
Haxor, Crocket R. Tubbs, Davey the Hat, Petey Pistachio,
Paper-Bag Head, Paper Bag-Head, Heidi Plainsight, Millicent the
Uncouth, Emo Pat, Russ Jackal (SquareWolf by Night), Frogpants
Louie, Baron Vermin Von Flopsweat, Kerchief Candyglow, the
Oregon Tail, Mama Salad, Lap One, Startlekins the Unwieldy,
Bertha Sneezeshroud, Shinylegs, Trash-heap the Silent, Gordon
Soondead, Gordon-in-Waiting, Labrat McGillicutty, Purrmaster
Nottacat, Broad Jump, Bread Jump, Bed Jump, Sump Pump,
Fraidy Fred, Frayed Freddy, Pippin Sheepspawn, Snot Smuggler,
Fun Guy Yuggoth, Fuzz Fountain Cortez, Tartan Cabertoss,
Skip Turtleback, Genghis Flan, Bear Bodkin, She Who Must Not
Be Named, Thing One, Thing Three,[90] Rice Cat, Ozymandias
O. My, Ms. McGruffit, Squirrel Version 3.5, Mr. McCoocoo,

90 No one talks about what happened to Thing Two.

Em Em Em, Mick Donald, Nature Rat, Steven M. Inecraft, Ender Squirrel, Simon the Squidherd, Fuzz Master Flex, RubberLegs Andy—"

"Okay," Ana Sofía said. "That's good. You can stop now."

"Sorry," said Doreen. "Sometimes I just get so excited about how cool squirrels are. Did you know no two squirrels ever have the same name? And their bite is fifty times stronger than a human's? And yesterday I saw Fuzz Fountain Cortez jump ten feet straight up and grab the edge of a squirrel-proof bird feeder."

The squirrels started squeaking so hard they fell off the tree house walls and onto the floor, rolling on their backs, holding their shaking bellies.

"Are they okay?" asked Ana Sofía.

"They're just laughing. 'Squirrel-proof bird feeder' is one of their favorite jokes."[91]

"Well, if Fuzz Fountain Cortez can jump up five times her body-length, maybe you're capable of the same—which would be . . . holy fire, Doreen, that would be more than twenty-five feet vertically! That must mean you can leap even farther horizontally. This video starts to prove that you do in fact have the *proportional* powers of a squirrel."

---

91 It's a classic. One squirrel says, "A squirrel-proof bird feeder," and the other says, "A friendly dog," and the first says, "A cat." Cats are hysterical just in and of themselves, because they climb up trees and then literally get stuck up there. I mean, why would they climb up if they can't get down? Solid squirrel humor.

Ana Sofía pressed PLAY. The video had been shot yesterday, as Squirrel Girl raced to catch the escaping hot-air balloon and save the supposed baby.

"That's me!" said Doreen. "Or . . . her-me anyway. That's Squirrel Girl. Hey, her-me is pretty fast. Tippy, did you know I could run that fast? I— *Whoa . . .*"

The video had just shown her leap from the building's roof to the balloon, a distance that seemed impossible, even with fuzzy-squirrel-catapult help. And yet, she'd done it.

"Look how the video cuts between multiple cameras," said Ana Sofía. "It follows you from the rooftops to the balloon, and several of the angles show that there were cameras mounted in the balloon as well. This whole deal was a set-up to film you, Doreen. This MM guy is watching you."

"Creeee-py," said Doreen. "But awesome video."

"Chkkt-chek," said Tippy-Toe.

"Yeah, let's watch it again," said Doreen.

Tippy-Toe chittered throughout the second viewing, giving feedback to the squirrels about how to improve their teamwork and giving names to various moves so they could practice them later.

By the third watching, Doreen's mood, which had begun high and excited like a kid at the top of a waterslide, now had slid down, down into a wet cold mud puddle of apprehension. Who had set this all up? And why?

"This *is* creepy," Ana Sofía agreed. "Something isn't right. And whoever set up a fake baby-napping and filmed it isn't done yet."

"It's like a Super Villain move, you know?" said Doreen. "But a Super Villain is Super Hero territory, not Squirrel Girl territory. I wish I had, like, a real professional hero I could call up and be all, *Hey, Hulk, any advice?*"

"We can figure this out," said Ana Sofía.

"I guess," said Doreen. But all the hop and fuzz had gone out of her.

Tippy-Toe scampered up to her shoulder, put a tiny cold paw on her cheek, and sniffed. It was the sort of sniff that implied, *Don't worry, I have a plan.*

19

TIPPY-TOE

One of the first things my mother taught me as a pup was how to hop from one tree to the next. But now that I was planning to hop from one city to the next . . . well, I had to wonder whether I'd twitched a little too far left and come down with noggin rot. My dear fuzzed mother wasn't pushing me into this leap. But Doreen needed a confab with her own squeaks, and she couldn't just hop to the burrow a few blocks down and have a chitter. Her squeaks were in New York City, and Doreen couldn't call them until she had their numbers.

She didn't ask me to go. She didn't need to. When I see a problem, I take care of it.

The journey took the better part of a day, even piggybacking on oil-oozing and smoke-coughing buses. Making it to New York City was only the first part of the problem. Now, how to find these Avengers? At the bus depot, I put my nose in the air and sniffed. Even with its machine and human stink, I could smell a huge cluster of trees to the north. And where there are lots of trees, there are squirrels. And where there are squirrels, there is information.

I staked out an unoccupied tree in the corner of the park. A male gray scrabbled up the trunk to a branch just below me. Manners said to wait for the local to acknowledge me first, but I was in a hurry.

"This some kinda leaf masquerade, squeak?" I asked, trying not to sound impatient.

There was a rustling, and the gray scampered up to my branch, perching a respectful distance away.

"Huh?" the gray noised. "Clear the chitter-fog and I'll say straight, duchess."

"Looks like you're pretending to be branchspawn, all quiet and skulky, I mean," I said. "You tryin' to hide?"

"Naw," he said. "I mean, you seen me, right? So I couldn't 'a been hiding."

"Right," I said.

"So . . . yeah," he said, twitching his tail all shy-like. It felt like he was going to ask me out on a date. "How you doin'?"

"Peaches and nuts, Amster cat. How you doin'?"

"That's some slick chitter, squeak," he said. "You Jersey?"

"Shucked it on the first, sly," I said. "You got a name, or should I just keep callin' you Cat?"

"Respect, Jersey, respect," he said. "You can call me Frizz."

"That tuft grow on you like fuzz or dropped puptime by your mother?"[92]

"Full name Frizzwicket Lieberman, but Mom only used the whole bit when I was in trouble."

"Respect for respect then, Frizz. For you and your mother. But how is it you lead with that? You know me? What chitter you heard?"

"Just what comes on the chitter-train, squeak. Jersey squirrels puttin' the groundies in their place, right? Saving babies? Caging the sharp-toothed garbage? That scamper true, Jersey?"

"All but the groundies, Frizz. Dogs dealt with, babies saved. But the groundies, squeak? They're mates. Partners, shuck? We're working together now."

"Nuts," he said. "They agree to that? No threat?"

"No threat," I said. "Common interest."

"More respect to top the hoard, then," he said. "You on the chew in the city, or breaking?"

"On the chew," I said. "Gotta find the Avengers peeps. The humans."

"Their nest is no hidden hoard to me, natch," he said.

"I figured," I said. "Point me the way for an acorn?"

"No charge, cousin," Frizz said. "I'll take you there myself."

I followed him through the park, which had more trees than

---

92 Sometimes this Jersey squirrel dialect is tricky! Here I think she's asking, "Did you earn that nickname, or is it the one your mother gave you at birth?"

I'd seen, more than in my dreams of our ancestral forest. Then he stopped in a tree across the street from a mansion on Fifth Avenue that hogged up an entire city block. It smelled of stone, steel, and electricity, which meant the humans had taken great effort to make it secure.

"You been in, Frizz?" I asked.

His eyes widened. "No, squeak. I mean, don't know how you do it in Jersey, but we stay outta human nests."

"Right, right," I said. "We do, too. But in this case, I'm doing a favor, see? For a human."

"No rot? Must be a pretty special human."

"She is," I said, scanning the building for an opening. "You should meet her."

"You talk? She chitter?"

"That's right," I said. "She understands. So mostly I chitter, she nods."

"That is peaches and nuts," he said. "Bring her next time you come, huh?"

"Will do," I said. The building was well protected with cameras, sonic fences, and automated energy weapons, but squirrels have ways of getting inside things. "Wish me luck, Frizz," I said, and leaped into action.

20

TEXT MESSAGES

SQUIRREL GIRL

Hey hi is this the famous super hero known as Black Widow?[93] I need some help

BLACK WIDOW

WILN

SQUIRREL GIRL

Ooh do Avengers speak in code that makes so much sense bc anyone could be spying.[94] So supersecret spy help needed here. Any tips on stopping an evil mastermind from releasing terrible gaseous vengeance?

---

93 You know who Black Widow is, right? Everybody knows Black Widow. Super spy, fellow redhead (respect!), penchant for tight black jumpsuits?

94 After the fact, I figured out that she wasn't actually speaking in supersecret Avenger code but just thought I was someone else. Turns out WILN = What in Loki's name. I guess the Avengers kinda have their own swearwords.

SQUIRREL GIRL

BLACK WIDOW

Parker stop texting me. Ur roommate's farts do
not qualify him as a super villain

SQUIRREL GIRL

LOL not Parker. Or is Parker more code? I'm
Squirrel Girl

BLACK WIDOW

How did you get this number

SQUIRREL GIRL

From a squirrel

Yeah so what would you do if a talking zucchini
in a hot-air balloon threatened to poison the
neighborhood

BLACK WIDOW

Stark if this is you I'd start wearing the armor to
the bathroom

SQUIRREL GIRL

???

BLACK WIDOW

BECAUSE NOWHERE WILL BE SAFE

SQUIRREL GIRL

Nowhere is safe? I was planning to stake out the gas stations but if nowhere is safe then maybe you're saying the danger isn't in one place but moving around?

BLACK WIDOW

Enough Stark one word to Pepper from me and u r in the doghouse

SQUIRREL GIRL

Doghouse? Um I'm not sure I totally get your code but I'll look into It

BLACK WIDOW

I'm blocking you Stark or Parker or whoever this is. U r probably the one who ate my yogurt too even though it was clearly labeled and on my fridge shelf. Mess with BWs yogurt and you get STUNG

SQUIRREL GIRL

I think you're kidding? But thanks for the supersecret advice. I assumed gas meant gas station but you're right nowhere is safe from this mysterious super villain. And I'll be vigilant and keep an eye on the dogs. K thx BW!

[text not received; user blocked]

21

TIPPY-TOE

Breaking into the Avengers Mansion, evading their numerous and ridiculous security measures, and accessing a contact list on a cell phone took more energy than I anticipated. I was curled up in the tree house in Doreen's yard with no more than an hour of sleep in me, when . . .

"Tippy. Tippy!"

Even half-asleep, I recognized the voice. It was Davey Porkpun, so called because of the jokes he tells. Bad jokes, mostly about pigs, bacon, and ham. I was not in the mood for jokes. I was in the mood for peace and quiet. I pretended to remain asleep, but when I felt the heat of his paw above my shoulder, I knew he was about to poke me. My eyes snapped open and I grabbed hold of his wrist just before he made contact. He startled.

"This had better be good," I said, releasing his wrist.

"It is," he breathed.

"Like buttered peanuts good," I said, flexing my tail.

"Green husks and monkey biscuits, not *that* good! Maybe as good as bacon on—"

"No jokes," I added quickly.

"Right," he said, but his eyes darted up and to the left in that way they do when he's trying to come up with a joke he thinks I haven't heard before.

"Focus, Davey," I snapped. "Why the branch stampede? What's up?"

His eyes popped back to mine. "It's the sharp garbage—er, the dogs," he said. "There's a good piece of rot dropping. They're snapping and growling something fierce."

Doreen had asked me and the squirrels to keep an eye on the dogs. The ones that, despite everything dogs had ever done to squirrels, we had actually helped.

"Something sour in the pile," I said. "I'll sniff it myself. Let's scamper."

To his credit, Davey kept up with me as I raced through the neighborhood. I could hear the dogs before I saw them, crooning and snarling like their paws were caught in a trap. The sound was nasty enough to make my fur stand up along my spine. Then I saw the body. One of my people, a tree squirrel, lying limp just beyond the borders of the bug-free lot. Tree squirrels don't just lie still. When we don't move, something is seriously wrong.

"That's Speedo!" said Davey.

Speedo Strutfuzz let out a weak cough, and I sprinted to his side, eyeing the bite marks marring his fur.

"Which sharp piece of garbage did this?" I hissed.

"Black stripe," Speedo muttered. I tensed to spring, ready to pay the animal back in kind, but Speedo put his paw on mine. "Naw, Tippy. Wasn't nasty. There was a . . . nail or something . . . on his back. He was in pain. I tried to . . ."

"Punish he to whom the teeth belong," I growled. "That is the law. If the black-striped garbage has the teeth that hurt you, he will be punished."

"Peaches, Tip," Speedo said, taking labored breaths, "but this pup . . . may be just the tooth of a greater monster."

Speedo's eyes fluttered closed, and though his chest still rose and fell with breaths, my heart twinged.

Davey carefully parted Speedo's fur to examine his injuries. "He got a branch-snap in the rib, but the leaks are gummed over already."

"Stay with him," I said.

I scaled a tree and looked down. The dogs had gone crazy, whimpering and growling, snapping and biting at anything and everything, including themselves. Except the dark mound the groundies had used as their community toilet. Even in their madness, it appeared the dogs had enough sense not to eat that. But all the other piles of refuse had been torn up. My tail twitched. If I fell into that mayhem, I would not survive.

The morning sun was cresting the buildings. The sunlight glinted against small pieces of metal in the dogs' backs, like giant robot bees had stung the beasts and left their stingers behind.

There was a yelp as one of the dogs rammed its head into the red concrete wall of the abandoned restaurant. The animal staggered and shook its head, but then snarled and used its head again to ram the wall.

Before the creature could ram the wall once more, I leaped from the tree and onto its back. I have ridden on dogs before, but always to distract them from hurting one of my clan. I told myself that this was still the case, because crazy dogs are bad news for squirrels. But the truth was, I could tell the dog was suffering. And I actually cared. About a dog. I sighed. Doreen had done this to me.

The dog bucked. My hind paws grasped handfuls of the dog's fur, and I stayed right where I was. Close up, the metal thing on its back looked like a large silver tick, six metallic legs digging into the flesh of the animal. Sparking arcs of electricity popped off of the tiny machine, and my mount twitched and jerked with each one.

I grabbed the tick and pulled. The dog howled. The spark of electricity fizzled through me, my hairs standing straight up. I've chewed through live electrical wire. I could take it. But my body's involuntary jerk that came with the zap still sent me flying. The tick came with me.

I landed hard on an open spot of asphalt, the impact noodling my noggin. I struggled to my feet just in time to be struck by something that sent me flying again. Canine teeth nicked my tail, and then I landed on what felt like mud. The smell of it sharpened me up, and I almost gagged when I realized I had come down on the potty pile. The dogs were leaving me alone. But still, gross.

I shuddered, leaping from the pile, to the fence, and up to the neighboring tree faster than I realized I could move.

"Whoa," Davey said. A handful of other squirrels had arrived during my dog and potty show and together had managed to pull Speedo up into the safe branches. "That was amazing."

"Not my first dog ride," I said, a little dazed. I was still gripping the metal device. It was hot in my paw.

"Naw, Tip. That dog you helped? It *saved* you," Speedo said, awake now and propped up against the trunk.

"Bug nuts," I said. "Chitter straight, Speedo." I looked back to where the animal now lay, collapsed in an exhausted heap while his brothers and sisters continued to pace, twitch, and howl.

"Clear chitter, squeak. When you tumbled, the other dogs were on straight scamper for your tail. But black stripe batted you away from them," Davey said.

"Hoarding his nuts, maybe," I said. "Wanted me first."

"Maybe," Speedo said, wincing as he sat a little straighter. "But I saw different. It seemed super peached to have that metal thing off its back. Grateful to you."

"It stinks like a summertime ham hoard," said Davey, sniffing me over.

"Sorry," I said. "I landed in the potty mound."

"No," Davey said. "I mean, yes, you do stink. But you smell like groundie droppings. That metal thing smells like . . . I don't know. Something else."

I took a sniff of the metal thing. Through the stink of my own fur, I could still tell Davey was right. The electric bug was like a shell with a rotten nut inside. It reminded me of something, but I couldn't quite put a claw on it.

"Chitter back to that mass migration of beetles last fall? When Sluggo ate one of the bugs?" Davey said. "Squeak's farts smelled like what's inside that thing."

"That beetle stampede was no migration," I said. I knew what he meant. Last spring an exterminator had puffed a house full of gas to rid it of bedbugs. "Those bugs were on the flee from fumigation. . . . Oh!"

"What's a fumigation-o?"

"Poison gas, meant to kill things," I said. "Bury this, fast." I handed the thing to Davey Porkpun.

"On it like bristles on a hog," said Davey, leaping to the ground.

"I'm going to tell Squirrel Girl about this," I told the rest of the squeaks. "Gather our best riders. I think we're about to have a rodeo."

22

SQUIRREL GIRL

Squirrel Girl sat on the flat roof of the Throat Rope Nest. Or the Garden State Institute for Business Management, which is what she discovered it was actually called while climbing up the front. She looked for the nice man in the throat rope through the windows to say hi again, but the building was dark. People didn't do much instituting for business management on Saturdays.

She sighed. She had told her mom she was going to study with Ana Sofía. This crisis wasn't specifically baby-related, but she couldn't bear it if her parents had said no. Still, she was surprised she'd been able to get out of the house before breaking down and confessing everything. Now she just felt yucky about the lie.

She checked her phone. 11:48 a.m. The talking zucchini said Saturday at "high noon." It sounded like a cowboy thing. She hadn't seen a cowboy since California, and that had been on

Halloween, so it probably didn't count. Maybe "high noon" was a Super Villain clue. Should she be on the lookout for robot cowboys, instead of robot zucchinis? Did "high noon" mean twelve o'clock, or *higher* than twelve o'clock? She sighed. It was a weird thing to say, even for a talking squash.

ANA SOFÍA
See anything yet?

DOREEN
When is it high noon

ANA SOFÍA
About ten min

DOREEN
But that's regular noon

ANA SOFÍA
High noon is the same thing but with cowboys

DOREEN
I know right? Do you think there will be robot cowboys riding little robot bulls

ANA SOFÍA
Maybe you are the cowboy in this scenario

DOREEN

Cowgirl

ANA SOFÍA

Cow squirrel

Squirrel Girl giggled, and then she heard a squeak. In the distance, a gray speck was leaping from treetop to treetop. She caught sight of pink ribbon.

Squirrel Girl jumped off the building, catching the top of a light across the street, and swung into a large oak.

The two friends met on the black-shingled roof of a house.

"*Ch . . . chk!*" It was rare to see Tippy-Toe out of breath, and it made her harder to understand.

"The what? The fur-teeth?"

Tippy held up a paw. "*Chk chuk CHIK!*"

"Poison dogs? What . . . wait—just tell me on the way! Let's go!"

Tippy-Toe rode on Squirrel Girl's shoulder. As girl and squirrel scampered from treetops to buildings, Tippy-Toe recounted the story of the dog with the metal tick, and how it smelled of poison gas.

The last time Squirrel Girl had been at the Burger-N-Bean Bowl, it had been bouncy with happy dogs, chasing one another's tails and sharing dog food. Now the lot was empty, except for a single black-and-white dog with its paw on Speedo Strutfuzz.

"Hey!" Squirrel Girl shouted, bounding toward the dog.
Speedo held up a paw.

"*Chkka,*" he said.

Squirrel Girl skidded to a halt. "You're okay?" she said.
The dog gave Speedo a soft lick on the back of his head.

Tippy-Toe scampered to Speedo's side and the two squirrels began chittering faster than Squirrel Girl could completely follow.

"*Chkkchtchktuckkckchikkcukcihkuchktchtchkk . . .*"

The squirrel chitters were interrupted by a high-pitched whine, as if a dozen competing public-address systems were turned on at once. It was loud, and everyone, including the dog, tried to cover their ears.

Six cat-size drones twitched from behind the bushes and hummed as they hovered over the Burger-N-Bean building. Each one looked like a crowd of tiny helicopters had crashed into one another from different directions and somehow kept flying. One of the spheres of whirling blades halted, revealing an eyeball-like camera lens inside.

"High! Noon!" All of the eye-copters simultaneously broad-casted the voice of Shady Oaks' new Super Villain. Squirrel Girl checked her phone. It was, in fact, exactly 12:00, but Ana Sofía's last text saying "Cow squirrel" was still on the screen, and she stifled a laugh into a snort.

"You've probably noticed that the dogs are gone," the metallic voice continued.

"*Chkcht!*" Tippy-Toe chittered at the flying eyes.

"I don't think he can hear you," Squirrel Girl said. "This guy likes talking way more than listening."

"And *why* are they gone?" the voice asked, sounding a bit like a whiny six-year-old Doreen once babysat in California.

"Debbie?" Squirrel Girl asked. "Debbie Pepperton, is that you? Come back to the light, Debbie! You aren't evil, no matter what your parents say!"

"The dogs are not dead," the voice continued, oblivious to Squirrel Girl's pleas. "Not yet. Each mongrel has a little metal device implanted on their backs that—*bzzzt*—has sent them running, mindless and confused. The devices contain pellets filled with highly concentrated chemicals. Those pellets will explode in exactly six minutes, or earlier if you attempt to destroy them. When they do inevitably explode, the chemicals will mix with the air to create clouds of toxic gas sure to kill any mammals in a thirty-meter radius. Also probably birds and fish. Maybe bugs. The point is, the dogs will be dead. And anyone near them will be dead. Can you stop it? Gotta catch 'em all! HA-HA-HA-HA!"

During the drone speech, Tippy-Toe had climbed to the top of the shuttered Burger-N-Bean building and now leaped toward the nearest eye-copter. She pulled her paws and tail in close and popped right through the spot where the two rotors had stopped. Almost immediately those rotors began to start again, but it was too late. Tippy-Toe was already inside. One by one, helicopter blades began dropping off, severed at the root by squirrel teeth. The drone wobbled, sparked, and—just as Tippy-Toe spun clear—crashed to the ground, exploding.

"I don't think that was Debbie Pepperton after all," Squirrel Girl said, leaping to catch another eye-copter. She batted it with her tail, and it crashed to the ground, twitching. She landed on top of the thing boots first, smashing it flat. The sleeve of her hoodie was torn where the blades of the eye-copter had hit.

"We need to find those dogs," Squirrel Girl said. "And fast."

"Chk chtta chk," Tippy-Toe said.

"I think I can pull the little robot ticks off them like you did," Squirrel Girl said. "Who else do you think has the strength?"

"Chk chuk," Tippy-Toe said, looking across the group of squirrels that had begun to gather.

"Right! But we'll need to bury them to stop the poison."

"Chika-k."

"Yes! Take the ground squirrels! Perfect. You guys grab, they bury. Squirrel teamwork!" Tippy-Toe started off, but Squirrel Girl yelled after her. "Any dog you can't get the tick off, herd it back here. I'll meet you and help out."

"Chk cha-chuk," Tippy-Toe said.

"Yes!" Squirrel Girl said. "Like cowboys. Like cow-squirrels!"

Tippy-Toe darted into the trees.

"Speedo?" Squirrel Girl asked.

Speedo Strutfuzz gave her a thumbs-up.

Squirrel Girl jumped to a window ledge of the old Burger-N-Bean building and scanned the neighborhood. The dogs were not trying to hide. They had left a mess in their paths and were barking up a storm. Now all she had to do was catch them before they exploded.[95]

First she found a brown terrier who'd gotten itself stuck between the bars of a bike rack. She yanked the tick out, quickly dug three feet down into someone's lawn, shoved in the bug, and covered it back up. She pulled apart the bars, setting the terrier free. It licked her chin in gratitude.

Then she followed the barking to three more dogs, who were chasing one another in someone's backyard. She tackled them, pulled out the devices, and buried the chemical pellets. The dogs went back to chasing one another, but in a happy way.

Barking led her back in the direction of the Burger-N-Bean. A group of squirrels had corralled a Doberman pinscher on the lot. Kitty Sloughwalker was riding it rodeo-style but spilled from its back before she could remove the device. She landed hard, chittering angrily. The dog came at her, teeth bared.

"Chuk chuk!" Big Daddy Spud called from a mound of earth. He threw a dirt clod at the dog, and the animal shied away from Kitty.

"Get ready!" Squirrel Girl said. She leaped into the lot, grabbing the upset animal and hugging it tight. With her teeth she

---

95 Before the gas-bugs on their back exploded, I mean. *So* glad this adventure doesn't have actual exploding dogs.

plucked the buzzing metal machine off the animal's back. Its sparks of electricity stung her lips and made them vibrate. As soon as she got the bug out, the dog went limp with relief, and she laid it down.

She spit the metal device toward Big Daddy Spud.

Spud caught it in his mouth and began to dig, dirt flying under his quick claws.

Fuzz Fountain Cortez arrived perched on a dog's head, tugging its ears to steer. Squirrel Girl plucked the little buzzing bomb off Cortez's mount and tossed it to Puffin Furslide, who buried it.

Tippy-Toe scampered in, reporting that she had taken care of two dogs all by herself.

"Time is almost up!" a distant tinny voice sounded. A couple of eye-copters, just out of reach, floated into view. "Ten . . . nine . . . eight . . ."

Squirrel Girl looked around, tallying reports from the squirrels.

"Is that all of them?" she asked. "I had four, plus Kitty's here, that's five. There was Cortez's . . . and Nic, Scummers, and Bear Bodkin each got one. With Tippy's two, that's . . . eleven. Twelve counting the first one with Speedo. Were there only twelve?"

"BOOM!" echoed the voice from the speakers in the drones. A muffled pop sounded from beneath the pile of dirt where Big Daddy Spud had buried one of the devices.

"We did it!" Squirrel Girl cheered, pumping a fist into the air.

"*Chka,*" Tippy-Toe said, not cheering.

Squirrel Girl's arms dropped. "What?"

"*Chka,*" Tippy-Toe said, looking off into the neighborhood.

"There were thirteen?" Squirrel Girl said. "Oh no."

She scampered up to the top of the building again, searching for clouds of gas, listening for screams or coughing, or anything terrible.

Speedo's black-and-white dog came galloping onto the construction site with Speedo on her back.

"*Chk chuk cha,*" Speedo said. "*Chk.*"

"Davey Porkpun?" Squirrel Girl asked. "Where's Davey?"

Squirrel Girl, Tippy-Toe, and a handful of others followed Speedo and his dog to the playground at the park. In the sandbox was a tired-looking wiener dog, and poking out of the sand was the back half of a squirrel body, tail twitching.

"Davey?" Squirrel Girl asked.

Tippy pulled Davey out by his tail. Davey shook his head wildly, sand falling from his fur. "*Mmmm! Mmmm!*" he said, not opening his mouth. There was something in it. Something much bigger than an acorn. He tried to burrow back into the sand, but Tippy held his head.

"*Chkka chk,*" she said.

Davey's eyes widened. He looked around and then spit out one of the dog tick-bombs. It sparked, and he threw his body on top of it.

"Let me see, Davey," Squirrel Girl said.

She plucked the machine out from under Davey's body. It was slimy with Davey's saliva, and as she watched, its little red light flickered, dimmed, and went out.

"Huh," Squirrel Girl said. "I think you broke it."

"*Chka,*" Davey said, hanging his head.

"No, that's good," Squirrel Girl said. "We want it broken. Your spit probably short-circuited the poison bomb. Score one for stupendous squirrel spit!"

"*Chka cht,*" Tippy-Toe said.

"Yeah, you're right," Squirrel Girl said, tossing the machine to Tippy. "We should still bury it." She looked at the sandbox where two identical twin girls were sitting, wide-eyed and staring at her and all the squirrels.

"And that, children," Squirrel Girl said, "is our show for the day. Thank you, thank you." She bowed, and the little girls started to clap.

"Uh, don't bury it in the sandbox," Squirrel Girl whispered to Tippy-Toe as she bowed again. "Just in case."

23

TEXT MESSAGES

SQUIRREL GIRL

Hey this is Squirrel Girl you prbly don't know me but I need some help

STARK

Your name sounds familiar. Did we meet in Moscow?

SQUIRREL GIRL

Wait who is this?

STARK

Tony

SQUIRREL GIRL

???

STARK

Tony Stark[96]

SQUIRREL GIRL

Whoops my bad I thought I dialed a hero

STARK

Ha ha srsly tho if I didn't give you my number
how did you get it

SQUIRREL GIRL

A squirrel

STARK

Really?

SQUIRREL GIRL

Yeah. She found a cell phone on a nightstand in
the avengers mansion and took some numbers
off it but most of them I can't tell whose they are
bc she scratched the info into an acorn she was
carrying in her cheek

STARK

Yeah I've heard acorns aren't the best data
storage medium

---

96 Tony Stark, aka Iron Man. I always feel so sad for him and his awkward facial-hair choices so clearly trying to compensate for his lack of tail. :(

SQUIRREL GIRL

SQUIRREL GIRL

I'll just try the next number sorry to bother u

STARK

Wait maybe I could still help. What do you need?

SQUIRREL GIRL

It's ok I just had some tactical questions about fighting bad guys. Hero stuff.

STARK

I've fought a lot of bad guys I'm pretty smart I might have some ideas

SQUIRREL GIRL

No it's cool sry to bug u

STARK

We didn't meet in Dubai? Reno maybe?

* * *

SQUIRREL GIRL

Hi I have a tactical question can you help?

WINTER SOLDIER[97]

Winter Soldier is go

---

97 Really not sure who this Winter Soldier person is, but I'm assuming a yeti who works for the Avengers undercover?

SQUIRREL GIRL

You're not Iron Man right? You're a hero who knows about fighting bad guys?

WINTER SOLDIER

Confirmed I am not Iron Man. How did you get this number?

SQUIRREL GIRL

A squirrel. So I've got a situation

WINTER SOLDIER

I'm listening

SQUIRREL GIRL

Some crazy super villain gassed a bunch of dogs and made them chase squirrels and put a zucchini in a hot air balloon and pretended it was a baby so I'd save it and is being generally creepy but the police might not believe me

WINTER SOLDIER

No police

SQUIRREL GIRL

Maybe I'm in over my head? How should I deal with a bad guy?

WINTER SOLDIER

Give me the address

SQUIRREL GIRL

SQUIRREL GIRL

Address?

WINTER SOLDIER

Coordinates. Be exact. Make sure he's there.
Then get out. Erase these messages and
dissolve your phone in acid and leave town. Say
goodbye to no one. Change your name. Gladys
is a good choice or yolanda. I'd recommend
something with a y but up to you no judgment
either way

SQUIRREL GIRL

Um

WINTER SOLDIER

Don't stay in any motel longer than one night.
Keep moving eat on the go but don't neglect your
greens. Dark greens rich with vitamins like kale
or spinach you get it

SQUIRREL GIRL

This is all a little more intense than I was
expecting

WINTER SOLDIER

Never contact your family again. That is if you
still have one no judgment here.

SQUIRREL GIRL

So

WINTER SOLDIER

Get a new wardrobe. Try a nice purple maybe. Chartreuse and gray isn't taken. Also you should shave your head and burn off your fingerprints. Maybe learn sumo or leg wrestling. Not my style but might work for yolanda. Or yvette.

SQUIRREL GIRL

I'm just gonna go now

* * *

SQUIRREL GIRL

Mr stark?

STARK

Hey you're back!

SQUIRREL GIRL

Yeah I got the winter soldier and he wasn't super helpful

STARK

He told you to change your name to yvonne didn't he

SQUIRREL GIRL

Yolanda

STARK

Knew it. So tell me the sitch. Is it hydra? Are the chitauri back? Kingpin at it again?

SQUIRREL GIRL

No actually I was just wondering do you have thor's number my squirrel friend didn't get that one. She-hulk would be ideal obvs but I bet she's prolly sooo busy being amazing and I don't want to bug her

STARK

Or you could just ask one of the smartest people on the planet who also happens to be an avenger and regularly saves the world

SQUIRREL GIRL

Great idea yes pls could u give me bruce banners number

Mr stark?

Tony stark? Iron man?

Hello?

Are you there? Hello? Helloooooooooo

Hellooooooooooooooooooooooooooooooooooooooo
oooooooooooooooooooooooooooooooooooooooo
oooooooooooooooooooooooooooooooooooooooo
oooooooooooooooooooooooooooooooooooooooo
ooooooooooo

STARK

I'm not giving you Bruce's number

SQUIRREL GIRL

K thx anyway!

24

ANA SOFÍA

*T*he cafeteria was blissfully quiet. Ana Sofía was having one of those days and had switched off her hearing aids.

She was so used to reading lips and deducing what people were saying she didn't always notice that the effort sometimes just wore her out.

Before she moved away, Honey had been Ana Sofía's best friend. Both Honey and her mom were deaf, and it was with them that Ana Sofía had chiefly signed. Honey's mother had explained that Ana Sofía had to use more brainpower than hearing people did in order to understand. That could be taxing. And when she felt exhausted, it was okay to take a break.

When Ana Sofía's father got tired, he got spacey. "Hmm, what?" he'd respond to everything. When Ana Sofía's mother got tired, she got sleepy, and half the time she fell asleep against Ana

Sofía's shoulder while they watched *Super Hero Action TV Live!* after dinner. But when Ana Sofía got tired, she got cranky. Like, melt-your-face-off-with-my-glare angry.

If Doreen had been there, she'd try to make her laugh. But Doreen wasn't at school. After the dog-gassing event, she'd confessed it all to her parents. They had made her stay home, half grounding her and half just plain worried about her.[98]

Ana Sofía had plenty of work to do on her laptop anyway. Sleuthing, that is. This mystery still had so many unanswered questions.

When the hot-air balloon had gotten loose from the Burger Frog grand opening, Ana Sofía had tried to text Squirrel Girl, only to discover her phone had no reception. She'd nearly trampled some poor guy in a frog suit as she ran to find a place with enough wireless signal to send the texts.

A cell-signal dead zone right in the middle of town? Something must have been causing interference on the radio waves. A mystery! So she'd set to gathering clues.

She'd installed an app on her phone that measured local reception and tagged GPS locations to the data. This past week she'd been running errands all over town. She picked up her dad's dry cleaning on the south side. She walked to school the long way, around the east edge of the park. She went with her

---

98 I was fine. When I'm exhausted, I get punchy. I have laughing-so-hard-I cry fits. Exhausted is when I come up with my best dance moves.

mom to the north side of Shady Oaks to get some paving stones for their garden. She attended her little brother's dance recital at West Elementary. Always with her phone on, the app running, measuring interference.

Now on her laptop in the cafeteria she plotted the data on a map of Shady Oaks. The new Burger Frog. The lot where they kept the wild dogs. The park with the squirrel traps. The hottest locations of radio interference were all places where MM had been. But the most interference right now was on the north end of town near a bunch of warehouses where nothing had happened.

Where nothing had happened *yet.*

An alert popped up on her screen. Another Squirrel Girl video! This time of the dogs and the attempted gassing. It'd been shot with several cameras. Clearly Squirrel Girl hadn't destroyed all the camera micro-bots. The video was edited like a music video with a thumping, heroic sound track. Text flashed across the bottom of the screen.

SPEED.

STRENGTH.

AGILITY.

DAY-SAVING.

THERE CAN BE NO DOUBT.

SQUIRREL GIRL IS A SUPER HERO.

A WORTHY FOE TO ANY SUPER VILLAIN.

Ana Sofía felt so uneasy she barely touched the cheese and crackers that made up her lunch.[99] In the video, Squirrel Girl did look like a Super Hero, even if Ana Sofía wasn't sure she could technically be one unless real professional heroes acknowledged her. Maybe the Avengers would see this and decide they needed Squirrel Girl in their Super Hero world-saving super team. Maybe even Thor was watching the video right that second.

Thor. Ana Sofía felt her cheeks grow hot and glanced around to make sure no one noticed.

Mike wasn't at her table today. Or yesterday. Maybe he'd finally gotten so annoyed with humanity in general that he dropped out of school. The Somebodies were gathered around their usual tables by the frozen-yogurt machine, but none looked her way.

Ana Sofía's uneasy tummy burbled when she thought about that last line in the video: *"A worthy foe to any Super Villain."*

Who was filming Squirrel Girl? Was it MM himself? What did he want?

Ana Sofía pushed up her sleeves and got to work, tracking the video-submitter's origin, tracing the account back to an IP address, and then narrowing down where and to whom that

---

99 Ana Sofía practically lives on cheese and crackers. Meat makes her troubled. Sauce makes her gag. The occasional pickle is her idea of an intense flavor experience. She's so awesome.

IP address belonged. It wasn't easy. This guy knew his stuff and was trying to make himself invisible. But Ana Sofía knew something about sorta being invisible herself. Not to mention a thing or two about computers.

Someone tapped Ana Sofía's shoulder. She looked up. The cafeteria was almost empty now; most of fourth-period lunch was heading back to class. Only the Somebodies were still lingering. One of their younger members, Lucy Tang, had tapped Ana Sofía's shoulder. Ana Sofía had known her in elementary school as a nice and somewhat shy girl. Getting into the Somebodies had made her bolder, more eager and anxious, and also a bit harder-edged.[100]

Lucy was talking. Ana Sofía sighed and turned on her hearing aid.

"What?"

Lucy huffed an annoyed breath. "I *said*, Heidi wants to invite you to sit with us."

Ana Sofía's already-uneasy stomach went queasy-uneasy. Her exhausted self dropped into ultra-exhausted. She followed Lucy, because you just didn't say no to a Somebodies summons, but she kept her eyes down because she was full of exhaustion and she didn't know how to turn it off. She noticed that Lucy wasn't wearing socks with her slip-on kicks. What was the point of

---

100 I think this is Ana Sofía's way of saying "less nice."

having feet if you didn't cushion them up in lovely soft socks? Some people just didn't know how to live.[101]

When she looked up, Heidi and all dozen-plus Somebodies were looking at her, curious but also laid-back cool, as if posing for the cover of *People Posing as Cats Magazine*.[102] "We've been watching the Squirrel Girl videos," Heidi said. Probably. Heidi didn't have a very expressive face. It was more difficult for Ana Sofía to figure out all her words. "Shady Oaks has our own Super Hero."

Janessa started talking before Ana Sofía looked at her, so she missed what she said. In such situations Ana Sofía could either pretend she'd heard and hope no response from her was expected, or she could risk bugging people by asking them to repeat it. Squirrel Girl mattered to her too much to pretend today, so she opted for the latter.

"What was that?" asked Ana Sofía.

"I *said*, I thought she was freaky at first, but freaky is cool, right?" said Janessa.

The swoopy-haired guys were nodding.

Two other people started talking at the same time, and then a third joined in, jabbering so quickly to each other, Ana Sofía only caught "Squirrel Girl."

---

101 Another fun Ana Sofía fact: She doesn't relish hugs. Try to hug her when she's not ready for it and she'll just stand there, arms limp, while her enormous brain thinks curses at you. But socks, she says, are hugs for your feet, and those are the best kinds of hugs.
102 *sigh* Also not a real magazine. Life is so unfair.

Heidi seemed to say something else . . . or had she just been smacking her lips as if to spread lip gloss? Then another swoopy-haired guy was talking but he was looking down and then at Heidi, so Ana Sofía missed that, too.

"Look, I can't follow this conversation, everyone talking over each other," she said.

Heidi held out her hand and gestured to Ana Sofía's phone. She handed it over. Heidi texted herself, then handed it back so they had each other's numbers. Then she inserted Ana Sofía into a Somebodies group text.

HEIDI

> Did u hear bout the skunk club? They legit went straight. Not trashing anymore and been tagging acorns all over as a sign that the town is protected by SG. They say they're squirrel scouts like they're an army or something. Now all my sister's friends at union high r calling themselves squirrel scouts too. Did u know that was a thing?

"Uh, yeah," said Ana Sofía, too tired to be polite. "It's *my* thing. I made it up."

Heidi looked around, as if getting approval from her brood. The others nodded. She began speed-texting on her phone again.

HEIDI

> We want u to make us squirrel scouts too and u can sit with us at lunch and come to parties at my house. Congrats ur in

Ana Sofía's glare turned into a gape. Wait . . . they were making *her* a Somebody? Everybody at Union Junior wanted to be a Somebody. And yet it was an honor that Ana Sofía had never even bothered to daydream about. Not in the way that she definitely never-ever-never daydreamed about playing air hockey with Thor and sharing crackers and just hanging out 'cause they were like such good friends they could just look at each other and laugh and laugh knowing exactly what the other was thinking. Not like that.

JANESSA

Yeah ur cool now

LANESSA

But just u not ur friend the one with buck teeth n chubby cheeks she look funny

A few others nodded seriously.

Ana Sofía was holding her laptop. And for just a moment she had a very real daydream. Not like the daydreams she definitely never-ever-never had about Thor where the two of them went bike riding along the coast and stopped at this little Ma-and-Pa sock shop and Thor bought a sock so big he wore it like a hat, and it streamed behind him as he rode, flopping around in the wind, and how they laughed and laughed!

Not like that. This daydream involved her knocking the Somebodies over their heads with her laptop. *I'll show* you *who looks funny.* . . .

She took a deep breath. She asked herself what Doreen would do. Her left hand made the sign of an *S*, her right hand a *G* tracing a flowing tail away from the *S*.

"This is the sign for Squirrel Girl," she said, just trying to start with something positive. No matter what Doreen said, being positive was way overrated. Still, she could see it would have a better effect than speaking those other not-so-positive words that were in her head at the moment. "Yes . . . you can be Squirrel Scouts. But it's important for Squirrel Girl that all those who represent her brand of awesomeness do so in a positive, heroic way. So you first, uh, need to learn the Squirrel Scout Creed. Repeat after me."

Ana Sofía made up the creed as she went, and sentence by sentence, they repeated after her:

As a Squirrel Scout, I solemnly promise to never judge someone by how they look. Or talk. Or walk. Or leap. I will defend the weak, the frightened, and the interesting. I will be a friend to the small and furry. I will be brave and silly. I will be honest, even when it's awkward. I will notice other people's awesomeness. And my own. And we will be awesome together. And also save the day whenever the day needs saving. Uh, amen.

"It's a work in progress," said Ana Sofía apologetically. "I'll have a better Squirrel Scout Creed next week, probably. But you get the general idea."

Heidi, it seemed, hadn't noticed any flaws. Her eyes were sparkling as she said, "I've never had a creed before."

"Really?" said Ana Sofía.[103]

Heidi stood up and imitated the Squirrel Girl symbol: letter S with the letter G swooping away, all tail-like. She was maybe five feet tall, but just then, she looked as powerful as a Greek goddess. She threw back her hair and grinned as she madly texted.

HEIDI

> I love being a squirrel scout! Im totes gonna uphold our awesome creed n teach others this awesomeness! And ur cheeked friend can sit with us too right fellow squirrel scouts?

The Somebodies read her text on their phones, nodding. One by one they made the Squirrel Girl sign.

Seeing the power her words fired up in Heidi made Ana Sofía forget how tired she was. She kinda felt fairly awesome herself. She kinda felt almost a teeny tiny bit like a real Super Hero.

Thor would be so proud.

---

103 Ana Sofía has tons of creeds. Usually they're mash-ups of the little sayings her mom cross-stitches on pillows. Like, last week's creed was "Home is the thief of joy." Or it might have been "Comparison is where the heart is." Something like that.

25

DOREEN

*U*nion Junior's parent-teacher conference was in the gym. The sandy-sweet chemical smell of bulk discount cookies on the refreshment table mixed with the gym's shoe-rubber and stale teen-sweat odors. Doreen's keen nose picked up all of it, and she wished the wish of open windows.

Though after being grounded, it felt pretty amazing to be back at school, strange scents and all. Two days alone in her room, blasting songs through her headphones loud enough to fill up the lonely places. Sneaky windowsill visits from Tippy-Toe had kept her sane. Now she was so relieved to be around other people again she couldn't help bouncing on the balls of her feet.[104]

The teachers sat at tables throughout the gym and parents

---

104 Tippy says I might be more of a ground squirrel since they're social animals, while tree squirrels tend to be solitary. But she meant it in a nice way.

stood in line for their turns. All the lines reminded Doreen of an amusement park. An amusement park where the ride was to sit down in front of your Algebra teacher, who then told your parents all your faults.[105]

"At the beginning of the semester, she showed no interest in her work," said Mr. Herrmann. "Then her homework started to improve, but she was absent this week and I fear she's falling behind again."

"We won't let that happen," said Dor. "Right, Doreen?"

Doreen nodded. Her feelings about algebra had greatly improved since Ana Sofía helped her make sense of it, but dang it if it wasn't hard to get homework done while also saving the day two or three times a week.[106]

Then on to her English teacher, Mrs. Finlayson.

"Doreen really needs to work on her focus. When she finishes her work, she does it too quickly."

"You're so right, she is quick!" said Dor. "And so efficient. I love that about her."

"I guess . . ." said Mrs. Finlayson.

On to Biology teacher Mr. Rodriguez.

"Obviously bright but very . . . talkative."

"Oh yes, very bright," agreed Maureen. "And yes, so talkative!

---

105 I'm pretty sure this amusement park will never be a thing, and I'm okay with that.
106 I totally get why real Super Heroes are adults. I mean, they are, aren't they? I don't see Captain America battling invading alien hordes while also studying for a Biology quiz and writing an essay on symbols in *Lord of the Flies*.

We never lack for conversation. Doreen is our lifeblood!"
Maureen kissed Doreen's head.

"Yes . . . but . . ." said Mr. Rodriguez.

History teacher, Mrs. Nelson.

"It's an awkward age; I'm sure she'll grow out of it."

"No hurry, if you ask me!" said Dor. "Every year I think: this
is my favorite age for Doreen yet. But then she surprises me by
getting better and better."

"That's sweet," said Mrs. Nelson, dabbing her eyes. "You're
right. Doreen is special. I forget sometimes that they're . . . they're
all special."

And Mrs. Nelson broke down crying.[107]

Maureen and Dor beamed, all their wonderful opinions about
Doreen confirmed.

Doreen was trying to catch sight of Ana Sofía and finally
spied her with her parents over by the PE teachers.

"BRB," said Doreen. "I've gotta warn Ana Sofía about the
bulk-discount chemical cookies."

The crowd was thick. Doreen tensed her leg muscles,
crouched, and very nearly sprang right over their heads.

No. She stopped herself just in time. It was confusing, switch-
ing between Doreen and Squirrel Girl.

---

107 When some people get tired, they cry a lot. Also I had a friend in California who,
whenever we had a sleepover and stayed up too late, got *sooo* gassy. Exhaustion comes in
many forms!

Instead she scampered through the crowd. She was pretty good at threading through spaces seemingly too tight for a fourteen-year-old girl.

As she passed by the Computers teacher, Mrs. Lin, she overheard her say, "Mike has been missing so much school lately. Is he okay?"

Curious, Doreen slowed down to listen. A woman who must have been Mike's mother was sitting upright in the folding chair before Mrs. Lin. She was tall and skinny, with rigid posture, pale smooth skin, and perfectly straight brown hair, dressed in a well-pressed pantsuit in a conservative navy blue.

"Mike is fine," said Mike's mother. "He is a little ill, so I have kept him home. But I want to assure you he is fine. No need to alert the authorities."

"Okay," said Mrs. Lin. "Will you tell him we miss him? He's my best student. Such a clever mind!"

Mike's mother said it again. "Mike is fine. He is smart and keeping up with his studies at home. I want to assure you that he is fine."

"Okaaay," said Mrs. Lin.

Sheesh, what a dull conversation. Doreen moved on and caught up with Ana Sofía.

"Hey, FYI, don't eat the cookies," said Doreen, signing the best she could. She knew all the noise in the gym would make it impossible for Ana Sofía to understand her. "They smell more like plastic and oil and metal than food. I don't know where the school bought them, but—"

"I have to talk to you," said Ana Sofía. "But it's so noisy in here." She held up a finger to Doreen and spoke to her mother. *"Mamá, me voy afuera por un ratito. Espérame, okay?"*

Ana Sofía pulled Doreen outside. Doreen took a big breath, filling herself up with delicious tree pollen, the fresh aroma of grass. Outdoor dirt just smelled cleaner than indoor dirt.

"The account that originally registered the block of IPs that posted the videos—the bank account, I mean, the one that paid the fees—belongs to Adam Romanger," said Ana Sofía.

"Who? What?" said Doreen. "Pee fees? I know what you said means something. It's like a secret code! I want to learn all the computer science stuff you know. Hey, maybe that'll be my major someday in college. Wait . . . Romanger? That name sounds familiar. . . ."

"Adam Romanger is Mike's dad. I think he's the one posting the videos."

"No way! Mike's mom is in there, but his dad isn't, and neither is Mike. He hasn't been to school in like a week, right?"

Just then Mike's mother exited the school. Her eyes fixed straight ahead, she walked across the parking lot, made a right turn at the sidewalk, and continued on.

"Something's—" Doreen started.

"Off about her," Ana Sofía finished.

Ana Sofía had to go back to her mother, so Doreen crawled

through the parking lot by herself. Completely inconspicuous. Unless someone happened to look over and wonder why that girl was crawling around a parking lot.

Tippy-Toe found her and crawled alongside her, head low to the ground and tail up. Doreen peered over the hood of a car, watching Mike's mother disappear into the night. Tippy-Toe leaped onto her head.

"Hey, Tip," Doreen whispered. "Will you follow that lady? Tell me where she goes?"

"Chk chukka chk?"

"No, the lady, not the robot. Wait, what?"

"Chuk-chk."

"The lady is a robot? How do you know?"

"Chuk chika cha."

"Whoa, you're right. And I was blaming that smell on the cookies. In that case, maybe we should both follow her."

Following proved to be difficult for Doreen. Sneaking after someone required her to move *slower* than the target. Doreen kept creeping from tree to tree way too fast, almost bumping into Mike's mother, and then having to crouch behind a bush and wait *for-ev-er* for her to walk another block.

DOREEN

Turns out Mike's mom is a robot. Following her. She's soooooooooooooooooo slow makes me want to scream

ANA SOFÍA

She's a robot for real?

DOREEN

Why can't evil people be faster? This is more irritating than accidentally eating a raisin

ANA SOFÍA

So ur parents are ok with u being super sleuth

DOREEN

Um txt u ltr

* * *

DOREEN

Hey Mumz sry I took off evil is afoot

MOM

Your father says to tell you that evil is not a foot but a butt. LOL ROFL

DOREEN

Evil is a butt! I'm using that

MOM

Just so long as evil isn't a head. Get it? Ahead? :) ;) LOL

DOREEN

I get it

MOM

Now your father is calling evil random body parts. :)> You're probably glad you're missing this

Wait why are you missing this? Where are you?

DOREEN

Following evil butts

MOM

But we still need to meet with your gym teacher and your art teacher. Is another baby in danger?

DOREEN

Probably somewhere? But there's this robot and I just need to follow her and see whats up bc she's my friends mom sorta? Sorta friend. Sorta mom

MOM

Your sorta friend's sorta mom is a robot?

DOREEN

That's what I'm trying to find out

MOM

Well now I have to know too. Ok but you stay back and don't engage. No SG promise?

DOREEN

Promise

MOM

Double promise? I mean it. I can be a mean mom if I need to

DOREEN

You don't need to I promise

And Doreen meant it. She really wasn't going to be Squirrel Girl. But as she perched in the sturdy maple across the street from the Romanger residence, she just felt so vulnerable. Like a shaved chipmunk. Like a tailless squirrel. Like half of herself.

Tail out. Hoodie up. But stay back, Squirrel Girl. Stay way back.

26

SQUIRREL GIRL

*T*he curtains of the Romangers' big picture window were not entirely closed, and between it getting dark outside and her excellent Squirrel Vision, Squirrel Girl could see two people on a couch watching television. The blue flickering lights of the TV lit up Mike's parents as they stared, expressionless, back at it.

"This feels creepy," Squirrel Girl whispered.

"Chk chukka," Tippy-Toe whispered back.

"Yeah, there's a creepy vibe coming from that house for sure, but I meant us, too, watching them here all sneaky-like. And really, we're the creepier ones, right? I mean, plenty of non-creepy people watch TV in the dark."

"Chkka chk," Tippy said.

"It is weird, right? How does anyone hold so still? They

haven't moved at all in, like, the what, fifteen minutes we've been here watching. That's probably unhealthy."

Squirrel Girl's hero phone buzzed, and she pulled it out from one of her utility belt pouches.

ANA SOFÍA

Find anything? Do not answer if currently battling evil

SQUIRREL GIRL

No evil just couchpotatoing which is kind of evil from a personal health perspective

ANA SOFÍA

Maybe MM just made it look like the account belonged to Mike's dad

SQUIRREL GIRL

The people watching TV don't look evil

ANA SOFÍA

That's the worst kind of evil that masquerades as not evil

SQUIRREL GIRL

But the dog bombs and the squirrel traps seemed so evil I guess I was expecting a volcano lair you know

ANA SOFÍA

No volcanoes in jersey. Yet

Tippy-Toe chittered softly, and Squirrel Girl looked up. The father had stood and was staring out the window.

"Oops," Squirrel Girl hissed, leaning farther back under the tree's canopy. "Do you think they saw?"

"*Chkka,*" Tippy-Toe said.

The probably-Mike's-dad figure pulled the curtains completely closed. Now even Squirrel Vision was no help.

"Do *you* have X-ray vision?" Squirrel Girl asked Tippy-Toe.

The squirrel made a clicking noise in the back of her throat in the way that meant, "Of course not. No one does. Don't be ridiculous."

"Yeah," Squirrel Girl said. "Me neither."

She jumped down from the tree and hopped across the street.

"*Chkka chk?*"

"I know, I know," Squirrel Girl said. "I'm not engaging. I promised my mom I wouldn't. I'm just going to knock. They're probably not robots really, right? We'll just make sure and go home and not be Peeping Toms anymore."

She knocked three times, put her hands on her hips, and smiled. Just like selling Girl Scout cookies back in California.

The door opened, and the dark-haired woman from the parent-teacher conference smiled back at her. Her smell was definitely not normal.

"Hello," the woman said. "Can I help you?"

"Hi," Squirrel Girl said. "I'm Squirrel Girl!"

The woman nodded. "Hello, Squirrel Girl," she said.

This was as far as Squirrel Girl had planned ahead in the conversation, and now she scrambled for reasons to explain why she had knocked.

"I'm . . . uh . . . going door-to-door," she said. "Looking for e . . . uh . . . eel. Um. Eels."

She had been about to say "evil," but realized that would definitely tip them off if they were evil and freak them out if they weren't.

The woman tilted her head. "For *eels?*" she asked.

Squirrel Girl scanned what she could see inside the house beyond the woman, looking for something, anything, that might be evil, or obvious proof of robots masquerading as parents, or Mike in trouble.

"Would you like to come in?" the woman asked.

"Why, yes," Squirrel Girl said. "Yes, I would, thank you."

Stay back, do not engage! Good, solid, parental advice. But something about a five-foot squirrel tail waving around behind her gave her so much confidence she just couldn't remember why she wasn't supposed to engage.

So when the woman stepped aside, Squirrel Girl walked in.

The living room looked almost irritatingly normal: Brown carpet. White walls. Sofa facing a flat-screen TV. Squirrel Girl's lip curled.

"Who is it, dear?" came a deep voice from the next room, followed by the very un-evil sound of a kitchen cupboard closing.

"It's Squirrel Girl, dear," the woman said. "She is going door-to-door looking for eels."

A pleasant-looking dark-haired white man appeared in the hallway, holding an empty drinking glass in his hand. "What a noble endeavor," the man said. "Though I'm afraid we have no eels here."

The man took a drink from his glass. From his empty glass.

And then she heard a scream.

"What was that?" Squirrel Girl asked.

"What was what?" the woman said.

The scream came again, and this time Squirrel Girl could definitely detect the edges of the word "help" in it.

"That," she said. "That scream."

"It is not an eel," the man said.

"We have no eels in the basement," the woman said.

The two parents shuffled back until they were standing in front of a closed door.

"Help!" the muffled sound echoed again, clearly from behind that basement door.

"Where is Mike?" Squirrel Girl asked. "Is Mike here?"

"Yes," said the father.

"No," said the mother, at the same time.

"Okeydoke," Squirrel Girl said, taking a step forward. "I'm just going to check."

The parents went rigid, their fingers splaying, arms locking straight at their sides.

"We can't let you do that," they said. With a ratcheting sound, blades slid from each of their fingertips, and they raised their hands up in perfect unison.

"Whoa, hold on," Squirrel Girl said, lifting up her own hands. "Can't we talk about this?"

Their wrists clicked and then started spinning. What had once been hands had turned into something like four industrial-size blenders.

"So, definitely robots," Squirrel Girl said. She darted down and leaped underneath the blades, rolling and popping up behind the two killer robot parents.

The robots swiveled around to their target nearly as fast as squirrels, hand blades still spinning. But with the movement the blades clattered into each other. There was a terrible sound of scraping, bending, and snapping metal. The robots pulled at each other, their hands intertwined and locked together by bent metal blades.

"While you guys figure that out," Squirrel Girl said, reaching for the handle to the basement door, "I'll just—"

The robots ejected their android hands at the wrists, the mass of twisted metal dropping to the floor. The father kicked the still-twitching hand blades at her. She ducked, just stopping herself from trying to catch the thing and throw it back, because ouch, too many sharp bits.

The robots marched toward her like handless zombies, arms out. Their mouths opened like they were going to speak, but then just kept going, their rubbery cheeks tearing as they gaped much wider than humanly possible. The mouths clamped shut then opened again as they shambled closer, like weird head-mounted versions of Pac-Man.

"Yeah! Definitely creepy!" Squirrel Girl shouted. Her work-out video training kicked in, and she instinctively enacted Commander Quiff's Blow Their Nose Kick.

The force of a leg that could propel a girl onto a rooftop slammed into one head, and then the other. The heads popped off and clonked onto the carpet.

"Gah! I'm so sorry," Squirrel Girl said. She crouched to the heads. "I normally don't behead people, really, not even robot people. You just freaked me out."

The heads chomped at her pointlessly a few more times, and then slowed to a stop, robotic eyes closing.

"Well," Squirrel Girl said. "That was—"

She was interrupted by a black loafer thumping into her tail. And then another. And then a pair of black pumps. Someone was throwing shoes at her.

She turned. The headless, handless bodies of the robots were twitching with the wincing sound of grinding metal. It wasn't some*one* throwing shoes. It was some*thing*. Two things. Two headless handless robot things. They'd expelled the shoes off their legs to reveal nasty pointed spikes instead of feet.

"You're not actually dead, are you?" Squirrel Girl said. "That makes me feel better about knocking your heads off."

The robots each bent at the waist, pushing the stumps of their necks together, wires snaking out like little tentacles toward each other. The two bodies joined into one freakish eight-legged spider thing.

"Okaaay," Squirrel Girl said. "I thought the chomping-head thing was creepy. . . ."

She looked for somewhere to leap, but the room was too small and the spider-bot was too big. It charged her, and Squirrel Girl scampered up the wall and wedged herself in the top corner of the living room. The robot swiveled in her direction.

"How can you see me?" Squirrel Girl asked. "You don't even have eyes anymore."

The spider-bot crawled to a spot just below her and stuck two of its spike-tipped legs into the wall. It heaved itself up and stuck the other two in, climbing.

"Right," Squirrel-Girl said. "Spider-bot. I guess climbing walls is a thing you do." She scampered aside, but not quick enough. One of the handless limbs whacked her leg, and she lost her grip. As she struggled to grab hold again, one of the spike-pointed limbs reared up to strike.

"Oh no, you don't," Squirrel Girl said, dropping just as the spike struck. She grabbed hold of the leg and, remembering when she told Ana Sofía that a squirrel's bite is fifty times more powerful than a human's, bit down. She cleared easily through chunks of rubber robot skin and found the thick metal skeleton. It began to bend between her teeth.

The leg shook, not like it was breaking, but like it was a wet dog trying to get dry. Squirrel Girl held tight, but the ride was the kind that made you regret everything you'd eaten that day. Hoping she timed it right, Squirrel Girl let go of the leg on an out-shake. She flew away from the spider-bot, spinning into the curtains of the big picture window and right through the glass. She tumbled across the front yard, her claws shredding the curtains wrapped around her as she rolled. She hit the trunk of the sturdy maple, tore herself free of the shredded curtains, and leaped to her feet.

"*Chkka?*" Tippy-Toe asked.

Squirrel Girl checked all her parts. "I'm okay."

The spider-bot crawled out of the Squirrel Girl–size hole in the window and twitched two stumpy forelegs at her.

"Ha!" Squirrel Girl shouted. "Sucka! You should have kept me caged inside! Outside is my world!"

She stood in front of the tree, put her hands up to her head like antlers and stuck out her tongue. "Nanna-nanna boo-boo, you can't get me! I'm freakin' Squirrel Girl, you trash heap. If the place has a tree in it, I *own* it!"

From the branches, Tippy-Toe chittered in alarm.

"Don't worry, Tip," she whispered. "I'm *taunting* it. I have a plan."

The robot charged. Squirrel Girl stayed where she was,

faking a frightened expression that probably wouldn't win any Oscars. Just before the robot reached her, she jumped, tucking and spinning over the evil-robot-parent-spider-thing as it slammed headlong into the tree trunk. The shudder of branches and cracking of wood woke the night.

The robot twitched, momentarily stunned, and then began lashing out at the tree as if the maple had attacked it. Branches flew and the tree creaked.

"Not the tree!" Squirrel Girl leaped to stop it, but already it was too late. The tree was tipping. The wrong way.

She gave it a hard push in the direction of the robot.

"TIMBERRR!" she shouted. The tree fell hard, bouncing down upon the robot, and then up and over onto a car parked in the driveway next door. A car alarm shouted a *BEEP, BEEP, BEEP, BEEP.*

All over the street, people were peering out windows and cracking open their doors.

"Oops," Squirrel Girl said. "Sorry!"

The robot twitched where it had been smashed and then pushed itself up again. Two of its legs were hanging limp, but it turned quickly enough and shuddered toward Squirrel Girl again.

"Sheesh! What does it take to turn you off?"

Sparks popped from the few exposed wires where the parent-bot's necks had joined. Squirrel Girl pounced. She landed hard on the robot's back and began tearing at the sparking spot, getting little jolts of electricity with every swipe. It was like licking a battery with her hands. A big battery. On the back of a runaway bull. And it wasn't working. She could see more wires through the crack, but her fingers were too short and her hands too big to get at them.

The robot ran wild, trying at turns to buck her off or reach onto its own back with one of its flailing limbs. It scampered onto the fallen tree and began to frantically smash its body against it and the car the tree was lying on. The car's windows shattered and at least one of the tires popped. A face in the house window was staring openmouthed at the destruction.

"Sorry," Squirrel Girl said again. "Robots, right?"

The robot scampered off the car on its three remaining spike-tipped feet, stamping holes in the driveway concrete, and then the sidewalk, and then the road.

"Tippy!" Squirrel Girl shouted from the robot's back. "Where are you?"

She heard a chitter and saw a flash of pink. Tippy-Toe was in a tree with a handful of other squirrels watching the robot as it tore into another yard, destroying what was once beautiful shrubbery.[108] At her call, Tippy scampered closer.

"I need," said Squirrel Girl, between the hard bucks of the spiderbot, "someone to . . . crawl in there . . . and chew wire!"

---

108 No kidding, this was like prize shrubbery, the kind of shrubbery that'd win a blue ribbon at a county fair. Such a tragic loss.

Tippy-Toe chittered something, but over the sound of the robot's rampage and the fire hydrant it just destroyed, Squirrel Girl could not make it out. Water shot out like from a cannon, soaking her hoodie. Sopping, it flapped low over her eyes.

"Can you—*whoa!*" The robot bucked hard as it trampled a mailbox, and Squirrel Girl almost lost her grip. "Can you do that?" she asked. "Chew wire? It might take . . . smaller ones. . . ."

Tippy-Toe looked back at a gathered group of her clan, among them Sour Cream and her wee triplets, the Chives.[109] On the sidewalk, the human neighbors had gathered. Among them a baby began to cry. Tippy sighed, gave Squirrel Girl a thumbs-up, and ran off to the other squirrels.

A few spider-bot bucks later, the Chives joined Squirrel Girl on the back of the robot. The tiny squirrels' claws slid around on the metal of the robot so Squirrel Girl had to hand-feed them, one by one, into the exposed electrical hole. They scampered in, and then, almost as if they had tripped a do-as-much-harm-as-possible switch, the robot turned directly toward the human crowd and began to charge.

"Aaah!" Squirrel Girl shouted. "Hurry, fuzzy friends!"

The robot continued its charge.

"Okay, okay," Squirrel Girl muttered. "I can stop this, I can stop this."

---

109 For whatever reason Sour Cream's kids insist on being known collectively as the Chives and don't have individual names, but to each their own, right? I don't judge.

She took a huge leap in front of the charging spider, propelled by her own legs and the momentum of the robot, skidding to a landing just in front of the gathered crowd. She had about two seconds before the robot reached her. It was actually pretty scary on this end. She could understand now why everyone was screaming. It'd been much more fun riding the thing.

She planted her feet, putting her arms up like she was just going to try to stop a charging football player and not an out-of-control robot spider. She clenched her teeth, closed her eyes . . . and the robot stopped. It clattered to a halt a foot in front of her, completely immobile.

"YEAH!" she shouted, turning to the crowd behind her, fists up. She expected a cheer, but they all just sort of stared.

"You're in shock," she said. "I get it."

Three fuzzy little forms emerged from the wreckage. Their hair, what was left of it, was standing on end.

"You did it, little friends!" Squirrel Girl said. "You saved the day!"

One of the Chives gave her a soft chitter. Tippy-Toe gathered them up and leaped away, taking them back to Sour Cream.

The gathered neighbors were talking to one another in low, urgent voices. Some were making phone calls—to the police, no doubt. Squirrel Girl looked back at the path of destruction the robot had made. Yards were torn up, at least two cars were totaled, and the road would have to be completely resurfaced.

Not to mention the unforgivable destruction of that sturdy maple. Evil robots were bad news.

"Omigosh," she said. "Mike! I completely forgot!"

She ran back to the Romanger house and leaped through the big broken window. In her excitement she tore the basement door right off its hinges.

"Whoops," she said. "Squirrel adrenaline, I guess."

"What?" a weak voice sounded from below.

She jumped from the top step straight to the basement floor.

Tied up in a wooden chair in the middle of the room was Mike. Squirrel Girl tightened her damp hood and swished her identity-distracting tail.

"I said," Squirrel Girl said in a voice she hoped sounded older and rougher than Doreen's, "I am here to save you."

"Oh," Mike said. "That's good."

Yay! Squirrel Girl was saving a real human person! Didn't that mean she was closer than ever to becoming a Super Hero? She cut Mike's bindings easily with her claws. He wasn't tied with ropes or chains, but with what looked to her like a bunch of shoelaces. She felt a little sad for Mike, who didn't have enough squirrel strength to break shoelaces.[110]

"You are safe now, citizen," she said, putting her hands on her hips.

"Thank you, Squirrel Girl," Mike said, standing. He didn't

---

110 Not to brag, but I'm constantly breaking shoelaces. And plates. Also shower curtains.

rub his wrists the way people did in movies after getting untied, so maybe he was tougher than she'd thought.

"Now to the task of finding your real parents," she said.

"My real parents?" Mike asked. "Oh, don't worry about them. They're gone."

Squirrel Girl dropped her heroic pose. "Oh no," she said. "Did those robots . . . kill them?"

"Excuse me?" Mike asked.

"I'm sorry," Squirrel Girl said. "That was indelicate. Did those robots . . . *eat* them?"

"No, no," Mike said, waving his hands. "My parents, my human parents, they're just on a business trip. They have to travel a lot."

"I'm sorry."

"No, it's good. Their jobs are really important. The most important. Frankly, I feel really sad for you and everyone else whose parents aren't as intelligent and important as mine."

Mike seemed to mean it. So Squirrel Girl tried to make her sad-for-you face look like a sad-for-me face.

"Someone sent those robot look-alikes to kidnap me while they were gone—probably their enemies, which all intelligent and important people have."

"By any chance did your dad set up lots of cameras around town to spy on me and put a talking zucchini baby in a hot-air balloon?"

"Not that I'm aware of," he said. "Though I guess that if that was intelligent and important he totally might have."

"Huh. When will your parents be back?" Squirrel Girl asked, eyeing the bizarrely empty basement.

"Oh, soon probably," Mike said. "I'll be fine."

"But you'll be alone," Squirrel Girl said.

"Yes, thanks to you."

"But . . . we should tell the police or—"

"NO!" said Mike. He took a breath and spoke carefully. "No. My parents trust me to look after myself. Obviously. Or they wouldn't have left me alone. You should go now. Squirrel Girl."

"Oookay," she said and started up the stairs. She popped her head back down. Mike was standing just where she had left him.

"FYI, your living room window, and, um, basement door are broken," she said. "Also maybe some walls and furniture. And that really nice shrubbery."

"Okay," he said.

"Right," she said, and scampered back up the stairs and onto the Romangers' roof. She sniffed the air. Victory smelled sweet. Also, a little like oiled metal and burned squirrel fur. But still, victory. Sweet.

27

TEXT MESSAGES

SQUIRREL GIRL

Hey is this a super hero?

ROCKET

No this is Rocket go away.

SQUIRREL GIRL

Rocket sounds like a hero name

ROCKET

Wrong. Hero names sound like me.

SQUIRREL GIRL

I got your number from the avengers tho so you must be special

ROCKET

Didn't say I wasn't special. I'm extra special. But those flarknards should not be giving out this number.

SQUIRREL GIRL

So u do know them! Do u have thor's number? Wait does thor even have a phone?

ROCKET

Sure yeah that hammer has an Asgardian cell chip built in.

SQUIRREL GIRL

Really?

ROCKET

Doubt it. You don't want to talk to him anyway. Asgardians ain't great on dialog.

SQUIRREL GIRL

How about cpt america? His costume has pouches one prob holds a phone

ROCKET

Yeah but then you got the whole human problem.

SQUIRREL GIRL

?

ROCKET

You know how humans are. They don't know
jack about squat.

SQUIRREL GIRL

I'm human

ROCKET

So you know what I mean. Just a bunch of
clueless hairless tailless krutackers down there
on Earth am I right?

SQUIRREL GIRL

I have hair

ROCKET

But barely.

SQUIRREL GIRL

I also have a tail

ROCKET

No glarking?

SQUIRREL GIRL

I don't know what that means. Is that a space
swear word? But yes I have a squirrel tail. Tails
are awesome

SQUIRREL GIRL

ROCKET

I know right? I feel bad for the poor naked bottom slobs without 'em.

SQUIRREL GIRL

Me too! You have a tail?

ROCKET

Straight up. You Earth people wouldn't keep mistaking me for a raccoon if I didn't.

SQUIRREL GIRL

Raccoon?

ROCKET

I AM GROOT.

SQUIRREL GIRL

wut?

ROCKET

I AM GROOT.

Groot, quit your yakking. The messaging program on the console uses voice recognition and I'm trying to talk to a girl with a squirrel tail.

I AM GROOT.

Aw that's okay, don't be so hard on yourself.

SQUIRREL GIRL

So ur an alien? Do you know anything about robots?

ROCKET

Only everything. You're lucky you got me and not any of those flark-nozzle Avengers

SQUIRREL GIRL

Have you ever dealt with evil robot parents?

ROCKET

Sure. They yours?

SQUIRREL GIRL

No a kid's from school and I'm trying to figure out who made them

ROCKET

You find them at a theme park?

SQUIRREL GIRL

No

ROCKET

The bots say anything about impenetrable vibroscreens or paving the way for the Kree Empire?

SQUIRREL GIRL

SQUIRREL GIRL

No

ROCKET

Is the kid dead?

SQUIRREL GIRL

No

ROCKET

It's him. He made 'em

SQUIRREL GIRL

Their son made them?

ROCKET

Yep.

I AM GROOT.

See? Groot agrees. Unless the kid is a robot, too. Is he?

SQUIRREL GIRL

I don't think so

ROCKET

Does he say BEEP a lot?

SQUIRREL GIRL

Not that I've noticed

ROCKET

Earth bots LOVE to say BEEP. But my bet is your boy is a regular meat-person, 'cause having robot parents is every human kid's dream

SQUIRREL GIRL

I don't think that's true

ROCKET

Well not yours, obviously. You have a tail. You're clearly well-adjusted.

SQUIRREL GIRL

I like to think so

ROCKET

But seriously go check out the kid.

SQUIRREL GIRL

Thx you've been super helpful

ROCKET

Tail pride, sister.

28

MICRO-MANAGER

*M*ike scanned through the columns of data his drones had collected during Squirrel Girl's three trials. He smiled. According to his analysis, he had a 98 percent chance of victory against her. He would have preferred 100 percent, but the hero's battle with the android parents had come unexpectedly early. It *had* been planned, of course, but for three days later and in a venue other than his own house.

The timetable had to be moved up. He needed to activate the endgame now. He had drawn too much attention to the Romangers already, and that was a no-no.

His parents—his real non-robot human parents—were life-long Hydra agents. Their relationship and marriage had been a research project by the Human Leverage Research division of Hydra, an attempt to prove the existence of such supernatural concepts as "love" and "domestic bliss." The experiment had failed, of course, and when it was shut down, his parents had been reassigned. His father had gone back to the subterranean nanotech manufactory in Cleveland, and his mother had returned to the Office of Viruses and Countermeasures in Rexburg, Idaho. Leaving Mike behind, alone.

He'd long wondered why Hydra hadn't gotten rid of him. He was a loose end from a failed project. But since he was not dead, his parents must have intervened. Though their domestic experiment failed, perhaps they had still felt some small kind of parental affection for him. The idea made him feel an embarrassingly warm and tingly sensation in his chest.

The last time he'd seen his mother, two years ago, she had said, "Hydra will probably ignore you. As long as you don't draw attention to yourself. Above all, be smart and be clever."

Mike shook his head, the disappointment he felt in himself obliterating that warm-glowy-chest thing. Having a Super Hero vs. robot fight in your home probably qualified as "drawing attention."

But his parents had left behind so many toys. His father's 3-D printers just sitting in the basement and in the family warehouse, each connected to spools of Hydra-issue titanium polymer. His mother's server farm and her workstations had not been wiped. All her programming libraries and self-learning code strings were still intact, ready to be uploaded to an accommodating computing platform It was irresistible. You can't leave a kid alone with toys and not expect him to play.

And frankly, he'd concluded, it must have been a test. Why

else would they have left it all behind if not *for* him? To see if he could prove himself equal in evil to his parents. And more than just a loose end from a failed experiment.

When Squirrel Girl had shown up the night of the parent-teacher conference, Mike had allowed the robot parents to battle her just as they had been programmed to do, despite it being the wrong day and wrong place. It was a calculated risk. He needed to see how well the Squirrel Girl fared in actual combat. *Now* he knew. *Now* he was ready. After his endgame with the rodent-girl, everyone would know his value. When Hydra came for him after that, it would not be to kill him. It would be to recruit him. He giggled with the thought and ate three Oreos in a row.

Blowing the cookie dust off his fingers, he logged in to the Hydra Hopefuls subgroup on the Baddit Super Villain forums, ready to post the announcement. His breath came faster; his fingers tingled. There was no turning back now.

Baddit / Hydra Hopefuls / Announcements[111]

SATURDAY SUPER HERO SMACKDOWN

submitted by micromanager

Big show this Saturday. Tune in to the Micro-Manager stream at 14:00 GMT

---

111 Okay, I read this part twice, and I kinda get what's going on. It looks like an online forum for Hydra hopefuls—like a website where potential villains come to chat and insult one another?

to see a Super Hero get smacked down. By the Micro-Manager. Me. If you
are actively recruiting talent, DO NOT MISS THIS.

44 comments / share / save / hide / report

HELLSTROM8
lies

MICROMANAGER
all true. stream at 14:00 to see

ANONYMASQUE
what hero?

MICROMANAGER
new one. its a surprise. check it out.

HELLSTROM8
proof of lies

ILLUMINASTY
trolloscam. front the info or bail. not going to waste my time watching a
powerless norm get spanked.

MICROMANAGER
powered target. and I'd watch my tone if I were you.

HELLSTROM8
oh snap. liar has bite.

SQUIRREL GIRL

ILLUMINASTY

wannabe dropping empty threats. so scary. till you say who the hero is, you are public poser number 1

MICROMANAGER

think I'm going to post name deets even here and risk dropping clues to net sniffers? rookie move

ILLUMINASTY

rookie is as rookie does, u poser

MICROMANAGER

get off my thread

ILLUMINASTY

make me, mickey mangler

MICROMANAGER

ok

ILLUMINASTY

. . . suddenly . . . my mind is not my own . . . must leave thread . . . LOL!!! even if you could do anything, you're a poser. scared. you've already shown that.

MICROMANAGER

not scared. smart. as in not dumb. As in smart enough to mask my ip and desynchronize my user id so people can't run traces to find out where I'm posting from. unlike some people

ILLUMINASTY

poser. even your bluffs are bogus.

MICROMANAGER
let's see, you're in the western US

ILLUMINASTY
ooooh. real close.

MICROMANAGER
Utah

ILLUMINASTY
what?

MICROMANAGER
Salt Lake County

ILLUMINASTY
hey okay

MICROMANAGER
looks like the city is called Murray? weird. you live in a city named after somebody's uncle

ILLUMINASTY
stop

MICROMANAGER
is that Vine street or whine street you're on?

ILLUMINASTY
dude stop I'm out I'm out

HELLSTROM8

going to a new thread

ANONYMASQUE

Can you provide metahuman power ranking on the target at least?

MICROMANAGER

sure. Greek holistic scale puts target at Delta minimum. estimated strength 2.5 Rogers, speed 0.22 Maximoff.

A1M80T

how were these figures determined?

MICROMANAGER

three-tiered trial, modified Arcade system with 20+ independent monitoring drones

---

A1M80T

Arcade system unreliable

MICROMANAGER

hence the mods

ANONYMASQUE

impressive then, if it holds true. would you be willing to share the data?

MICROMANAGER

for a fee. but if you're in recruitment for a credited organization I'd waive the fee.

ANONYMASQUE
lets wait until after the "smackdown" then we'll talk

MICROMANAGER
looking forward to it

29

DOREEN

Sunday morning, three days after the Battle of the Mysterious Robot Parents, Doreen was training to *Commander Quiff's Un-Mixed Martial Arts* in the basement. Victory. Her first big fight had ended in victory. So why did she feel kinda sick to her stomach?[112] She turned the volume all the way up. She punched the air. She leaped and kicked. She said "AAAAAGGGHHH!" But the feeling stuck there in her middle, stubborn and foreboding.

Her secret phone played a beat from "Run the World (Girls)," announcing a text from her BFFAEAE.

ANA SOFÍA

Have you seen it?

---

112 Like the nerves you get at the top of a roller coaster before the first drop. Except there's a big hole in the track below. And you ate expired sardines for lunch.

SQUIRREL GIRL

Seen what?

ANA SOFÍA

Nothing stay offline k?

SQUIRREL GIRL

Why whats going on? Is there a video of the last
sg fight?

ANA SOFÍA

It's nothing. Depressing stuff. You don't need to
get distracted when MM could strike again any
minute. Promise me you'll stay offline

That was sorta like telling someone, *There's something huge and
alarming behind you, but don't look.*

Now Doreen's stomach felt like she'd swallowed a small pal-
let of bricks. And mortar. She stared at her phone, her thumb
hovering over the web browser. Ana Sofía found the existence
of lunch meats depressing. So whatever this was must not be
your average everyday depressing. It must be really, really super-
powered depressing. Showing tremendous inner control, Doreen
put her phone down and didn't touch it again.

Until . . .

Monday at school. Everyone was talking about Squirrel
Girl. Doreen's keen hearing picked up that name over and over,

muttered from the back rows of classrooms and in conversations between classes.

But the way they were saying Squirrel Girl—it wasn't the same happy, excited tone you'd use to say "Black Widow" or "She-Hulk" or "free ice cream." It was more like the tone you'd use to say "garbage fire" or "infected hangnail" or "Great-Aunt Phyllis's pickled yams."[113]

After third period, Doreen cracked. She went to her locker, searched *squirrel girl* on her phone, and clicked a link to a video.[114] A popular vlog on TuberTV called BrosInTheKnows had posted an episode titled "What the Freak Is Squirrel Girl?" on Saturday. So far, the episode had 123,879 views.

KEVIN C: It's disturbing. This girl does in fact seem to have an actual biological squirrel's tail.

KEVIN B: I mean we've seen freaky, but this is beyond freaky.

KEVIN C: Do we know how she got a squirrel's tail? Is she a failed human-animal hybrid experiment? Some mad doctor

---

113 TBH, I don't mind pickled yams, but I remember one holiday my cousin Drake ranting for like an hour about how gross Aunt Phyllis's pickled yams were, so yam disgust must be a thing people have.
114 No, Doreen! This is Future Doreen warning you not to do it! The internet can be a black hole of meany-pantsery! Run away!

made her in a grotesque underground lab and released her on New Jersey as a cruel joke?

KEVIN B: Apparently some people are actually calling her a hero.

KEVIN C: Show me where in that last video she's a hero. She destroys a tree, two cars, the road—

KEVIN B: *Squirrel Girl.* I feel like we're being punked. Are we being punked?

KEVIN C: Somebody is. And that someone is Squirrel Girl. A hundred bucks says she has a mommy or bestest girly pal who tried to convince that weird mutated chick that she could be a hero.

KEVIN B: Seriously, try to think of a "hero" that would be even less useless than a girl with *squirrel* powers.

KEVIN C: Mouse Girl.

KEVIN B: Sloth Girl.

KEVIN C: Twig Girl.

KEVIN B: Real-Life Girl.

[laughter]

Apparently the first video had prompted several other TuberTVers to take aim at Squirrel Girl, because there were oh-so-many related links. And Doreen kept clicking them.[115]

The TuberTV channel Earth News Report spent ten minutes ranting:

> Squirrel Girl is not just another run-of-the-mill wannabe hero practicing dangerous vigilantism, but actually a troublesome new villain on the scene, masquerading as a hero. The so-called hero videos were clearly preplanned setups. As if Squirrel Girl just happened to "save the day" in the exact location where multiple cameras were recording her "heroics" from every angle.
>
> Others have already pointed out the many troubling aspects of the "Squirrel Girl vs. Robot Spider" video. But this reporter finds the older video, "Squirrel Girl vs. Carjacker," even more disturbing. First she stops the car by causing it to flip and crash in a crowded intersection. It was a miracle that no bystanders were injured. Or the *baby* that was *inside the car.* And then once she *supposedly* saves the baby, what does she do? Puts it high in a tree. A tall tree comes in at number seven on Earth News Report's list of Top Ten Worst Places to Put a Baby. Number one is *a live volcano.* Indeed, such irresponsible actions makes this reporter question whether

---

115 Stop! Past Doreen, you've got to stop now! This is going to get monumentally more depressing than lunch meats in any form!

she was, in fact, attempting to save the baby or if she was the original kidnapper all along.

What do villains do? Destroy property: check. Operate in secret: check. Have strange and disturbing powers: check. Show off their purported strengths to the world: check. So I ask you, what is Squirrel Girl?[116]

Someone called FancyPantsTV created a music video, overlaying the insulting pop song "I Be Smart" to the fight. The video was edited to look like the robot spider won, and cheering sound effects were laid over the part where Squirrel Girl seemed to be defeated.

And the mockery wasn't limited to TuberTV. An image search pulled up a still frame of Squirrel Girl falling butt-first. It had turned into a meme, hundreds of contributions shared across social media.

NO WONDER SHE'S THE BUTT OF SO MANY JOKES

APPARENTLY SQUIRRELS DON'T ALWAYS LAND ON THEIR FEET

AW, NUTS!

THE TAILBONE'S CONNECTED TO THE FUNNY BONE. . . .

SHE'S A GIRL. WHO LOOKS LIKE A SQUIRREL. GET IT? GET IT?

WE NEED SQUIRREL GIRL TO SAVE THE DAY!*

---

116 Um, are you asking me? Then the answer is NOT A VILLAIN.

*SAID NO ONE EVER

Doreen knew she should stop.[117] But she couldn't seem to help it.[118] For so many years Squirrel Girl had been her secret, silent self, her daydream identity, her core. Now thousands of people knew that name, had seen her at what she'd thought was her best. And according to these comments sections, they hated her.

ANONYMOUS
Squirrel Girl is a meme, a one-note idea that somehow we're supposed to take seriously?

ANONYMOUS
Like why does Squirrel Girl even exist? what is the point?

ANONYMOUS
Squirrel Girl is either a really bad Halloween costume or a really good prank

ANONYMOUS
Squirrel Girl honestly thinks she's a hero? Captain America is a hero. Spider-Man is a hero. Squirrel Girl is a Joke.

ANONYMOUS
Weirdo

ANONYMOUS
Freak

117 Yes, stop! That's what I'm trying to tell you.
118 Argh!

ANONYMOUS
Squirrel-shaped waste of space

Doreen had sat down at her locker, hunched over her phone, obsessively clicking link after link, making search after search. She didn't know how long she'd been there, but her tail was sore in her pants. She was aware of someone standing beside her.

"You okay?" Ana Sofía asked.

Doreen nodded.

Because of course she was okay. She was always okay. She was Doreen Green, age fourteen, freak weirdo squirrel-tailed girl who . . . who . . .

Doreen shook her head.

"You can't pay attention to the internet," said Ana Sofía. "It's full of sad little trolls with no life beyond mocking those who actually try to do good things, while craving the pathetic attention they get from slinging their nastiness around. Anyone who really knows you wouldn't believe that garbage."

"Hey, Ana Sofía!" Lucy Tang came stalking up the hall. "You lied to us. Squirrel Girl isn't a hero. She's a joke."

Ana Sofía's jaw clenched with annoyance, but her cheeks burned with embarrassment. "I couldn't understand you."

"Squirrel Girl!" said Lucy, leaning closer. "She is a JOKE!"

Ana Sofía's cheeks burned darker. "No, she is NOT."

"I stood up for you," said Lucy. "I told the rest of the Somebodies to believe in you and Squirrel Girl because my brother did. They trusted me and let you in the group. Now they're mad at me. Thanks a lot. Heidi says you're out, Ana Sofía, you and your dorky friend." Lucy turned and stalked away.

"Out? Of your inane club?" Ana Sofía hollered at her back. "We were never in! Because we didn't want to be! Not because of any other reason—"

Lucy was gone.

Ana Sofía made a noise of frustration and punched a locker. And then she just kept staring at it. Almost as if she wanted to pretend that Doreen wasn't there.

Doreen stood up and waited till Ana Sofía finally looked at her.

"Are you disappointed in me?" Doreen asked.

Ana Sofía shrugged. People who walked by mostly ignored Doreen, but no one ignored Ana Sofía. And there was no kindness in their eyes.

"Maybe I'm not," Doreen signed, "a Super Hero after all."

"Doreen," Ana Sofía said, "don't be naïve. You were *never* a Super Hero."

The hallway was empty now. Just the two girls, looking at each other.

"I'm just gonna go home, okay?" said Doreen.

She shouldered her backpack and left.

Ana Sofía didn't follow. Doreen kinda thought she might. Or text. Or something.

A few blocks from the school, a gray squirrel chittered to her from a branch.

"Hey, T-Toe."

The squirrels were upset, Tippy-Toe reported. Miranda Creepsforth had been chittering about how before Squirrel Girl, there were no squirrel death traps. Before her, there were no pits or exploding gas bugs in squirrel mouths. They had trusted her, the first big human they had ever trusted. And then she had knocked down a maple tree and sent young squirrels to risk their lives against a dangerous robot.

"I get it," said Doreen. "I'm trouble. You better stay away from me, Tip. You don't want your clan to toss you out, too."

She walked away. Tippy-Toe didn't follow either.

Doreen climbed the front steps of her house, one at a time. She dragged herself to her room, fell face-forward onto her bed, and reached up to click on the radio.

"I'm soooo aloooooone," sang the radio.[119]

"Truth," she said into her pillow. It sounded like "Mmmf."

Sad music. Doreen totally got it now. Before, she'd never understood why anyone would bother with music you couldn't

---

119 Looking back, maybe this was a cry for help from the radio. After all, it spends all day by itself in my room.

dance to or at least leap around to in a mosh pit.[120] But right then, all she could bear was slow, depressing ballads in minor keys with lyrics about how everything was pointless.

"*Mmmf,*" Doreen said into the pillow. "*Mmmmmmmfff...*"

After a while, she changed the station to see if a fresh beat might cheer her. The pop tune's bouncy rhythm stabbed her brain with such agony she pulled the radio's cord right out of the wall. And the outlet along with it.

Music usually scooped up her frantic, broken pieces and smoothed her all together again, soothing and cool. But now, every part of her insides were so raw and aching even the slight beat caused pain.

Several silent hours later, the light from the windows dimmed into evening, sliding toward night. She was still lying down, her tail over her head.

Her parents sat on the edge of her mattress. Doreen knew it was them because she could smell them, even through her tail.

"I made a mistake," Doreen said into her pillow. "You were right. I'm too young. I can't handle being Squirrel Girl. This *suuuuuucks.*"

"Doreen . . ." said her mother.

---

120 Though I can't ever mosh for fear of hurting someone. Ooh, maybe the Avengers Mansion has a mosh pit. I bet, like, the number one benefit of being part of the Avengers is having people you can knock around in a mosh pit without worrying you'll break bones. With Hulk, I could totally cut loose!

"I'm not a hero. I'm not Squirrel Girl. And I can't go back to school ever again. My plan is to lie here till I dissolve into a puddle."

"Even in the depths of despair she's making plans," said Dor. "Such a clever girl."

Doreen twitched aside her tail and blinked up at them. Her face felt soggy from pillow crying.

"Did you see the . . . stuff . . . online?"

"We did," said Maureen. "Sweetie—"

"It doesn't matter. It's all over," said Doreen.

"All that talk about Squirrel Girl?" said Maureen. "That's not about *you*. You're not her, right? You're a fourteen-year-old ninth-grade student at Union Junior High."

"Yes, you did a good job keeping her identity secret," said Dor.

"If only Thor had a secret identity, that poor man . . ."

"I'm not Thor," said Doreen. "That MM villain guy thinks I'm a joke. He says everyone knows I'm a joke. And he was right."

"And that's another reason for a secret identity," said Maureen. "Your real self, Doreen Green, will always be safe no matter what people say about Squirrel Girl."

"But I think . . ." She swallowed what she was going to say: *I think Squirrel Girl IS my real self.* "I can't believe . . . For a while there I really thought I could be a Super Hero."

"You could," said Dor. "We've always known that."

Doreen rolled her eyes. "You saw the videos."

"Yes sirree, I sure did," said Dor. "All of them. And while a few people from the internets have landed on my Folks Who Will Never Get Invited to One of My Barbecues list, well, I have to say, I enjoyed seeing you in action so much I think I'll add those to our family videos. Still, just because you *could* be a hero doesn't mean you have to be."

"It's okay, Doreen," said her mother. "No pressure. You don't have to be Squirrel Girl. You're young, you can wait. Take your time. Be a kid. Then when you're an adult, see how you feel."

Doreen nodded. She sat up and hugged her parents with her arms and her tail. And she did feel a little better. But a part inside her, that core self she'd always called Squirrel Girl, shriveled up just a little. Ached quite a lot. And seemed too far away to ever reach again.

30

MICRO-MANAGER

*M*ike steepled his fingers together as he waited for his program to run all the online commentary about Squirrel Girl. One by one he watched increasingly hateful and aggressive comments about his opponent scroll by. He preferred not to use the internet as a tool for work. For research and for Baddit, certainly, but to depend on the net as your own weapon was unwise. Too hard to control.

Nonetheless, he had planted several seeds of doubt about Squirrel Girl onto the net. His data had shown that her powers seemed to get a boost from either confidence or overwhelming ignorance. He must begin their final battle with the upper hand, and that meant doing his best to damage that confidence.

The internet had taken his seeds and grown an entire garden of mockery and ridicule. It was, in many respects, what he had wanted. But his drones were now reporting no further sightings of Squirrel Girl. Had she been scared away by all the hatred? Perhaps he had done his job too well. Defeating his opponent through shame was all well and good, but it didn't make for an exciting victory video. He needed scouts from Hydra to see his work in action.

He grabbed the tablet sitting beside the monitor and opened a telnet session to one of the hidden servers back in the Romanger house. After the conflict with Squirrel Girl and the robot parents, he had moved most of his operations off-site to the warehouse his parents had once purchased for materials storage. But the databases that managed the AI and personality profiles for his aerial drones were still in the house. They weren't particularly important, as he had no plans to change the drones' primary operational parameters, so he hadn't bothered to relocate them yet. Besides, he'd booby-trapped everything there anyway, so if the authorities discovered his hidden server room, the house would blow up in their faces.

He accessed the subroutines for the second-generation aerial drones he still had monitoring the neighborhood. That particular model had been installed with a front-mounted Tesla coil weapon that shot short-range electrical bursts. The weapon was intended for use against meddling vermin but would work equally well as a charring tool. If, for example, he wanted to burn some graffiti into various locations around town.

Mike uploaded an image of the phrase I SUPPORT SQUIRREL GIRL and instructed one of the drones to etch it onto three locations where Squirrel Girl had been seen in the past. He committed the change to the drone's behavioral profile and leaned back, closing the laptop.

"There," he said. "She will see the graffiti and think she still has supporters. Perhaps then she will come out of hiding long enough TO BE DESTROYED."

Mike Romanger, the Micro-Manager, began to laugh. He had planned a long evil laugh, but was interrupted mid *MWA-HA-HA* by a beep on his computer followed by the message COMMAND NOT UNDERSTOOD. PLEASE REPEAT.

He threw Oreos at the monitor until he ran out of Oreos.

31

DOREEN

*D*oreen kept her phone by her bed that night in case Ana Sofía texted. She didn't. And the temptation to scour the internet for more horrible commentary on freaky Squirrel Girl was so great that, in the morning, an exhausted Doreen turned over her phone and laptop to her parents.

Her mom called the school to report her sick. Doreen did in fact feel sick. To her stomach. In her head. Her muscles even ached as if she'd been chewed up and spit out. Maybe the Avengers had seen the videos. Maybe She-Hulk had laughed at a Squirrel Girl meme. Maybe the ground would split open beneath her and mercifully swallow her whole.

It wasn't like she'd never been made fun of before.

But back in California or in Canada, whenever kids whispered about her or made up oh-so-clever nicknames like Chunky Cheeks, Blab Mouth, or Big Butt, she used to think, *This isn't really me. Doreen Green is only half of me. They'd like me if they knew the real me, if they knew Squirrel Girl.*

But now . . . *Joke. Freak. Squirrel-shaped waste of space . . .*

She stayed in bed for two days.

The third day Maureen made her daughter get out of bed at least. Doreen got as far as her backyard. She climbed into the tree house—using the ladder even, like a normal girl would. It was there that Ana Sofía found her.

Doreen smelled her first—homemade soap, cheesy crackers, and that other scent that was all Ana Sofía. She peeked out the tree house window and saw her standing down there in the yard, looking up, just like that day after the Skunk Club when Ana Sofía had spied her leaping into a tree. This time Doreen didn't jump down.

"Can I come up?" Ana Sofía asked.

Doreen shrugged.

Ana Sofía climbed up and sat. "I thought you might like to see this."

Ana Sofía showed Doreen a text on her phone.

HEIDI

Everyone's mad at u so dont come to my party tonight but I wanted to say I miss being a squirrel scout

"Heidi?" asked Doreen.

"The de facto leader of the Somebodies. She's . . . well, she's

Heidi. But it's not just her. This kid Richie at the high school wrote a mean thing about Squirrel Girl in the school paper, and last night every garbage can for blocks got dumped on his front lawn and someone spray-painted acorns all over his house."

She showed her another text message, this one from a Skunk Club member.

ANTONIO
Peeps alwys sell us short 2. Tell sg da sc gt her bck

"Someone carved 'I support Squirrel Girl' into a few buildings," continued Ana Sofía. "And now there's even more acorn graffiti than ever. I'm not saying vandalism or trashing somebody's home is a good thing, but you've still got . . . I don't know . . . fans out there."

Doreen nodded. She supposed that should mean something to her, but it did nothing to budge the elephant-size weight of shame and loneliness pressing on her heart.

Ana Sofía hugged her knees to her chest.

"I should have gone after you, right?" she said. "When you left school. I should have followed. Or texted you. Or something." She sighed. "I haven't had a lot of friends. Not really. Honey hasn't e-mailed me back in a year. And with most other people . . . well, I feel like a service project. In third grade the teacher even assigned different girls to be my friends, like because I'm deaf I'm not capable of making friends on my own. I don't know, maybe she was right."

"You are my friend," said Doreen. "If you want to be, you are. But I feel like . . . you wanted to be my friend because of Squirrel Girl. She was the interesting part of me. And if there is no Squirrel Girl anymore . . ."

"Like, what will we talk about if we don't talk about fighting injustice and saving the day?"

"Yeah . . ."

"Socks?" offered Ana Sofía.

"Nuts?" said Doreen.

"Math?"

"Squirrels?"

"Thor?" said Ana Sofía. "I mean . . . I didn't mean to say Thor; that's weird that I just said Thor. . . ."

"When I'm done being grounded," said Doreen, "do you want to go sock shopping at the mall?"

Ana Sofía smiled. "Sure. And maybe you could play for me some of those bands you're always going on about."

"You like music?"

"Oh yeah," said Ana Sofía, "as long as it's got a really good beat."

Doreen grinned. "Me too. Totally me too."

"Chok-chok!"

Tippy-Toe came in through the tree house window so

quickly, she did a tuck-roll through the air, zooming straight for the thick trunk of the tree. But the moment before she hit it, Doreen caught her like a baseball, as no doubt the squirrel had trusted that she would. Tippy-Toe was chittering so fast all her squirrel words sounded like the static between radio stations, just a constant *chhhh.*

"Whoa, slow down, Tip!" said Doreen. "What's going on?"

Tippy-Toe opened her tiny maw, took a shuddering breath, and tried again.

"Chet chikka-chik chutty chut chek—"

"Oh no!" said Doreen. "Tippy says that Davey Porkpun has disappeared. He does that sometimes, especially after eating really old chocolate. He'll go out wandering for a day or two, but always comes back right as rain, so they wouldn't be worried. Except his sister, Sour Cream, and her kids, the Chives, are also gone."

"Well that's kinda alarming, right?" said Ana Sofía. "I mean, I don't know squirrel domestic habits, but Tippy seems upset about it. What could have happened?"

At that exact moment, almost as if it'd all been perfectly timed to be especially dramatic (though of course it hadn't) a voice echoed from somewhere. Or not somewhere—from *everywhere,* all at once.[121]

"SQUIRREL GIRL," said the tinny, robotic voice. "THIS IS

121 We figured out later that he was broadcasting from his tiny micro-bots above the neighborhood all at the same time. Creepy.

THE MICRO-MANAGER. IT SEEMS YOU HAVE FALLEN OUT OF FAVOR WITH YOUR PRECIOUS FRIENDS AND SUPPORTERS. MWA-HA-HA."

He didn't laugh. He actually said "Mwa-ha-ha." Doreen found it infinitely creepier than a real evil laugh.

"YOU HAVE ONE CHANCE TO REDEEM YOUR NAME."

"What's that voice saying?" Ana Sofía asked, so Doreen did her best to sign it.

"BATTLE ME! AND RECEIVE THE GREATEST HONOR ANY HERO CAN ATTAIN—TO LOSE TO THE MICRO-MANAGER, THE NEWEST, MOST POWERFUL SUPER VILLAIN ON THE SCENE."

"Aw, man. All this time I hoped it was 'Muffin Master,'" said Doreen. "But anyway . . . no thanks, Mr. Manager. That sounds like a terrible idea."

The voice kept talking, no doubt prerecorded. "IN CASE YOU LACK THE PERSPECTIVE AND WISDOM TO CHOOSE THE HONOR OF BATTLING ME, HERE IS FURTHER INCENTIVE."

The Micro-Manager relayed a series of random numbers and letters.

"What the fudge cake?" Doreen said, pausing her signing so she could type the number-letter sequence on Ana Sofía's laptop as fast as he spoke them.[122]

---

122 I'm a scary-fast typist, actually. I have to slow it down in Computers class so I don't freak the teacher out. Or, you know, break another keyboard.

"ARE YOU ACTUALLY A SUPER HERO, SQUIRREL
GIRL? OR ARE YOU JUST A GIRL WHO LOOKS LIKE A
SQUIRREL? IF YOU ARE A HERO, YOU WILL FIND ME AND
FACE ME. GO AHEAD AND BRING ALONG AS MANY OF
YOUR LITTLE VERMIN FRIENDS AS YOU ARE WILLING TO
SACRIFICE. IT WILL NOT BE ENOUGH. I HAVE A SURPRISE
HOSTAGE THAT WILL MELT YOUR FURRY HEART. I
KNOW HOW WEAK YOU ARE WHEN IT COMES TO *TINY*
CREATURES. HURRY, SQUIRREL GIRL . . . BEFORE IT IS
TOO LATE. MWA-HA-HA-HA-MWA-HA-MWA— *AHEM.*"

The voice stopped.

"Whoa," said Doreen. "What in the triple fudge—?"

"Look!" said Ana Sofía. She had pasted the number-letter
sequence into a web browser. The address pulled up a video. The
image was dark, with a little daylight filtering through a high window. The blackness implied vastness, some huge open space. A
single light buzzed on, and Doreen could make out a gray squirrel
hanging facedown. A cord attached to his tail was slowly lowering
him. A few feet below, a robotic jaw with jagged sharp teeth was
squeaking open and snapping shut, open and shut, open . . .

The little squirrel was quivering, brown eyes wide, teeth
bared in terror.

"Davey!" said Doreen. "The Micro-Manager captured little
Porkpun! What a jerk! Judging by the speed he was lowering and
the distance to the jaws, how much time do we have, Ana Sofía?"

"Fifteen minutes, tops."

"Chik-chuk," said Tippy-Toe.

"You're right, Tip, he must have Sour Cream and the Chives, too. That's probably what he meant by 'surprise hostage' and 'tiny creatures.' He's using baby squirrels as bait to get me to go fight him! What a complete and total jerk! I can go out there and—oh." Doreen frowned. "Yeah. I'm not Squirrel Girl anymore. I can't save anyone. I'm not a—"

"You are, Doreen," said Ana Sofía. "I was wrong. I was feeling sorry for myself and I was mean. You *are* a hero."

"I'm not sure. . . ."

"I am. Try a taunt. See how it feels."

"Okay. Um, that Micro-Manager is going downtown without a bus pass!"[123]

Ana Sofía nodded. "Try some more," she said.

"Hey! Dirty bum! Prepare to get wiped by the paws of justice!"

"Maybe something less gross," Ana Sofía said.

"I'm here to kick butts and eat nuts. And I'm ALL OUT OF NUTS!"

"That's the ticket," Ana Sofía said.

Doreen grinned. "But . . . everyone thinks I'm a freak and a weirdo. I'm nothing like the Avengers."

"Right now you need to do some heroics," said Ana Sofía. "Later, *after* the day-saving, we can decide if you were actually qualified to save the day or not."

---

123 I made that up on the spot. It's a pretty good one; I think I'll add it to my list of taunts to use on evil dudes.

"Right. 'Leap before you look' is my motto, after all. I mean, I *have* to help Davey no matter what, right? Tippy, do you think any squirrels would be willing to search the neighborhood? You don't have to say I'm involved if they're mad at me."

Tippy-Toe sneezed a sneeze that sounded like "affirmative."

"Hey, start at the warehouses by the river, at the north end of town," said Ana Sofía. "There's a ton of radio interference there, and it might be caused by Muffin Master and his equipment."

Tippy-Toe sneezed again and then leaped out the window, squeaking all the way.

"I think that Rocket guy was onto something," said Ana Sofía, stuffing her laptop into her backpack. "I'm going to Mike's house, see if he's there, look for clues. I mean, not that I think I'm a legit detective or anything—"

"Except you sorta are," said Doreen.

Ana Sofía smiled. "Yeah, I sorta am."

"Awesome! So I'll go—wait." Doreen smacked her forehead. "Ow! I shouldn't do that. I hit hard. But I forgot that I have a babysitting job tonight—"

"Go get out of your babysitting job and meet up with Tippy-Toe. Text me when you figure out exactly where he is." Ana Sofía put a hand on Doreen's shoulder. "Be safe, Squirrel Girl."

Ana Sofía climbed down the ladder and exited out the back gate. Doreen leaped out the tree house window onto the lawn. And landed face-to-face with her parents.

They were both frowning.

Doreen took a breath so deep, her tail curled tighter in her pants. "I know I'm grounded. But . . " She pulled up the video of Davey on her phone. "This is the kind of stuff bad guys do. They're going to hurt my squirrel friend, and probably his sister and her kids. And this is the sort of thing that Squirrel Girl does. She saves squirrels. And babies. And zucchini sometimes, but that's not like a regular thing. Squirrel Girl defends the weak and stops bad guys. And Mom, Dad . . . I don't need to wait till I'm older to know. I know now. I *am* Squirrel Girl."

Dor wiped his eyes. "My baby girl."

"We heard that voice broadcast," said Maureen. "The Micro-Manager? I don't know that villain. It's like he exists just to fight you, and that scares me. It scares me down to my bunions, Doreen. We're just trying to protect you. Meanwhile, you're trying to protect others."

"I wish you could wait till you're older," said Dor. "I mean, you bet we knew from the beginning that you were special. You can't have a tail like that and not be special. But so soon?"

"I need you to believe in me and support me as Squirrel Girl." Doreen took their hands and smiled. "But, like, right this second, so I can save Davey and his kin."

Maureen and Dor looked at each other, sighed simultaneously and went in for a family-of-three hug.

"Okay, go ahead," said Dor. "Save the day."

"But keep Doreen safe," said Maureen. "I want you to have your private life, a normal life."

Doreen tied her bear-eared hoodie around her waist. She smiled, her long front teeth exposed. "I was never gonna be normal, Mom. But I was always gonna be Squirrel Girl."

And she ran, just a tiny bit faster than humanly possible. It was daylight, after all, and she wasn't Squirrel Girl right now. She was Doreen Green, on the scene, in a hurry like any normal teen.

She took the Santinos' front steps three at a time (rather than leaping up the whole set) and just kept herself from knocking hard enough to split the front door.

It opened almost immediately.

"Hey, Mrs. Santino! I know I'm early, but I—"

"Doreen!" said Mrs. Santino. Her dark hair, normally pulled back into a smooth bun, was loose and sticking out like a wild, slightly crunchy lion's mane. "Have you seen Dante? HAVE YOU?"

"Have I seen Dante? Like, today? No. I just got here—"

Mrs. Santino's hands were shaking. "We were in the park. He was chasing after some squirrels. Lately he's been so fascinated by squirrels."

"Oh no . . ."

"I looked away for just a moment, I swear. When I looked back, he was gone! But I saw . . . something. Out of the corner of my eye. Not a person. Something crawling."

"Was it made of metal?"

"Silver! Yes, I think it was silver! I searched the entire park over and over, even though I know he didn't wander off. He was taken! The police are searching now, they told me to wait at home. But I don't think they believe me that a silver crawling thing kidnapped my baby!"

Now Mrs. Santino was gripping Doreen's arms so hard she'd probably bruise a normal girl. Her eyes were wide, wet, and fixed on Doreen, pleading . . . something. Perhaps Mrs. Santino didn't know it, but she needed Doreen to be a hero. She needed her to save her day.

"I believe you," said Doreen.

Mrs. Santino nodded.

"Stay here and wait for the police. I'll go look around for Dante, okay?"

Mrs. Santino nodded again. But she wouldn't let go.

Doreen's stomach was so tense it felt like a walnut in there, hard and small and tight. In her mind, she measured how much lower Davey Porkpun was than before, how much closer to those insane snapping metal jaws.[124]

So she called her mom.[125]

---

124 Who builds something like that? Seriously?

125 I'm sure real Super Heroes call their moms sometimes, too. Like Captain America would take his mom along with him, if she hadn't died in 1962 or whatever. She'd put on a star-spangled helmet, hop in the sidecar of his motorcycle, and shoot S.H.I.E.L.D. lasers at bad guys, shouting, "Leave my boy alone!" I bet you my last acorn that Cap's mom was totally awesome.

"Can you come sit with Mrs. Santino?" she said. "I think she needs to not be alone."

Doreen left. She ducked into the neighbor's shrubs. Up went the hoodie. Out came the tail. If the Micro-Manager had stolen Dante Santino, the most adorable baby in the world, he was indeed going downtown without a bus pass. He was going to pay, and nothing was on sale. And no matter how gross it was, she was going to wipe the floor with that dirty bum.

But most of all . . . she checked her utility belt. She was, in fact, all out of nuts.

It was time to kick butts.

32

SQUIRREL GIRL

Squirrel Girl jumped onto a nearby roof.

"Come on, friends," said Squirrel Girl. "Let's scamper!"

Leaping from rooftop to rooftop, she made her way closer to the river. The squirrels within range of her voice followed the girl with the giant tail. There were dozens of them. Then a hundred. Then more. Brown, gray, red, and black, they raced behind her, leaping in unison, seeming to flow behind her like a tremendous sweeping squirrel tail.

She hopped down and ran on the ground. They couldn't keep up with her running speed, so they jumped aboard the Squirrel Girl Express. Squirrels crawled up her, held on to her legs, rode atop her arms and head. Their little claws dug in to keep from falling. People pointed and shouted.

"Look! It's her!"

"It's Squirrel Girl!"

"Is she a hero? Or a villain?"

"Are you sure that's her? She's so hairy."

"That's not hair. That's squirrels! She's covered in squirrels!"

"Why, she's no girl at all! She's just a fuzzy conglomerate of rodents!"

At first she waved at the people, but the two squirrels sitting on her hand almost fell off, so after that she just focused on running. Through the neighborhood toward the river, where the air smelled like water and oil.[126]

She was just a couple of blocks away when she detected a change in the chittering of squirrels.

A message was being relayed from Tippy through the squirrel network. Tippy-Toe had discovered the Micro-Manager's lair. The old Fly By Knight warehouse, dark, covered with graffiti, and seemingly abandoned.

Typical. Evildoers loved a nice, large, secluded warehouse even more than a solid laser gun.

Even more squirrels were waiting with Tippy-Toe in the warehouse's shadow. Just tree squirrels, though. Big Daddy Spud's ground squirrels apparently hadn't forgiven Squirrel Girl for her mistakes in the robot-spider fight. The reminder gave her

---

126 Two things that don't mix, just like evil and justice, like villainy and Squirrel Girl, like nuts and raisins. Or nuts and nougat. Just leave the ding-dang nuts alone, okay?

a pang in her chest, and she seemed to smell again the singed fur of the squirrel younglings.

The squirrel passengers leaped off Squirrel Girl. She texted Ana Sofía the exact location, then held out her hand. Tippy-Toe leaped up onto it.

Squirrel Girl took a deep breath. Some part of her, a center, a core, still felt off-balance. Her heart still hurt. Her tail felt cramped, even though it was free.

"Who am I, Tip?" she whispered.

Tippy-Toe perched on her shoulder, put her tiny paws on Squirrel Girl's cheeks, and looked into her eyes. *"Ckktkkt." You are Doreen Green, age fourteen, over five feet tall and not an inch mean. You are also Squirrel Girl—Super Hero, with both powers of squirrel and powers of girl. And you are my friend.*

Tippy-Toe caught Squirrel Girl's tear on her little claw. She rubbed her front paws with it and used it to press the fur on her head into a damp Mohawk. She adjusted her pink bow, bared her teeth, and made a dangerously fierce expression.

"Kkt."

"Right on." She lifted her fist. Tippy-Toe knocked Squirrel Girl's middle knuckle with her own tiny squirrel fist. "What do you think, Tip?" she asked, checking the time on her phone. Davey had perhaps three minutes left. "Sneak attack or full-on assault?"

"Chetty-chik."

"You're right, the Micro-Manager must know we're here. He's expecting us. No use sneaking." She turned to face the gathered squirrels, standing tall, fists on hips, tail swooping impressively behind her. *"Chuk chetty chik!"* she said.

The squirrels stopped chittering and looked at her with their glittering black eyes.

"In that building is a great big jerk," Squirrel Girl declared. "He's the one who built the squirrel traps. He's the one who made the dogs go cuckoo and tried to gas the neighborhood. And now he has some of our own clan—and maybe even our favorite baby, Dante." The squirrels gasped. "I know. I won't ask you to risk your lives in there for me or any squirrel or human. But I know you will anyway, and not just for your own clan, but for truth, justice, and the squirrel way. Come on, furry warriors!"

Squirrel Girl marched up to the single metal door leading to the interior of the warehouse. She drew back her foot but before she gave it a kick, she decided to try the door handle. It was unlocked.

"That's helpful," she said, walking into the darkness of the warehouse followed by a stream of furry friends. "He left the door open for us. Maybe he isn't that bad after all."

There was an electric hum and the door slammed shut behind them, narrowly missing Puffin Furslide, who jumped just in time to save his tail.

"Or maybe he is," Squirrel Girl said.

She tried the door, but it had bolted shut. She was trapped in a dark warehouse. Goose bumps rose across her arms; the hairs on her tail stood up.

A light snapped on, shining like a spotlight on a balcony mounted high on the far wall. There stood Mike Romanger.

So it *was* Mike! That Rocket was clearly an intelligent, trustworthy individual.

"Hey, Mike—" Squirrel Girl said, quickly adding "-ro-Manager." Doreen might be on a first-name basis with Mike, but Squirrel Girl wasn't.

"Hello, Squirrel Girl," the Micro-Manager sneered. He was speaking softly, but his voice was loud, simultaneously broadcast from a hundred tiny speakers. "It is impressive how you've dealt with my minions. You are a truly powerful opponent. But the Micro-Manager exists in a realm beyond *your* definitions of power."

He spoke as if he was auditioning for a play, or reading a poem he'd written in English class.

"Huh," Squirrel Girl said, looking around the space. No sign of Dante. Maybe Mrs. Santino had been wrong? "Where's Davey Porkpun?"

"Don't try to distract me with nonsense," the Micro-Manager said. "It won't work."

"The *squirrel*," she said. "From the video? Or am I in the wrong warehouse?"

"Ah, yes," he said. "The bait." He tapped at a tablet computer strapped to his forearm.

Another light flickered on, illuminating Davey Porkpun dangling from a metal claw by his tail. Directly below him was something that looked like a cross between a bear trap and a hungry hippo. It was a toaster-oven–size metal-toothed chompy thing, and it was facing up, as if ready to chomp whatever fell into its mouth. A mouth which, despite the video she'd seen, wasn't chomping at the moment. Squirrel Girl glanced at Tippy-Toe and gave her tail a twitch. It was what Tippy herself did just before doing something particularly sneaky, and Squirrel Girl hoped she got the message. Tippy nodded and backed into the darkness.

"Hey, Micro-Manager," Squirrel Girl shouted, "what do you call that toaster-oven–size metal-toothed chompy thing? Because I'm calling it a toaster-oven–size metal-toothed chompy thing in my head, and that phrase is taking up too much of my brain space. You must have a name that you use for it."

"It is," he said, pausing for dramatic effect, "the *gnashmouth!*"

He pushed a button on his tablet and the gnashmouth began chomping with loud, angry clicks.

"Isn't that a band?" Squirrel Girl shouted over the noise of metal clashing against metal.

"What?" the Micro-Manager shouted back.

"Gnashmouth. Isn't that a band?"

"WHAT?"

"I said," Squirrel Girl shouted again, "isn't that—?"

The Micro-Manager stabbed his finger at his tablet, and the gnashmouth went silent.

"I *said*," she said, though not quite as loudly as last time, "isn't that a band? Gnashmouth?"

"No," he said. "I researched it. The only other thing by that name is someone's *World of Battlecraft* character."

"Are you sure?" Squirrel Girl said. "'Cause that sounds like a band name. If you had a band, what would you name it? I like Fuzzy Vengeance. Or the Murray Ditko Players. Or the Good, the Bad, and the Squirrelly. Or—"

The Micro-Manager rolled his eyes. "You're a bona fide freak, you know that, right?"

"Yeah, you said all that before, and so did those dudes on TuberTV. That word—"freak"—it kind of pings around in your brain, makes it hard to think."

"If the shoe fits, buy a spare pair, freak girl," he said.

"But in all that chitter-chatter online and meany-time finger pointing," she said, "I almost forgot one thing."

Squirrel Girl paused dramatically. The Micro-Manager pressed his lips together. She raised one eyebrow. He sighed.

"WHAT?" the Micro-Manager finally asked, furious to be the first to break the silence.

"That I'm awesome."

He frowned but quickly recovered with a spoken "MWA-HA-HA! You are absurd. Now! To the doom. You must save your furry friend before—"

"Which furry friend?" Squirrel Girl asked.

The Micro-Manager gestured to the metal claw hanging above the gnashmouth, which was now empty.

"What?!" he sputtered.

Tippy-Toe chittered from near her feet. Davey Porkpun stood beside her. His tail was bent a little funny, but otherwise looked okay. He waved at Squirrel Girl, and then at the Micro-Manager.

The villain stomped his foot. "NO! MORE! DISTRACTIONS!"

He stabbed at his tablet again. Four glass tubes lit up near the ceiling of the warehouse. They were like triple-size fluorescent lightbulb tubes, but they were hanging vertically, and inside each one was a tiny terrified squirrel. Sour Cream and the Chives. The squirrels were keeping themselves from falling with their own paws, but the inner surface was clearly slick. Squirrel Girl could see them slipping. They would not be able to hold on for long.

"At the bottom of each of those tubes is an electrified mesh," the Micro-Manager announced. "A bug zapper. A vermin roaster. They fall, they fry."

"Tippy!" Squirrel Girl shouted. There was no time to distract or trick the Micro-Manager now. They needed to get to the Chives and Sour Cream before they fell. "See if you can—"

"By all means," the villain interrupted her. "Use your little friends. And I will use mine."

Hundreds of tiny red lights lit up across the warehouse walls. Bladed rotors began to whirl, and one by one each flying robot detached itself from a wall. These weren't the giant eyeballs from the dog-gassing thing. They looked more like regular four-rotor drones, except on the front of each they had a kind of metal antenna sparking electricity. And there were hundreds of them. They filled the air, hovering like an evil storm cloud between Squirrel Girl and the tube traps.

"Let us see how flesh and fur fares against the metallic microbot menace of the Micro-Manager!" he shouted. "MWA! HA! HA! HA!"

The micro-bot army began to descend. Squirrel Girl tightened her hood.

"All right, furry friends," she said. "Let's go nuts."

Almost faster than human eyes could follow, she ran. Weaving in and out of the spaces between the micro-bots, squirrels would leap one by one into her hand, and one by one she would hurl them at a target.

"Fuzzball Special!" she shouted.

It was Fuzz Fountain Cortez that she threw first, and the squirrel tore right through the center of a micro-bot's body without even looking back. Then Bear Bodkin and Kerchief Candyglow each hit their targets, using their momentum to smash the machines hard into the wall of the warehouse.

Calendar Earl, Bubo Nic, and M. Scummerset Maugham scampered onto her hand, interlocking their legs and tails.

"Triple-Play!" Squirrel Girl yelled, throwing the bundle of squirrels. As they flew, the three expanded, keeping their tails linked. Spinning where their tails held, they became a flying disk of claws and teeth. They tore straight through five micro-bots, only stopping when they hit the opposite wall, bouncing off separately to attack three different targets.

Squirrels were everywhere. While the micro-bots outnumbered them at least five to one, it seemed like each squirrel was in two or three places at once. The flying robots would track one target, lose it, track another, and then bump into one another, tangling blades just like the evil robot parents' hands had.

In the midst of all the movement, something not moving at all drew Squirrel Girl's attention. On the floor, a few feet away from the gnashmouth, a gray pink-ribboned squirrel lay, faintly twitching. A mass of micro-bots, sensing an easy target, gathered together in a dense mass of blades, closing the distance.

"Oh no!" Squirrel Girl shouted. "Tippy!" As she bunched her muscles to leap toward her friend, Tippy-Toe suddenly rolled onto her feet and darted away. In that same instant, a dozen squirrels dropped from above, raining doom upon the micro-bots that had gathered together. They tore into the wires and gears, riding the micro-bots until just before they crashed into the floor, shattering into pieces.

"My BSFFAEAE is a genius," Squirrel Girl said.

From the tubes hanging from the ceiling came a frightened squeak. One of the Chives was slipping. The baby squirrel was halfway down the tube. In seconds she would hit the mesh at the bottom and be electrocuted.

Squirrel Girl tore through the micro-bots, ignoring the blades that ripped her hoodie and scratched her arms and hands. She ran to just below the tubes and leaped up, but the tubes were just too high. She fell back to the cement floor.

"You'll find the tubes are exactly six inches higher than the highest you've ever jumped," the Micro-Manager's voice sounded from speakers all around. "Get ready for roast squirrel!"

The baby squirrel squeak was louder now, more desperate. Squirrel Girl rolled under an attacking micro-bot and ran to the wall of the warehouse. She dug her claws into the wall and climbed. Maybe she could climb all the way up, somehow move across the ceiling, and drop down over them. But it would take time, and just then two more baby squirrels lost their grip, beginning to slide.

She had to jump, now.

Higher than the highest you've ever jumped . . .

"The highest I've ever jumped *so far*," she whispered.

It didn't matter if she could leap that far. She simply had to.

"So far!" she screamed as she pushed her legs against the wall and leaped, sailing right past each of the tubes. She scraped her sharp claws against the glass tubes as she passed, cutting through them.

One by one, the bottom half of each glass tube dropped away, and one by one Sour Cream and the Chives dropped out of their prisons. They landed directly onto flying micro-bots, ready to exact their revenge with teeth bared.

Dozens of micro-bots still buzzed in the air, and Squirrel Girl was bleeding from not a few scrapes and cuts. But she had leaped farther than ever before, and the kidnapped squirrels were safe. It felt to her like the trouble was almost over now.

"I am a rock star!" she said. "I heroed all over your Super Villain boo-tay."

"I expected no less," the Micro-Manager's voice echoed from all around. "Now with the tedious trapped vermin out of the way, we can move to phase two."

"Phase two?" Squirrel Girl asked.

CLANG! The Micro-Manager's platform and the back wall of the warehouse began to lower, emitting a hiss and a screech. The wall, it turned out, was not a wall, but a floor-to-ceiling door. And behind the door were hundreds more flying robots. Only this time they were the bigger ones, the eyeball ones, all covered in spinning blades. It was enough to make Iron Man wet his iron pants a little.[127]

"Chek kut," said Tippy-Toe. It was the squirrel's opinion that the new swarm was too much for their troops. They had rescued the captured squirrels, mission accomplished, and now it was time to scram!

Squirrel Girl agreed. She pulled on the bolted warehouse door and the hinges slowly started to bend. It might take her a minute, but she thought she could—

---

127 *Allegedly* wet his iron pants. I don't want Iron Man to sue me or anything.

"Oh wait, did I forget to mention the surprise hostage?" said the Micro-Manager. One more spotlight turned on, pointing way up in the newly opened space.

A hundred-foot pole. On top, a metal disk twenty feet in diameter. It reminded her of those "squirrel-proof" bird feeders, only times a hundred. A flying drone circled above, filming and projecting the image against a wall.

A glass box perched on top of the metal disk. Inside, the sound silenced by the thick glass, sat a crying baby. Not a zucchini disguised as a baby. But a real, actual human baby with olive-tone skin and straight black hair and a dimpled chin, wearing his favorite fuzzy striped onesie.

Dante Santino.[128]

"No!" said Squirrel Girl.

"Now, now, he came of his own free will," said the Micro-Manager. "I sent a thief-bot to the park to snatch a few of your precious squirrels for bait, and this human crawled eagerly after them. And I thought, sure, why not? Because you know what Super Villains do? They *escalate*, that's what they do. Ha-ha! There's no going back after baby-napping! I am so completely a Super Villain now!"

"Let the baby go!" Squirrel Girl shouted. She was trembling all over, with rage, with fear, her muscles bunched up tighter than tight. This was all her fault. Dante had chased after

---

128 OMGosh! The Micro-Manager is srsly the jerkiest jerk of Jerk World!

squirrels because she'd always had some around whenever she was babysitting.

"Don't get lazy!" the Micro-Manager said. "You're the *hero*. Saving babies is *your* job, not mine."

"Apparently your job is being a giant jerk face!" Squirrel Girl yelled eloquently.

The Micro-Manager frowned. "That was mean."

He lifted his arms into the air. "Phase! Two!" he shouted, and the second wave of micro-bots, like an impenetrable swarm of lethal eyeballs, surged straight at Squirrel Girl.

33

ANA SOFÍA

*M*ike's house was surrounded with the yellow DO NOT CROSS police tape Ana Sofía had only ever seen on TV shows. The damage done in the Squirrel Girl vs. robot parents fight must've been bad enough to lure in the officers from the county. The smashed cars and broken trees were gone. The busted front window was boarded up. Surely Mike had been taken away by Child Protective Services.

But still, Ana Sofía knocked on the front door. When no one answered, she turned the knob. It was unlocked.

"Mike?" she called out. "Mike, are you here?"

The house smelled stale and abandoned, like a box of crackers left open overnight. She ducked under the police tape and went inside.

She was no forensics expert, but the slashes in the walls and furniture looked like they'd been made by the rotating blades of transforming robot parents.[129] Her heart was slamming in her chest. Maybe that barstool there was actually a robot that would suddenly transform and attack an intruder. Or that beaded curtain might actually be tentacles that would reach out and—

Mike wouldn't do that, would he? He'd always been sorta nice to her. Well, not *nice*-nice. When he wasn't ignoring her, he was complaining about something. Frankly, she agreed with all the horrible stuff he said about their town and other people. Or she had.

And then there'd been that time when someone had stolen her lunch. She didn't even say anything, just sat at their cafeteria table reading and not eating. But he'd left and come back twenty minutes later with a bag from a nearby market: a box of crackers and a block of cheese. He'd set it in front of her without a word.

Heart pounding, she opened doors and peeked inside. Boring bedrooms. Boring bathroom. The garage was more interesting. No cars, just piles of random stuff: bike tires, cases of car stereos with the innards removed . . . Wait—all the stolen stuff that'd been disappearing from around the neighborhood the past couple of years. Had that been Mike all along? Scavenging parts for his robots?

Ana Sofía found the door to the basement stairs. She grabbed

---

129 She's so smart. Also I'd told her that's what had happened.

the rails and slid on her hands all the way down. One big open room. Boring.[130]

Now to find the secret Mike was hiding down here. Hopefully hiding. There had to be something helpful—pretty please with cheese on top—or she was wasting time while Squirrel Girl was engaged in a highly dangerous and possibly life-threatening battle.

But there seemed to be nothing. What would Squirrel Girl do? What would Thor do?

No, wait . . . what would Ana Sofía do? Something super-sleuthy, she decided.

Ana Sofía sniffed the air for the dusty-sharp scent of electricity. She felt the wood-paneled walls for heat. She noticed a place on the green shag carpet that was slightly more worn. She investigated the wall panel, found a hidden latch, and pressed it. The panel swung inward.

"YES!" Ana Sofía said aloud. "I found your secret!"

The secret room was bedroom-size, windowless, chilly, and filled with humming servers. Against one wall, a large machine was whirring away.

A 3-D printer! Only this was to a normal 3-D printer what a tank was to a bicycle.

As she watched, it finished a creation: a palm-size micro-bot

---

130 Another reason I love Ana Sofía: we are both interested in interesting things. Boring things, we agree, are just so boring!

that turned on and flew up a tube, presumably going outside and away to join the battle against Squirrel Girl. The printer was already starting to build another micro-bot. Ana Sofía looked for a way to turn it off and found nothing. She heroically picked up a metal bar and gave it a few whacks. The machine didn't even pause.

In the back corner, Ana Sofía found a computer station. "Here we go," she said. She connected her laptop and began to type, trying to hack her way through security. It took her a few minutes, but she slid in and found a file with the operating code for the drones.

A previously dark monitor lit up with flashing text:

INTRUDER BREACH. 60 SECONDS TO SELF-DESTRUCT.

"Dirty Fuzzmuppets," Ana Sofía muttered. The code was complicated and dense. Ana Sofía was certain she could make sense of it if—

45 SECONDS TO SELF-DESTRUCT.

Her heart was pounding so hard the motion of it distorted her vision. She noticed in a parallel database table all the data the Micro-Manager had collected on Squirrel Girl and the squirrels. Physical limits, top speeds, personality profiles. Holding her breath because she was so nervous it actually hurt to breathe,

Ana Sofía merged the squirrel personality data with the data that drove the drones' AI subroutines.

10 SECONDS—

She ran up the stairs and out the front door so fast she might've had temporary squirrel powers. The police tape tangled around her ankles and she fell face-first onto the front lawn. Behind her, she felt a low *BOOM* and seconds later, the bright yellow of fire eating the house from the inside out.

She saw neighbors come outside to look, cell phones in hand to dial the fire department. So Ana Sofía ran down the block to a pocket park and collapsed behind a tree, breathing hard.

Something was wrong, though she couldn't place it at first. Why was everything so still?

Aha. There were no squirrels. Anywhere. The neighborhood was empty of little fuzzy-tailed shadows twitching about acorns and justice.

All the squirrels had abandoned the neighborhood, and even now perhaps were locked in mortal combat with micro-bots in a warehouse by the river. Along with Squirrel Girl.

It wasn't till she reached for her cell phone that Ana Sofía realized how badly she was shaking. But she took a deep breath and bravely sent out a group text.[131]

---

131 Ana Sofía rates group texts on her evil-things list somewhere near foot fungus, marinara sauce, and public flogging, so this was a big deal.

ANA SOFÍA

Squirrel scouts! I know those online videos made SG look like a villain but it's lies. She is a hero, a super hero even. I believe that and don't care what anybody else thinks. Right now she's fighting the real villain. He calls himself the micromanager and he's the source of most of the thefts in our town. Just one guy being crummy turned this into a crummy place. One person can be powerful for good or evil. U r powerful too. What will you do? He wants to destroy SG bc she stands in his way. I won't let him! If any of u are still squirrel scouts meet me at the old Fly By Knight warehouse by the river and 14 St. It's time to defend the weak the frightened and the interesting. It's time to be brave and silly. It's time to prove ourselves SQUIRREL SCOUTS!

34

SQUIRREL GIRL

*T*hey were losing.

Most of the squirrels were still on their feet, but they were hurt. They were tired. Squirrel Girl couldn't even get near the giant pole and Dante. The micro-bots were everywhere.

Tippy-Toe was on Squirrel Girl's shoulder.

"Chk-chukka!" she chittered.

"Yes," Squirrel Girl said, kicking a drone out of the air. "More help would be nice. But I lost all my human helpers."

"Chk-tik chuk," Tippy-Toe said. She leaped onto a passing drone, tore out some wires, and leaped back onto Squirrel Girl's shoulder.

"Where?" Squirrel Girl asked. Tippy-Toe nodded in the direction of the door they had come in, and she saw a handful of squirrels gnawing a hole in the corrugated steel of the door. The hole was big enough now that a squirrel could get through.

"Good, get everyone else out of here," Squirrel Girl said. "I don't want any more of you getting hurt. I can finish this by myself."

She believed it when she said it. If she had enough time and enough space, she was convinced she could smash every drone in the building before she died. Not having the squirrels around to worry about, not having to be concerned with their safety, might make things easier. In a way. Her dying seemed inevitable. But her victory did, too. She had to save Dante. Any other outcome was simply incomprehensible.

A twitching drone flew near her. She punched through the blades, grabbed it, bit it in half, and threw the pieces to the ground.

"Good." The Micro-Manager's voice echoed through the speakers in each drone. "Give in to your anger."

"I'm not doing that!" Squirrel Girl shouted, smashing another drone. "I don't even know what that means! And don't quote *Star Wars*! You'll, like, sully it with your nasty self!"

While she was punching two micro-bots out of the air and swiping at two others with her tail, a fifth flew in low and cut her calf with its whirling blades.

"Ow, ow, ow!" Squirrel Girl yelled. She fell to the ground, but managed to land with her butt on the drone, smashing it.

Tippy squeaked an alarm. A cluster of some fifty drones were diving straight at Squirrel Girl.

From the corner of her eye Squirrel Girl could see Tippy and the other squirrels running back from the hole to help her, but they were too far away. This was it, then. She was going down in one last clash. She whirled around, eager to take down as many as she could before they took *her* down, but her claws only sliced through empty air.

"What?" She stumbled forward. "Happened?"

Most of the drones had stopped and fallen to the ground. One dove a few inches, backed up, and then scampered away. Others darted around erratically. They were quick but didn't attack or move in formation.

"Chukka?" Tippy-Toe asked. A drone hovered down to stare at Tippy's tail. She swiped at it. The drone dodged away easily, and then returned to stare at her tail again.

"Yeah, super weird," Squirrel Girl said, getting to her feet.

"CHK! CHK! CHAK!" Suzie Skunkkiller yelled. A micro-bot had grabbed the acorn she had been using as a shield.

Other drones were attempting to scamper up the walls. Having no legs, they weren't very good at it.

"Chk," Tippy said.

"I know," Squirrel Girl said. "It's like they're trying to be squirrels."

"AAAAGGH!" the Micro-Manager shouted. He was pounding at his tablet. "The firmware is corrupted!"

"You know what?" Squirrel Girl said to Tippy. "I think Ana Sofía did this. That girl is awesome."

"Fine!" He tapped on his tablet, tore it from his arm, and threw it on the ground. The drones exploded, littering the floor with pieces of plastic and metal, nothing left airborne but black smoke.

Squirrel Girl kicked through the debris toward him. "Give up and bring down that baby, or I'll shell you like a nut!"

"Are you kidding?" He pulled a phone from his pocket and held it to his mouth. "Engage Sparta Protocol. Authorization: crawl, crawl, crawl."

The ground beneath their feet began to shake.

"What was that?" Squirrel Girl asked.

"That," he said, "is the endgame."

He dropped out of sight. It was as if the floor opened its mouth and simply swallowed him whole. Squirrel Girl rushed forward, limping on her wounded leg. Now she could see a circular metal hatch right where the Micro-Manager had been standing. She scratched at it, leaving marks on the metal, but got nowhere in terms of opening it.

"Get that baby down!" she yelled.

The ground shuddered again.

"Phase three." Mike's voice came from a single loudspeaker mounted to the wall just above her. After the impressively creepy boom of his voice coming from several hundred flying robots, this sounded sad.

Squirrel Girl was at the pole, trying to climb up. It was slick and straight, and no matter how hard she jumped she couldn't get more than halfway up.

"So are you going with 'phase three' or with 'the endgame'?"

Squirrel Girl yelled back. "It'd be less confusing if you just picked one. Personally I'd go with 'endgame.' It sounds more fun."

"Most of my micro-bots, the flying ones, were never designed to do anything but observe people and chop meat," the loudspeaker sounded.

"Gross!" Squirrel Girl shouted as she leaped at the pole for the twentieth time. "Those are gross things to be designed to do!"

"My ground troops, though," the Micro-Manager continued, "they were designed to chew up concrete and stone. To march through the world and grind it to dust."

"*Chkka,*" Tippy said. She was looking nervously at the trembling floor.

"They will emerge from the foundation of this building and wipe the neighborhood clean. Then the state. If I'm lucky, the world. You know what they say. ABE. Always Be Escalating."[132]

"Check it out, Tippy!" Squirrel Girl said. She didn't dare leave till Dante was safe.

Tippy-Toe and the other squirrels scampered to the hole in the wall, filing out one by one.

"You made me do this," the Micro-Manager said. The rumbling from beneath her changed pitch. "If you'd just been good and died earlier, the city might have been saved."

"How about if I play dead?" Squirrel Girl said. "Then will you shut the drones off and lower the baby?"

---

132 Who exactly are "they" in this sentence? I certainly never say that.

"Before the day is out, this entire neighborhood will be rubble. And it will be all your fault."

"The squirrels and I *will* stop them, you know," Squirrel Girl said, sliding uselessly down the pole, her claws making a *squeeeeak* against the metal. "We'll smash them like the others. You should turn them off, get that baby down, and call it a day."

She gave up and started to climb up the wall of the warehouse. Maybe if she got high enough, she could leap horizontally to the platform Dante was on?

"I have to admit the squirrels might have a chance against my ground drones with you fighting by their side," said the villain on the loudspeaker.

The hatch he had disappeared through clicked and slid open, a platform rising to reveal a giant multiarmed robotic figure. It looked like a cross between Iron Man and several small construction vehicles plus some NASCAR stickers. The helmet slid open, uncovering Mike's face.

"Unfortunately," he said, "you will be otherwise occupied. I saw how easily you defeated my spider-bot. Trust me when I say that was child's play compared to my deathcruncher."[133]

Squirrel Girl gulped. Her mouth was dry. Her heart fluttered like a hummingbird's. She'd barely survived phase two. There didn't seem to be much hope she'd survive phase three, aka the

---

133 Legit scary name. And probably also someone's *World of Battlecraft* character.

endgame. She could almost hear the entire internet laughing at her: *She's just a girl with squirrel powers. What can she do against a Super Villain with an army of killer robots plus something called a deathcruncher?*

Through the glass box, she could almost make out Dante's muted cry.

35

TIPPY-TOE

I was the only squirrel still inside the warehouse when the giant robot boy attacked. Three of his fists pounded the ground, cracking the concrete floor. I could hear the calls of my cousins from outside, but inside was a monster bent on destroying my best friend.

Squirrel Girl leaped from the wall at him, claws- and feetfirst. He batted her away. She rolled across the floor.

Her groans sounded more like *ouchie-ouchie-but-I'm-okay* than *tell-my-mother-that-I-loved-her*, so I jumped onto her shoulder and asked, "What's the plan?"

Another blow from the robot boy shattered the concrete floor. We separated, dodging, and then came back together.

"You need to go!" she shouted.

"You can't do this alone," I said. Metal projectiles flew

from one of the creature's arms, but we twisted, missing both.

"I have to save Dante," Squirrel Girl said. "I'm his freakin' babysitter, like I won't! But out there? Those robot things are going to destroy the whole town."

Puffin Furslide poked his head through the hole and shouted something, but I couldn't hear it over the noise of the metal claw scraping a wall, barely missing Squirrel Girl.

"Go, Tippy," Squirrel Girl said. "Find Ana Sofía, she can help you save the city! You and your clan are mighty!"

She leaped onto one of the attacking arms and scampered to the robotic suit's head. Just like a squirrel would.

"I'll join you as soon as I take care of this," she shouted.

I felt uneasy leaving her, like I'd just eaten a nut two winters buried, but I darted out the hole after Puffin.

"We've been hearing something like a buried beehive," Puffin said, pressing his head to the ground. "Like a hundred buried beehives."

Suddenly a metal spider thing was upon me, slashing. As I dodged, Bear Bodkin caught it and Puffin tore out the electronics from its underside with a bucktoothed bite.

"Where did that come from?" I asked.

"There," Puffin said, pointing to a sinkhole just beyond the foundation of the warehouse.

"We need to plug that—" I started to say, but just then, three more holes suddenly opened into the ground, all in a straight line along the base of the building. And out of each one came crawling more of those metal bugs. From the rumble beneath my feet, I anticipated hundreds more. My heart sank.

"Tippy-Toe!"

I turned to see Big Daddy Spud perched on a post. Behind him preened over a hundred groundies. "We thought you could use a paw."

"Praise the leaves, you are a sight for beady eyes," I said.

"Got a plan?" Spud asked.

"Take your top-branch diggers to fill the holes," I said. "Slow those rot-bottomed bugs down." I turned to the assembled tree squirrels. "Cortez! Stand our top-branch scrappers beside each hole to protect the groundie diggers. A bug gets through, give it tooth and claw."

Fuzz Fountain Cortez nodded and darted away.

Throwing dirt into the holes wouldn't be enough to keep all the ground drones buried, I knew. I needed to plug them with something bigger. I searched the group for a squirrel with likely talent.

"You! Groundie with the teeth! What's your name?"

"Chomp Style, ma'am," said the ground squirrel.

"You chew, Chomp Style?" I asked.

"Four-time log-gnaw champ, ma'am."

"Solid bark. See that tree?" I pointed to the tall oak growing just outside the warehouse fence. "You and a crew are going to chew that trunk front to back."

"Ma'am?"

"Honor to the tree, Chomp Style, but if we don't knock over this one tree we might lose all the trees in this town."

"On it," Chomp Style said, and galloped to the tree.

"Everyone who's just standing around swishing their tail, shadow Chomp Style. Chew together. Stop when the wood creaks and leans."

Cletus the marmot hung back. "I'm not much for the chew," he said, flexing his paws. "Never had much call for it."

"Natch. No chew for you, Cletus," I said. "I need you to thump."

Cletus smiled. Cletus liked to thump.

One of the metal bugs broke through the line of scrappers and hurtled toward us. I crouched, ready to pounce on its back, but Cletus planted his feet and let the thing ram into his head. It bounced back, twitching, and while it did, Cletus tore its head off.

Cletus and I scampered to the tree, where the chew crew already had the thing almost tipping.

Chomp Style spat out a chunk of wood the size of my head. "One more bite ought to do it," he said.

"Perfect," I said. I scanned the tree, calculating the distance from the warehouse and the angle it would need to fall to plug those holes. I scratched an X into the bark with a claw.

"Thump it, Cletus," I said. "Thump it like there's honey inside."

The marmot smiled, took a few steps back, and then charged the tree.

There was a splintering noise as he hit, and at first I worried it was Cletus's skull. But then the tree began to tip.

"Everybody move!" I shouted to the front lines. "Out! Out! Now!"

The squirrels scattered, and the masses of bugs they'd been holding back in their holes surged forward, free to move for a single second before the tree crashed on top of them. The ground shook from the impact, and as the dust cleared I could see the tree fell nearly exactly where I wanted it. All four of the holes were capped with a ton of solid Jersey oak.

The crowd cheered, but I knew it wasn't over. At best I bought us time, and the tiny robotic chainsaw sound I heard muffled beneath the oak told me that it might not be much time at all.

I leaped onto the fallen tree. Through the wood, I felt the vibrations of an army of robots cutting and digging.

"Squirrels!" I shouted, and without being told, my army gathered before me. They were dirty, some were wounded, but they were fierce. I spoke to them in the old tongue, with large words and deep meaning. I needed them to know this moment was *important*.

"The enemy is not vanquished! Even now they dig. Even now they cut through this tree! They destroy it as they would the world! But will we let that happen?"

"NO!" my assembled family yelled.

"This is where we hold them," I shouted. "On this abandoned field, this is where we fight! Whether we crush them by acorn or shred them by claw! Remember this day, squirrels, for it will be yours for all time!"

"*CHK-CHA!*" the army responded.

"Squirrels, what is your profession?"

"NUTS AND DEATH!" came the reply.

"This day we rescue an ignorant world from destruction!" I said. "We protect a world that would call us vermin! Why do we do this? Because we are mighty! Because we are valiant! BECAUSE WE ARE SQUIRRELS!"

"SQUIRRELS!" shouted the assembled crew.

The tree splintered then, and thousands of robot bugs spilled out from the shattered wood.

"Give them nothing, but take from them EVERYTHING!"

And we held them, we three hundred squirrels. We held our own against that robot army. For a time, it looked like we might actually win. But when Cletus twisted an ankle and fell, the tide turned. It was all we could do after that to stay alive.

I thought if we could survive long enough for Squirrel Girl to come, she would help us turn things around. But she didn't come, and that meant she was in trouble, maybe as much trouble as we were in. Was she even still alive? Minute by minute our numbers were dwindling. A squirrel is basically live energy wrapped in a fur coat. But when that energy depletes, it's gone, and we have no choice but to sleep till we revive. All over the battlefield squirrels lay limp as corpses, too tuckered out to even twitch.

"They've stopped coming out!" Davey Porkpun shouted, and

it was true. The hole in the oak that had spewed forth robot bug after robot bug was finally empty. But it was too late. There were only a dozen or so of us still able to fight and at least two hundred of the metal wretches to dispatch. While I grappled with three at once, a dozen charged past me.

"Tippy!" Big Daddy Spud flattened one of my opponents with his bulk. "A group broke through our line!"

"I know!" I said, gutting the other two. "We'll have to chase them down later. There's too many here—"

Spud grabbed my wrist and pointed my paw in the direction the group of robots ran. "They're heading straight for the day care, Tippy. There are babies there. *Babies.*"

And then I heard the distant sound of crunching and knew they must have begun drilling through the day-care wall.

"Babies," I whispered. "Why is it always babies?"

Spud and I were tackled from behind by a pair of the crawler drones. Spud grunted as his head hit a rock, and then he lay still. My attacker had one of its sharp legs jabbing into my back, pinning me to the ground. As I wriggled to get free, I saw Fuzz Fountain Cortez tearing her way toward me through the waves of robot bugs. I twisted, getting leverage with my tail, and managed to roll both the bug and me over.

"Go!" I shouted to Cortez, pointing in the direction of the day care. "Save the babies! I've got this!"

As if to punish me for my arrogance, the robot snapped its pincers at my throat, missing my neck by only a hair. My bow was not so lucky. The pink ribbon that Doreen gave me the day we met slid off my neck, caught the breeze, and flew away.

"You did NOT just cut off my bow," I snarled.

The metal insect buzzed self-importantly, and I grabbed its head. I imagined it was an acorn, and that I was very hungry. The robot did not buzz for long.

I looked down the street toward the day care, fearing it was already too late for the babies.

And then, from the fringes of the battlefield, I heard the call.

"The dogs are coming! The dogs are coming!"

For a brief moment my heart sank with the thought of another set of enemies, but then I saw them. The feral dogs from the lot, in battle formation, with Speedo Strutfuzz riding atop the back of the black-striped leader.

"Thought you could use some more fur in the game," Speedo said from his black-striped mount.

"The day-care center?" I asked.

"Still standing," he said. "The dogs stopped the digger drones. But looks like we've still got loose bots about, and if we don't hook and crack them all, they might head there, too."

"Then it's time to send the rest of this garbage to the scrapyard," I said.

Speedo nodded. "Let's give 'em shell, squeaks," he shouted to the assembled dogs. "Charge!"

The animals tore into the crowds of robots, chomping and snarling.

"Open a hole," I yelled to the squirrels. "Catch the dogs' scraps!"

Even with that extra help, it seemed useless. We were overwhelmed. Until—

"Tippy-Toe!" someone yelled from beyond the battlefield, but this time in human language. I scampered to the sound of Doreen's human friend, the one who calls herself Ana Sofía. With her were three groups of people: one that smelled like scented lotion, another carrying swords and smelling of oiled leather armor, and the last carrying baseball bats and smelling of paint and trash.[134]

"Tippy, I brought the Squirrel Scouts. We're here to help."

"We took care of the attacking army," I said, "but we have to hunt down and break apart every last straggler or the town won't be safe!"

Ana Sofía stared at me, uncomprehending.

"Did that squirrel just talk to you?" one of the girls asked Ana Sofía.

"Yes," Ana Sofía said.

"What did it say?"

Ana Sofía sighed. "I don't know."

I pointed at the robots, and then at the neighborhood around us.

---

134 The Somebodies, the LARPers, and the Skunk Club! All working together! Seriously this story should be a Very Special Holiday Television Event or something. I know I have chills.

"What?"

I did the pointing again before realizing I had something better. I had the hand language that Ana Sofía and Doreen sometimes used. I struggled to remember a few signs.

Catch—robots—run away, I signed.

"What is it—?"

"It's *she*, not *it*," Ana Sofía said, "and I don't . . . Wait."

She crouched down to my level and watched me. I made the signs again. Ana Sofía gasped, her eyes widened. And then slowly, she smiled.

"I think she's signing!" Ana Sofía said. "Do it again, Tippy."

Robots—run—find, I signed.

I was so intent on my signing that I did not see a charging micro-bot until it leaped at me, pincers wide. Before it landed the attack, however, it was pinned by an aluminum sword.

"Have at thee, craven insect!" one of the humans in armor shouted, and then smashed the robot with a booted foot.

I gave the human a thumbs-up, and he gave me one back, smiling.

"Okay," Ana Sofía said. "I think Tippy is saying that some of these robots have escaped and are in the neighborhood. We need to find them and smash them. Is that right, Tippy?"

I gave Ana Sofía a nod.

"You know what to do, Squirrel Scouts," said Ana Sofía. "Charge!"

"Yeah!"

"We shall vanquish the metal demons, forsooth!"

"This is so *awesome!*"

The humans surged forward. Behind me the dogs leaped and snapped, destroying the remaining robots. For a few seconds, I just breathed and watched, so in awe even my foot-claws tingled. Last year, I would have been just fine if all humans and all dogs just disappeared and left the world to us. But today, humans and dogs were working with us to save that world. Now if they all disappeared? I think I'd miss them.

A little.

36

SQUIRREL GIRL

She shouldn't have laughed at him. Because when it came to phase three,[135] the Micro-Manager didn't mess around.

Squirrel Girl couldn't seem to concentrate. It was hard to anticipate his moves, hidden as he was inside that hulking death-cruncher suit. She tried to leap; he knocked her down. She tried to run; he stopped her with a sticky net shot from a robot arm. She cut through the net with her nails and tried to attack; his armor didn't break. She eventually managed to worm her teeth into the joint of one of his extra robot arms and pop it off, but the electrical shock she got for it nearly knocked her out.

She started to get tired. Deathly tired. And that made her feel punchy.

"You know, you totally could've been a hero," she said,

---

135 I still prefer "the endgame" to "phase three," but whatevs.

dancing around to make herself harder to hit. "A Super Hero, even. You're smart. You're clever. You're . . . You have great taste in polo shirts. . . ."

A rocket exploded, and she rolled out of the way just in time. She could smell burning hairs on her tail. Never had she felt less like a Super Hero. She crumpled to the floor.

"What I am is maddeningly disappointed," he said. "I'm broadcasting this fight live, you know, and I'd hoped for more of a show. After all this, you're going to simply go belly-up. And oh dear, *wut will happen to dat poor wittle baby . . . ?*"

He clicked a button. There must have been a microphone inside the glass box, because Dante's cry, previously muffled, now was suddenly loud and fierce, broadcast through a speaker on the wall. Squirrel Girl could hear in the baby's cry exactly how scared he was. Her throat closed off; her feet and tail turned cold.

"And there's nothing you can do," said the Micro-Manager.

Something clicked on inside her, some hot, fierce center. Her vision focused. Her senses exploded. She knew, without question, that she had it. Whatever it was that gave squirrels the ability to outsmart anything that was supposedly "squirrel-proof." To adapt to any climate, any place on Earth. To survive. To win.

She leaned into that place. Her squirrel-ness. Or maybe it was her girl-ness. It was definitely her Squirrel Girl–ness.

She felt unbeatable.

Still down on all fours, she looked up at the Micro-Manager. And she smiled.

"W-what?" he asked.

"I hope you have a bus pass," she said. "'Cause you're going. Down. Town."

Squirrel Girl attacked.

She bit. She scratched. She leaped and grabbed and scampered and twitched and dug and climbed, chatting all the while. Eventually she tore off another one of his arms.

"I have so many good phrases," she said. "I keep forgetting. Which do you like better: 'Are you a frog? Because I think you're about to croak' or 'I'm not your mama's squirrel-tailed super—' "

"STOP TALKING!" the Micro-Manager screamed.

Two of his robot suit's four arms were on the warehouse floor, twitching uselessly.

"Okay, time for some real talk," Squirrel Girl said, darting between his legs and scampering up to cling to his back. "Which of those arms do you miss most?"

"I don't need the pincer arm to destroy you!" he shouted, slamming his back against the wall in an attempt to squish her. He'd tried that already four times, and each time all he managed to do was dent the wall.

"Ooh, the pincer arm was a good one," she said, leaping off his back, onto his helmet, and then back to the ground. "You almost got my tail with that one."

The building shook with the force of his robotic suit slamming against the wall. She rolled backward into the center of the room, coming to a rest next to the unpowered gnashmouth.

"Hey, gnashmouth," Squirrel Girl said, talking to the inactive chopper. "No hard feelings, right?"

The robot-suited villain took a step forward. A panel on the suit's chest slid open.

"ELECTRO-BOMBS!" he shouted.

A half dozen sparking metal spheres shot out of the suit, arcing toward her.

The shouting was a thing he'd been doing throughout the entire fight. Not to communicate over the noise, but to announce his moves or weapons by name. She'd tossed out a couple of good ones near the beginning of the fight,[136] but after his "ARACHNO-POUND," "STEEL VENGEANCE," "DOUBLE STEEL VENGEANCE," "ROBO-RAKE," and now "ELECTRO-BOMBS," she was beginning to worry that maybe she was supposed to keep doing it, too.

"Um," she said, "CATCH AND RELEASE!"

She caught one of the electro-bombs, intending to throw it back, but as soon as she touched it, she was shocked, hard.

"YOW!" she yelled, dropping the thing and leaping away from where all the other bombs had landed and were now popping with electrical arcs.

"I am unstoppable!" the Micro-Manager yelled from within the helmet.

---

136 Fuzzball Special was my favorite.

Squirrel Girl was pretty sure that wasn't true, but who was she to slam his hopeful self-love?

The gnashmouth started chomping again, apparently repowered by the electro-bombs. There was nothing for it to chew, since Davey Porkpun was long gone. It just sat there, chomping the air.

She tore the base mount from the ground. She hefted the base, pointing the mouth, still gnashing, at the Micro-Manager, like a super-fat jousting lance.

"What are you doing?" he asked.

"REVENGE OF GNASHMOUTH!" she shouted, charging the giant robot suit.

The Micro-Manager put out his hand to swat away his attacker, but the gnashmouth chomped it off at the wrist.

Squirrel Girl skidded to a halt. Both she and the Micro-Manager stared at the arm stump, shocked.

"Oh, man," she said. "That didn't, like, take off your real hand, did it?"

He shook his metal head. But the fact that his fleshy hand was safe inside the suit didn't appease his rage. He screamed and swung his other arm at her. Instinctively she blocked with the gnashmouth lance, and off went his robot suit's other hand.

"Golly," Squirrel Girl said, looking at the gnashmouth in amazement. "It's super-mega-ultra chompy. You did a good job with this thing."

He tried to kick her, and his robotic knee came off in the teeth of the gnashmouth. After that, it was all downhill for the Micro-Manager. The gnashmouth lost its charge and stopped chomping right around the time the Micro-Manager lost his suit's left foot, but by then he had already given up.[137]

Mike just sort of slumped to the ground as Squirrel Girl hopped about, pulling off his remaining bits of armor.

"Lower that pole down and let me get the baby," she said, "or I'll—"

"Mwa-ha-ha," said Mike, though she could tell that he wasn't really into it. "I'd hardwired the baby trap controllers into that." He pointed to a crumpled blackened mass that had been part of deathcruncher. "You foiled your own heroics!"

"Well, crap," said Squirrel Girl. She squinted up the pole. Her center was still white-hot, live as a wire, sparking with confidence. "Squirrel-proof bird-feeder-slash-baby-cage, eh? We'll see about that."

She left Mike sitting on the floor, the remaining pieces of the heavy robot suit on his legs keeping him pinned down, and she climbed the warehouse wall. On the slick parts, she pounded her claws into the corrugated metal to keep going up. A hundred feet up. And even more, up to the ceiling so that she was higher than the baby cage.

---

137 Not verbally, though. He never actually said "I give up." That would've been super helpful. FYI, it's tough to know in villain fights when it's officially over. Sometimes I'm still fighting for a bit before I realize they're not really trying anymore and it's *soooo* embarrassing.

Perched there, she eyed the stand. Inside that thick-walled see-through box, Dante had curled up, his back rising and falling in sleep.[138]

"That glass is bulletproof, FYI!" shouted Mike from the floor.

"Bulletproof and squirrel-proof are *not* the same thing," she whispered.

She shut her eyes and told herself, "Leap before you look, Squirrel Girl." And then, screaming "For the love of *nuuuuuuuts!*" she leaped as hard as any girl or squirrel had ever leaped.

Only once she was in the air did she look. It was a good thing she'd jumped first, or she might not have had the courage. The distance was far. Impossibly far? Not for Squirrel Girl, apparently, because she managed to swipe the edge of the giant disk with her fingertips. Good thing she'd done *Commander Quiff's Fightin' Fingertip Workout.* She gripped with those eight mighty fingertips till she could pull herself up onto the disk and finally to the glass box.

With her claws, she cut a hole in the top of the glass, lifted Dante out, and tucked him inside her sweatshirt. "Poor baby, poor sweetie baby!" She swung over the edge of the platform and slid down the pole all the way to the floor.

Mike was staring wide-eyed. "What *are* you?"

"You know who I am," she said. "Say my name!"

"S-s-squirrel Girl," he blurted.

---

138 Poor little fella; when he gets exhausted, he just conks out.

"Dang straight," she said. She kissed sleeping Dante's head. He smelled like lemon-scented baby shampoo. "So, how do I shut off the robots out there?"

"It's too late," he said, staring at one of the deathcruncher's amputated limbs. "They will have destroyed half the city by now."

"Hold on a sec." She dashed to the hole in the wall, and with Dante tucked into her arms, she kicked the opening wider so she could duck through.

The ground outside the warehouse looked like a battlefield, torn up and scarred, burned in places. But all the "dead" bodies were robots. The dozens of limp squirrels were still breathing.

A few drones remained, buzzing and clacking and scrambling around, arms whirling. Squirrel Girl started forward to attack, but she only got a couple of steps when suddenly it was over.

Tippy-Toe knocked one drone with her tail, serving it right to Skunk Club leader Antonio, who smacked it with his bat. Other Skunk Clubbers were attacking a drone with cans of spray paint. The drone gurgled and sputtered as the paint got into its gears. The baron and two other LARPers were cheering as they summarily hacked three micro-bots with their swords. Vin Tang shot another drone out of the air with a bow and arrow, while the he-giant Derek Facepunch, wearing his iron gauntlet, punched a drone approximately in its face. The Somebodies were emitting high-pitched shrieks as they stomped on the last small cluster of drones as if they were cockroaches.

Ana Sofía looked around, put her hands on her hips, and let

out a big breath. "Good work, Squirrel Scouts! I think we just helped save the day!"

"Huzzah!"

"Long live the queen!"

"We smashed the punks till they cried out for their robot mommies!"

"*Chektt!*" Fuzz Fountain Cortez leaped onto Ana Sofía's shoulder and nuzzled her cheek.

"Wow," Squirrel Girl said. "Looks epic!"

Tippy-Toe made a tiny salute. "*Chk!*"

"Your squirrels were awesome, Tip," said Squirrel Girl. "Hey, Scouts! Hey, Ana Sofía!" She moved closer to Ana Sofía so she could see her face clearly. "You kill all the bugs?"

"'Tis certain, my liege," said the baron.

"Yeah, I think so. You good?" asked Ana Sofía.

"Yep, and I saved this human baby, who I've never seen or babysat before today at all."

She handed Dante to Ana Sofía. He nestled into Ana Sofía's arms, snuggly and sleepy. Fuzz Fountain Cortez cooled off Dante's damp forehead with sweeps of her tail.

"*Aw,*" said Squirrel Girl, Ana Sofía, the Skunk Clubbers, the LARPers, the Somebodies, and the squirrels all at the same time.

"Movies have taught me to never leave a Super Villain alone, so BRB," said Squirrel Girl.

Mike was still slumped there, but he looked up with something like hope in his eyes.

"Is it all gone?" he asked.

"Yep," she said.

He smiled and sighed. "Well, at least there's that."

"Yeah, good news all arou— Wait. I don't think we're talking about the same thing. When you say 'is it all gone,' what is the 'it' that you mean?"

"The neighborhood," he said. "The city. All that mess the drones were supposed to destroy. I imagine the Avengers will take care of the bots before they hit New York, but at least I have this victory."

"Riiiight," Squirrel Girl said. "See, when I said yes to that question, I was talking about, like, all *your* stuff. The drones, the robots, you know? *They're* all gone. Smashed."

He stared at her, uncomprehending for a moment, then closed his eyes and slumped fully to the ground. "I've failed," he muttered.

"Um," Squirrel Girl said, crouching at his side. "Well, yeah. Evil is a butt."

"What?"

"What I mean is, uh, evil doesn't win."

"Sometimes it does," he said, turning to look at her. "If you're good at what you do. I thought I was pretty good."

His eyes started to fill with tears. Squirrel Girl had already felt bad for him generally, but now she felt like a heel for smashing up his awesome robot suit. She had to remind herself he had wanted to kill her. And innocent squirrels. And an entire city. Not to mention the baby.

Still, he was sad.

"Hey, look," she said, "you *were* good. That suit? That was freaking awesome! Everything you made was awesome! This is Tony Stark–class stuff."

"I'd hoped it was better," he said.

"Well, uh," she said, "better than what he was doing at your age, I promise you that."

"It doesn't matter," he said. "I'm ruined. My life is over."

"Are you kidding?! You've got like, at least fifty more years. Right? How long do humans live?"

"All I ever wanted was for someone *really* evil to say *good job, Mike. I'm so proud of you. You're everything we hoped you'd be.*"

"Really? That's all you ever wanted? Never like, a pony, or to be an astronaut, or to have a tail or anything?"

"Don't make fun of me," he said.

Squirrel Girl held up her hands. "I'm not, really. It's just that's a kind of a, I don't know, nonstandard life wish. But I get it, ponies aren't for everyone. Allergies, amirite?"

"And now that will never happen," he said.

"I don't know," Squirrel Girl said. "It might. I mean, assuming you don't change your ways and decide *helping* people feels better than destroying them."

"No, not now. Everybody knows. The entire villain community

saw this," he said. "Saw you beat me. They're probably watching right now, unless they got too bored." He pointed to the last remaining loudspeaker. Right below it was a small wall-mounted camera.

Squirrel Girl scampered up the wall until she could stick her head in front of the camera. "Hey, creeps," she said. "You're on notice. Behave yourselves."

She tore the camera off the wall, crunched it into a ball, and leaped back to the ground. "They're not watching now," she said.

"It's too late. This was my shot. No way my par—uh, Hydra will take me in now. If I was good—really good—Hydra would be here already to recruit me into an unmarked vehicle driven by green-cowled lackeys and from there into an underground lair where they would train me to be the next whiz kid of Super Villainy. A thousand bucks says S.H.I.E.L.D. gets here first, which will be Hydra's way of saying *no thanks, you can have this one.*"

"What does Hydra know anyway?" she said.

"Only everything."

"You don't need anyone to tell you you're great for it to be true."

"Yeah, I'm not sure about that," he said. "But thanks. I guess."

With a clatter, the outer door dropped off its hinges. Ana Sofía stood in the doorway with a big pair of bolt cutters. Behind her, a dozen squirrels were babysitting Dante, rocking the sleeping baby softly on their collective furry backs.

A distant, high-pitched whine grew louder, and louder. Squirrel Girl gave Mike a look.

"That's not yours, is it?" she asked. "That machine noise? There better not be a postgame to your endgame."

He shook his head. "Not mine. I'm finished."

"You do still have to go to jail, you know," said Squirrel Girl. "Or juvie. Is that what they call it for kids?"

"They have a special one for Super Villains," he said. "I wish I could go to that one."

Ana Sofía took a step into the warehouse and cleared her throat. "Oh, hello. Squirrel Girl. Looks like you saved the day."

To keep Squirrel Girl's identity secret, Ana Sofía was pretending like they weren't best friends. Her tone was stiff and self-conscious, like she was giving a school presentation, and Squirrel Girl couldn't help giggling.

"You bet, friend—friendly neighborhood stranger girl with bolt cutters," said Squirrel Girl.

"Ana Sofía, is that you?" Mike said, looking up. "Don't tell me you're with this freak. You were actually okay."

"Mike, you kidnapped a baby," said Ana Sofía.

"That's right, I did! I *escalated*. There was no going back. I was almost a Super Villain."

"Well, I'm a Squirrel Scout. Best of luck, Mike."

As the distant noise got louder Squirrel Girl thought it might belong to a helicopter. She became absolutely certain it belonged to a helicopter when a big black helicopter landed on the gravel outside the warehouse.

Through the windshield she spotted a shock of red hair that looked remarkably Black-Widowish. Then the pilot hopped out. There was no "ish" about it. Black Widow was here, wearing a black leather jacket, black jeans, and black combat boots.[139]

Moreover, riding shotgun was golden-haired, breast-plated, hammer-wielding Thor.

Squirrel Girl heard a small sound escape Ana Sofía's throat, a sort of *eeeeh* ending with an *ugh* followed by a choke and a whimper.

Thor stepped out of the helicopter, which suddenly seemed much smaller next to him. He shouted, "We have arrived!" and raised his hammer in the air.

Unfortunately the helicopter's blades hadn't quit rotating yet, and his hammer and fist thrust right in the middle of them. The blades stopped abruptly and with a screeching sound that couldn't have been good for the vehicle's mechanical bits.

"Thor, honestly," said Black Widow. "I can't take you anywhere."

He smiled sheepishly and shrugged. "Is yon disturbance settled?" asked Thor. "Didst we miss the battle?"

---

139 I bet one day Black Widow was all, *You know what, I love black!* And then she just threw out all her non-black clothes 'cause once you know, why settle, right?

"Yeah," said Black Widow, "appears Squirrel Girl here and her friends took care of business."[140]

Thor laughed. "'Tis a pity to miss a battle, but arriving in time for the victory celebration nigh makes up for it!" He caught sight of Ana Sofía, his eyes lowering to her knee-high star-spangled blue-and-gold socks. "Fair maiden! Thy socks. They. Are. Glorious!"

"Thanks," she said, her voice a little scratchy. "I like socks."

"As do I!" Thor shouted. "Socks are one of the greatest treasures of Midgard, and woe betide any who claim otherwise!"

While Black Widow knelt to examine the remains of some of Mike's robots, Thor began to give a brief history of the origin and fashion of socks across Earth's past two millennia. He stood an arm's length away from Ana Sofía,[141] his eyes on her, his head still. That made it much easier for Ana Sofía to read his lips, but Squirrel Girl suspected he didn't know that. Thor was just Thor, and his attention right then was all Ana Sofía's. And Ana Sofía's cheeks were a deep purple.[142]

Black Widow spoke to Squirrel Girl while deftly removing the guts of a battle drone. "No joke, he has like an entire dresser full of socks in the Mansion. He says he can't get away with

---

140 She knew my name! She knew my name!
141 Though, TBH, Thor's arm's length is a good size longer than your average arm's length
142 I think they were more "maroon."

wearing them in Asgard, so as soon as he lightning-bolts himself to *Midgard* he pulls on his favorite *woolies.*"

Ana Sofía cleared her throat but when she spoke her voice was merely a squeak. "I've always thought socks are like hugs for your feet."

Thor laughed a big, booming laugh of satisfaction. "Indeed! You have hit upon it exactly!"

Black Widow touched a device in her ear and spoke.

"Coulson, it's definitely Hydra design. Slightly adapted. My best guess—this kid had access to Hydra equipment and set up his own shop. I want to talk to him. And we'll need a clean-up crew. I don't want so much as a bolt of this stuff getting into the wrong hands."

Two black SUVs rolled up, grinding gravel beneath their enormous bulletproof tires, each bearing gray S.H.I.E.L.D. logos on the sides. Four dark-suited men and women emerged. Without pause or word, they extracted Mike from the remains of his robot suit, handcuffed him, and marched him toward one of the SUVs.

"He wants to go to Super Villain jail!" Squirrel Girl called after the S.H.I.E.L.D. agents. "Not just regular juvie!"

Mike glanced at her, the edges of a smile forming on his face. Then he was pushed into the car, the door shut, and the Micro-Manager was gone.

As Mike's SUV drove away, three trucks pulled in, these disgorging people in gray coveralls who began to gather up the defeated drones and take pictures of the battlefield.

"Victory is yours!" Thor bellowed.

Squirrel Girl and Ana Sofía both jumped. Ana Sofía turned her startled movement into a little happy dance, and Squirrel Girl couldn't help giggling again.

"So the Micro-Manager kidnapped that baby—" Squirrel Girl began.

"Sayest no more," saidest Thor. He plucked up sleeping Dante from his rocking bed of live squirrels. "I will restore the suckling to his matriarch. Anyway, babies love me."

He cooed at Dante's little face.[143]

Thor stepped back and began to swing his hammer from the strap on the handle, so fast it was a blur. The air crackled and hummed.

"Tonight I shall eat shawarma in your honor, fair maidens," he said, nodding at Squirrel Girl and Ana Sofía. He snuggled Dante close against his breastplate and then he shot into the sky with the sound of thunder.

Black Widow snorted. "He's such a show-off."

It was Squirrel Girl's opinion that if one had a magic hammer and could fly up a lightning bolt or whatever, then showing off was totes permitted. Ana Sofía was still wiggling in a little happy dance, so she seemed to agree.

"Let's get this stuff back to HQ," Black Widow was saying to another agent. "And call Stark. He's going to want to take a look."

---

143 At this point, I was surprised Ana Sofía didn't just keel over dead.

"Tony Stark? Iron Man?" said Squirrel Girl. "Isn't he just your errand boy?"

"Errand boy?" said Black Widow. "He's an Avenger."

"But . . . but I thought . . ." Squirrel Girl pulled up her text exchange with Tony Stark on her phone and showed it to Black Widow.

The super spy read the texts, pursing her lips as if trying to keep a straight face. A chuckle escaped her throat. Then she started to laugh. She laughed so hard the S.H.I.E.L.D. agents called for backup and set up a perimeter. She laughed so hard she didn't make any noise at all.

37

TEXT MESSAGES

Tailed human!

SQUIRREL GIRL

Tailed alien!

ROCKET

Got two questions.

SQUIRREL GIRL

Shoot

ROCKET

Shoot where? I'll fry their tentacles off! I'll blast them into the next quadrant!

SQUIRREL GIRL

I meant shoot as in go ahead and ask

ROCKET

JK

I AM GROOT.

Easy, easy, I WAS just kidding. Really. Sort of.
Anyhoo, Squirrel Girl, I tapped the streams of
your planetary network to get vids to confirm you
actually have a tail and caught some d'ast fine
fighting against robots. That you?

SQUIRREL GIRL

Prbly I kinda fought a robot army earlier today

ROCKET

That micromanager glarkface used the term
"always be escalating." Any chance he got that
from the "heights of villainy" motivational lecture
series?

SQUIRREL GIRL

Yeah actually my friend found that exact
audiobook on his warehouse computer

ROCKET

BWAHAHAHA! I totally made that. Groot and I
were trolling Thanos with it for months!

314

SQUIRREL GIRL

I'm not sure if that makes you evil or not

ROCKET

Not evil. HILARIOUS. The other thing. Did I see you do a patent pending Blow Their Nose Kick?

SQUIRREL GIRL

Yeah I learned it from this video workout called commander quiff's unmixed WAIT A MINUTE ARE U SAYING THAT U

ROCKET

Me! Well, me and all the hidden camera video I have of Peter Quill "dancing" in his quarters. Thought I'd edit it into an instructional video, sell it online for quick credit or two and make fun of "Star-Lord" at the same time. Score!

SQUIRREL GIRL

Wait that was u who said iron man was the avengers poor untalented errand lad? Cuz I believed commander quiff all these years and only just found out that iron man has actually been a legit super hero this whole time

ROCKET

icntblev kjod

SQUIRREL GIRL

SQUIRREL GIRL

??

ROCKET

Srrr laffg to hard voice rec nt wrkkkg

SQUIRREL GIRL

You nerd! I texted him and turned down his help like a million times! He totally could've been my pard!

ROCKET

kjsd fdsk

SQUIRREL GIRL

Well thank mr quill for me anyway bc his moves helped me win the fight

ROCKET

There's a first time for everything I guess.

SQUIRREL GIRL

And thx for all the super helpful advice. Stay cool tall bro

ROCKET

Yours in battle, tail sis.

38

MIKE

*M*ike Romanger was waiting in the interview room at juvenile hall. He was itchy. The orange jumpsuit they had given him was too stiff. The inner lining felt like it was made of dead cockroaches, and he wanted to scratch all the time.

The door opened, and a woman in a business suit came in. She smiled, as if she could hear how his heart had started to pound at the sight of her. She shut the door and sat in a chair opposite him.

"How did they find you?" Mike asked, slumping in his chair. How many times had he imagined seeing her again in a moment of supreme villainous triumph? And now, here, in his ignominious defeat? He slumped even slumpier.

The woman placed a small metal disk on the table between them and gave it a quick tap. The fluorescent lights above them flickered.

"There," she said. "Now they won't hear anything we don't want them to hear. So glad you got sent here and not to S.H.I.E.L.D.'s Raft. Private conversations are a lot easier to manage in a facility like this."

"They sent *you* to kill me?" Mike asked. "That seems cruel, even for Hydra."

"You did draw attention to yourself," she said.

"S.H.I.E.L.D. grilled me," he said. "I didn't tell them anything. I don't think they were even listening. They don't think I'm a threat."

"They are shortsighted," she said. "Fools often overlook the seemingly ridiculous enemy. Blinded by prejudice, they entirely miss the power."

Mike narrowed his eyes, unsure if she was comforting or insulting him. "I'm a loser. You know it, Dad knows it, the whole world knows it."

"I'm not here to kill you," she said.

"Probably be better if you were," Mike said, his posture, as previously mentioned, definitively slumpy.

"I'm here to recruit you."

"What?"

"My bosses were impressed with your performance, Son," she said. "So was I."

"With my defeat?" Mike said. "With my failure? What do you guys need, a crash-test dummy or something?"

"You're not the only one who has been paying attention to this Squirrel Girl," she said. "Superficially ridiculous and yet legitimately powerful. A rare and perfect combination."

"I was supposed to beat her," Mike said, slumping harder than he'd ever slumped.

"You nearly did," she said. "That you lasted as long as you did is impressive."

"What do you mean?"

"As I said, we've been watching her. Our scientists have been able to determine no upper limit to her squirrel powers. In fact, I am beginning to suspect that Squirrel Girl"—she leaned forward and whispered—". . . is *unbeatable.*"

39

DOREEN

School the next day barely happened. That is, people showed up. Classes were held. Students sat in desks. But the teachers were unable to impart very much information over the constant whisperings of their pupils.

Everyone had seen the videos, shot outside the warehouse and posted by a member of the Skunk Club. Mike Romanger taken away in handcuffs. Ana Sofía chatting with Thor. Her Squirrel Scouts battling robots. And of course Squirrel Girl saving a baby!

It felt like months till at last the lunch bell rang and the masses raced to the cafeteria.

When Doreen and Ana Sofía arrived at their lunch table, the crowd parted to let them through and then closed in around them again. But instead of a confining cage, to Doreen it felt more like an accepting hug.[144]

"Ana Sofía, what were you—?"

"Where was—?"

"How did you—?"

"Hey, Ana Sofía, can you tell us—?"

"QUIET!" said Doreen, jumping onto the table. "She can't understand you with all that background yakking. One at a time, sheesh!"

Utter quiet. Then a few raised their hands. Doreen called on one.

"Ana Sofía," asked a shy seventh-grade girl, "do you *know* Squirrel Girl?"

"Um, yeah," said Ana Sofía. "Not completely, of course. She has secrets. But we've talked."

"Is she cool? Do you think she'd come to my birthday party?"

"Uh . . ." Ana Sofía smiled. "I can't speak for her, but I think that she prefers to keep private except when she's, you know, fighting crime and saving the day. Which I suspect she plans to keep up. So maybe we'll all see her around."

Doreen called on Vin Tang.

"Ana Sofía," he asked, "will you go out with me Saturday night?"

144 Not up there with a full-body squirrel clan hug, but still very nice.

"Oooo," said the crowd.

Ana Sofía blushed.

"Maybe," was all she managed to reply.

Vin grinned hopefully.

"So, yesterday was awesome," said Heidi in her lazy way, though her eyes were sparkling. "Good job, everybody. Ana Sofía, you and your friend are re-invited to join us at *our* table."

The two friends looked at each other.

"Thanks, but that's okay," said Doreen.

"Yeah, we're good here," said Ana Sofía.

"Okay, cool," said Heidi.

The crowd dispersed, even more amazed than before. Someone had turned down the Somebodies!

The two girls sat at their table and signed to each other.

"How are you feeling?"

"The most awesome ever," said Doreen. "Are you going to go out with Vin?"

Ana Sofía shrugged, her blush under control. "Probably. Are you going to go join the Avengers if they invite you?"

Doreen shook her head. "They're cool and everything, and maybe the Avengers Mansion does have a mosh pit and an all-you-can-eat nut bar. But all the adults I know are way more boring than you and the squirrels. Besides—"

Doreen's *other* phone buzzed with an incoming text. As she read it, her stomach seemed to drop into her shoes, her heart broke through her ribs, her fingers tingled, her toes froze, and her mouth grinned in both uncontrollable joy and confused panic. She'd just gotten a text from —

SHE-HULK

This is She-Hulk. Is this Squirrel Girl's phone?

SQUIRREL GIRL

WHAT ARE YOU SERIOUS how did you get my number

SHE-HULK

A squirrel

SQUIRREL GIRL

For real?

SHE-HULK

No I got it from black widow. I saw your videos and I know you don't need my approval but I wanted to say good job

SQUIRREL GIRL

I can't believe ur texting me why ru texting me ur like the strongest person on the planet

SHE HULK

strongest lawyer on the planet for sure

SQUIRREL GIRL

> U R EARTH'S MIGHTIEST LAWYER U R SHE FREAKIN HULK

SHE-HULK

> And you're Squirrel Girl. Stay strong k?

SQUIRREL GIRL

> I will I totally will

ACKNOWLEDGMENTS

Squirrel Girl first leaped onto the pages of a Marvel comic book in 1991, created by Will Murray and Steve Ditko. Since then many incredible creators have carried on her story. If you haven't read any Squirrel Girl comics, Ryan North and Erica Henderson's *The Unbeatable Squirrel Girl: Squirrel Power* is a great place to start. You won't regret it!

Oodles of gratitude to Cece Bell and Andrea Shettle for being beta readers and helping us make sure that Ana Sofía is awesome. If any errors remain, they are entirely on the heads of Dean and Shannon. Margaret Stohl, you make great things happen. Max, Maggie, Dinah, and Wren—you are everything!

Much love for the fantastic crew at Disney, including Tomas Palacios, Emily Meehan, and Mary Ann Zissimos, and the super team at Marvel, including Sana Amanat, Sarah Brunstad, Emily Shaw, Adri Cowan, and Charles Beacham.

And thanks to all you Squirrel Scouts out there. Your enthusiasm for this character is contagious. Let's go nuts!

Turn the page for a sneak peek at
Squirrel Girl's next awesome adventure.

SHADY OAKS NAMED LEAST DESIRABLE PLACE TO RAISE A FAMILY

Litter, graffiti, thefts, and packs of feral dogs helped land our township in last place in the annual *New Jersey Today* poll.

MYSTERIOUS TAILED GIRL SAVES BABY

"She tore that car door right off," says a local man. "Saved the baby from the backseat of the stolen car and caught the carjacker to boot. I tell you, I've never seen the like."

"SQUIRREL GIRL" SAVES THE DAY!

An amateur Super Villain heads to jail after Shady Oaks's local Super Hero Squirrel Girl foils his nefarious plot.

SQUIRREL GIRL STOPS CONVENIENCE STORE ROBBERY

"I didn't know what hit me," says the alleged thief. "Turns out it was a giant squirrel tail. Man, I'm telling all my buddies to avoid Shady Oaks. This neighborhood is protected now."

ALLEGED CAR-RADIO THIEF RESCUED FROM EXTREMELY TALL TREE

When asked why he was in such a tall tree, the suspect responds, "Squirrel Girl told me to spend some time up here thinking about my life choices."

COUPON COUNTERFEITING OPERATION SHUT DOWN

County police discovered a coupon-counterfeiting gang when the alleged criminals made a panicked 9-1-1 call: "They're everywhere! They've taken out the lights! Hundreds of small black eyes staring at us! Now they're throwing acorns! Save us! Save us!"

SHADY OAKS CRIME AT ALL-TIME LOW

Local residents credit their own neighborhood Super Hero, the unbeatable Squirrel Girl, and her squirrel friends for the sudden drop in crime.

SHADY OAKS TO GET A SHOPPING MALL

With crime low and consumer confidence high, businesses are starting to invest in long-overlooked Shady Oaks.

1

SQUIRREL GIRL

*T*he night was as cool as glass. Streetlamps cast orange cones of light onto the pavement, but everything in between them was darkness. Darkness so thick, you could gnaw on it.

Squirrel Girl perched atop a streetlamp, twelve feet above the quiet suburban street. Not the kind of place where you'd expect to run into a laser-blasting maniacal villain. Squirrel Girl's bushy tail twitched. Her keen eyes raked the darkness for any sign of that dastardly ne'er-do-well.

Then, her phone buzzed.

Finally! All this waiting was getting super boring. She went for the phone, scooping it out of a pouch on her utility belt. But a bunch of loose cashews spilled out of the pouch, and she fumbled the phone.

"Dang it," she said, diving headfirst off the streetlamp. She caught the cell just before it could crack against the sidewalk, twisting to land on her feet.

On her phone was a text from Ana Sofía Arcos Romero, her BHFF.[1]

ANA SOFÍA

Are you hidden?

Squirrel Girl checked her surroundings in a super-sleuthy sleuth way. She was standing directly under the streetlamp, orange light falling over her as bright as a fire.

She leaped up into the shadowy branches of an oak tree in someone's front yard.

SQUIRREL GIRL

Yep of course I'm the most hiddenest. Soooo sleuthy. Very stakeout

ANA SOFÍA

Good cuz u know sometimes u forget to hide and the bad guys see u and no more element of surprise

---

1 That means Best Human Friend Forever. By the way, this is me, Doreen Green, aka Squirrel Girl. I'm just gonna read along with you and let you know my thoughts down here in the footnotes, deal?

SQUIRREL GIRL

Who me?

ANA SOFÍA

Anyway the Squirrel Scouts on the north end of
the park saw Laser Lady going down Bungalow
Row so she might be coming your way

SQUIRREL GIRL

Ooh is that what we're calling her cuz i was
thinking maybe Light Emitting Desperado?
You know, cuz it would be LED? Or Smashlight
maybe? Zap Mama?[2]

ANA SOFÍA

She kinda named herself already. In the way that
she's running around shouting I AM LASER LADY

SQUIRREL GIRL

Good way of making sure no one messes up
your name

ANA SOFÍA

Maybe I should try it. Mr Hanks calls me Annie
Sophie. The pain is real

---

2 Or Luster Lass, Lumen the Undying, Captain Incandescent, Flicker Filly, the Inexcusable
Glare, Sun Bunny . . . If it were me, I would just go as "Shine," but I would also pretend
to be Australian, because with the accent people might think my name is "Shoin," which
would confuse and discomfit them, and that's what crime is all about, right?

> I'm so on board with u walking into first period
> and shouting I AM LASER LADY and u know
> what that's a pretty good name now that I think
> about it

A voice cut against the cool-as-glass night, sharp as a diamond. Squirrel Girl wasn't sure if normal humans would be able to tell what the distant voice was saying, but her slightly-better-than-your-average-person's hearing most definitely identified the words "I AM LASER LADY! FEAR ME!"

Squirrel Girl leaped from the treetop to the next one, and from there to a streetlamp, but the shouting faded. She sniffed the air but smelled no trail. In the next tree over, someone was waiting. A small, furry brown someone with a fetching pink bow tied around her neck. Tippy-Toe, her BSFF.[3]

"Chkkt-tik," said Tippy-Toe.

"You got that right, Tip," said Squirrel Girl, landing on the branch next to her. "Wandering around a neighborhood pointing lasers at people *is* super annoying. Laser Lady might hurt someone."

"Chukka chik-chet."

"Yeah, Laser Lady is a pretty cool name. Per usual, we agree in all things."

---

3 Best Squirrel Friend Forever, of course

Squirrel Girl lifted up her human fist. Tippy-Toe tapped it with the knuckles of her tiny squirrel fist.

A call began to ululate, growing louder. A message was traveling down the chain of squirrels: Laser Lady had been spotted near the park. Tippy-Toe scurried up to perch on Squirrel Girl's shoulder.

"It's clambering time!" said Squirrel Girl as she clambered out of the tree and onto a roof. "Did you get that joke, Tip?"

Tippy-Toe shrugged.

"'Cause I was clambering?" said Squirrel Girl, who was in fact still clambering, this time up a chimney.

"*Chkt-chikka kit coff,*" Tippy-Toe said, which meant, "But clambering implies climbing in an awkward manner, and you're much too graceful for that."

"Aww," said Squirrel Girl, as she jumped off a roof. "Your compliment really takes the sting out of my failed joke."

And suddenly, there she was. The nemesis of this night. The hoodlum of this hood. The mysterious Laser Lady.

"Aha!" said Squirrel Girl, landing on the sidewalk directly in her path.

Laser Lady swerved her bicycle to miss Squirrel Girl. Because Laser Lady was riding one. A bicycle, that is. Squirrel Girl had never battled a villain on a bike before. Firsts were always a plus.

The bike crashed into a tree. Squirrel Girl managed to grab hold of Laser Lady's cape to keep her from crashing into the tree as well. Because Laser Lady was wearing one. A cape, that is.[4]

"FEAR ME!" said Laser Lady, tugging her cape from Squirrel Girl's hand.

She looked about forty years old, white, with brown hair in a trim bob. She jumped to one side, flipped her purple plastic cape back with a cracking sound, and pointed her laser directly at Squirrel Girl's face.

"Laser shot!" she said, firing a red beam into Squirrel Girl's eyes.

Squirrel Girl squinted. "Ugh, stop that! It's really annoying."

"Laser shot!" said Laser Lady, aiming the laser beam at Ana Sofía and the Squirrel Scouts, who were running toward them up the sidewalk.[5]

"She's been shining her laser-pointer thing at people in the park," said Ana Sofía. "She even shined it at cars."

Squirrel Girl gasped. "That could distract a driver and cause an accident!"

"That's right!" said Laser Lady. "I *could* cause an accident! So you should FEAR ME!"

While she said it, she was trying to climb back onto her bicycle, but her cape kept getting caught on the chain ring.

---

4 In my experience, capes are a lot more common among the Super Villain lot than bicycles. Which is a shame because bikes could totally be evil with the right look. SPIKES! CHAINS! EVIL HANDLEBAR STREAMERS IN SHOCKING COLORS!

5 Squirrel Scouts are basically anyone who thinks Squirrel Girl is pretty awesome and wants to help me stop evil. This group was mostly from my school, but you can be a Squirrel Scout, too; it's not an exclusive club or anything.

Squirrel Girl picked up the bicycle. Laser Lady tried to grab it, so Squirrel Girl held it over her head.

"Look, Laser Lady," said Squirrel Girl, "I'm sure it's fun to ride around on a bike and shine a laser pointer at people and shout *FEAR ME* and all—"

"It isn't about *fun*," said the would-be villain, jumping up and down, trying to reach her bike. "Sometimes you . . . you just want someone to . . . *fear* you . . . you know . . . what I mean?"

Squirrel Girl smiled as a way to show understanding but not answer directly because, no, not really interested in being feared, thanks. For one thing, she wouldn't get invited to parties.[6]

"Let's get down to the nuts and bolts of this," said Squirrel Girl. "Why do you want so much to be feared?"

Laser Lady lifted her laser pointer at Squirrel Girl. "LASER SHOT!"

But before the harmless beam of red light hit Squirrel Girl's face, Tippy-Toe leaped through the air, seized the laser pointer in her valiant jaws, and landed on the sidewalk.

Laser Lady's shoulder's drooped. Her bottom lip quivered. "No more laser! Now what am I going to do?"

"What do you think you should do?" Squirrel Girl asked. Because it was what her dad often said when she went to him with a problem.

---

6 Even so, I haven't been invited to that many parties in my life. Yet. Probably the invitations will start rolling in soon. But I was trying to empathize with Laser Lady's feelings first so she'd take my advice after. You know, like parents do.

"Stop . . . shining laser pointers into people's eyes?"

"Well, yeah. That's a really good start," said Squirrel Girl, still channeling Dad. "But back to the nuts! You want to be feared because . . ."

"I don't know." Laser Lady jumped and reached for the bicycle, jumped and reached. "I guess . . . it's better . . . than being ignored. I'm sick of being . . . ignored!"

Squirrel Girl nodded encouragingly. "I hear you, Laser Lady."

"You do?" Laser Lady stopped jumping. "Because today at work we were in a meeting and I kept trying to give my input, but every time I spoke, Todd talked right over me just like always. I'd say, *Maybe we could minimize the negative publicity* . . . and Todd would say, *WE SHOULD MINIMIZE THE NEGATIVE PUBLICITY* while pointing his laser pointer at the board, and everyone would say *Good idea, Todd! Great input, Todd!* till I just snapped! I grabbed Todd's stupid laser pointer and ran!" Laser Lady sniffed. "The cape was from last year's Halloween costume. . . ." She sniffed again. "Bride of Frankenstein."

"Todd sounds like a real gem," said Squirrel Girl.

Laser Lady looked up in surprise, and then belatedly hearing the sarcasm, she started to laugh. "A real gem—that's Todd."

"Obviously your pointer thing there is not a *dangerous* burn-holes-through-walls kind of laser," said Squirrel Girl. This conversation was suddenly super-interesting to her. She had known a "Todd" or two, after all. "But the pointer lasers are still mega annoying. Plus it's prolly not good for eyeballs. But you know what the real problem here is? Spoiler alert: it isn't lasers."

"Then what is it?"

"It's Todd," Squirrel Girl said.

"YES!" agreed Laser Lady.

"I think you need to tell him to back off. Tell him to stop copying you all the time and talking over you and stealing your ideas. That's way more annoying than a laser pointer."

"You're right! Thanks, Squirrel Girl!"

"Aw, that's what Super Heroes are for," said Squirrel Girl.

She put the bicycle back down—which was a relief, because even with proportional squirrel strength her arms had started getting tired. Laser Lady wrapped her cape around her neck like a shawl and pedaled away, dinging her little bike horn.

"*Chkt-cht?*" Tippy-Toe asked, holding up the laser pointer.

"Yeah, good idea—we don't want any other potential villains getting hold of this," she said, sliding it into a pouch on her utility belt.

Squirrel Girl turned to the Squirrel Scouts, adjusting to make sure her hood was up and all. The hood sported little bear ears—which on a girl with a huge bushy squirrel tail could easily be mistaken for squirrel ears—and was part of her Super Hero disguise.[7]

"We did it, gang!" Squirrel Girl said, her fist punching the air.

---

7 TDH I still can't believe they don't recognize me from school, even if I do hide my tail in my pants. They must be like "Doreen sure looks like Squirrel Girl, but I don't see a squirrel tail, so totes not her, I guess."

The Squirrel Scouts groaned.

"What?" said Squirrel Girl, her fist coming back down. "Is it constipation? Sudden group constipation? That sounded like a gastrointestinal groan."

The Squirrel Scouts looked at each other and seemed to share a general disappointment. Though from vastly different social groups at Union Junior and Union High, they'd come together to follow Squirrel Girl and fight bad guys. And hadn't that night been just oozing bad-guy fights and Squirrel Girl–ness?

"There was like zero punching," said Heidi, the blond leader of the Somebodies.[8]

"Yeah, I like the punching parts," said Antonio, his pale face hidden under a baseball cap.[9] "Remember when we got to punch all those robot drones?"

"And the stomping! Don't forget the stomping!" said his friend Robbie.

"I love stomping on robots," Lucy Tang said quietly. "It was very satisfying how they crunched under my boot."

"Yeah," said Vin Tang. He was skinny and black-haired, and

---

8 The Somebodies is . . . a popular group, I guess? I don't really get how that works. But Heidi's dad donated a frozen-yogurt machine to the school cafeteria, so for a long time that apparently meant that she and her friends got to decide who mattered? Middle school is confusing.

9 Antonio is basically the leader of the Skunk Club, who used to think making graffiti and tipping over trash cans was fun till I showed them that fighting Super Villains is way more fun.

a full head taller than his sister. "The robot-drone battle was the best."

"That was indeed magnificent, forsooth!" said the baron, a brown-skinned kid in a leather breastplate, a feathered cap atop his short Afro.[10] "A tale fit for kings to be retold long after our scarred hides are hanging on the Wall of Warriors."

"Forsooth," the duchess said sadly.

The Squirrel Scouts walked away, muttering to each other in disappointment.

"When Ana Sofía texted us that we'd be fighting Laser Lady tonight, I was all *yeah*, but now . . ."

"But now . . ."

"Yeah, but now . . ."

"Forsooth . . ."

Only Ana Sofía remained. She was wearing so many layers and scarves, Squirrel Girl could only see half of her brown face and her black bangs sticking out from under her hood. The girl did not like being cold.

"So?" she asked.

"At least it wasn't group constipation," Squirrel Girl said.

"Huh? I didn't catch that," Ana Sofía said, pulling her hood back an inch.

---

10 The baron leads the LARPers—Live Action Role Players. They like to pretend they're living in medieval times, I guess? Listen, when you spend most of your life hiding a squirrel tail in the seat of your pants, you don't judge.

Under the clear light of the streetlamp, Squirrel Girl recounted to Ana Sofía the life-changing conversation she'd just had with Laser Lady. Ana Sofía wore hearing aids, but without seeing someone's lips as they spoke, it was nearly impossible for her to parse the sounds and make sense of a conversation. Even then, Squirrel Girl had come to realize, lipreading wasn't a 100 percent accurate sort of thing. Neither of them were fluent in ASL, but they both knew enough that Squirrel Girl often punctuated what she was saying with ASL signs for clarity.[11]

"I think this is a new thing, Ana Sofía!" she said. "Talking criminals out of criming! Why didn't I think of it before? It's so much faster than all the fighting and whacking and punching and gnawing. Seriously, the Avengers should look into the talking thing."

"I'm not sure that would work every time," said Ana Sofía. "You tried to talk the Micro-Manager out of unleashing a droid demolition army on the neighborhood, but he did it anyway."

"Maybe I didn't try hard enough."

Tippy-Toe headed to the park, so the human girls started home, too, texting each other as they walked side-by-side.

ANA SOFÍA

Did u do your math homework

---

11 I've been studying ASL, but it's a complex language! Even my amazing squirrel powers don't help me learn new languages overnight.

SQUIRREL GIRL

Yep

ANA SOFÍA

Did u

SQUIRREL GIRL

Any second now

Did vin set a time for your date yet?

ANA SOFÍA

I don't want to talk about vin

SQUIRREL GIRL

He luvs u

ANA SOFÍA

stahp

SQUIRREL GIRL

Okay. Love you dude

ANA SOFÍA

I know. Love you too

**TURN THE PAGE FOR
A SQUIRREL-TASTIC
PREQUEL COMIC!**

MARVEL

The Unbeatable
Squirrel Girl

AS SEEN IN MARVEL COMICS

MEET CUTE

SINGLES

Five Years Later

DING-DONG

Doreen, it's your guests! It's time for your birthday party!

Yay!

Now remember, like we practiced, Doreen. Tail in the pants, we don't wanna give away any secrets.

Tail in the pants! No secrets!!

Hello, Kimberly! Hello, Ashley! Hello, Tyler and Cameron!

Hello Doreen's mom!!

Hey, guys.

Pickup in three hours, right?

You're welcome to stay.

Hah! Dorian, this is our first no-kids afternoon in months. They're alllll yours.

Sure you don't want to stay and--

Too late! I'm already fantasizing about quiet restaurants with actual ceramic plates, sorry!!

Thanks, Dor! You and Maureen have fun!!

Where are the crossover restaurants that give you both the classy ambiance and the charmingly snooty maître d', but also the crayons and the paper tablecloth you can draw on? "No idea," you whisper, as we both smuggle our crayons and coloring books past the charmingly snooty maître d'.

The birthday girl

"Iron man" versus "Iron man but he's disguised as spider-man so he's got the powers of both"

Follow the leader!

All right everyone, that's how you do it. Now it's Doreen's turn in front. Follow the leader!

Follow the leaper!

No no no, "leader"! Follow the *leader*. Doreen, no, listen to me, you can't--

Follow... the...

Oh no oh no oh no

WHOOSH

Leaper!!

Hello!!

THIS JUST IN: Five-year-old Doreen is unbeatably *adorable*, surprising no one.

Geez, it just hit me that the parties we go to as adults *never* have goodie bags that you get to take home at the end! ADULTS, I HAVE SOME BAD NEWS: somewhere along the line, *we totally lost our way.*

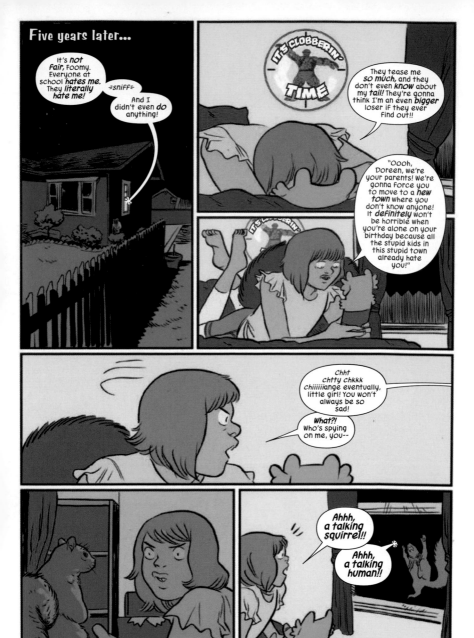

I am happy to report that close reading of Doreen's Thing clock suggests that it's *always* clobbering time. Please, govern yourselves accordingly.

This squirrel learns he can communicate with a new species for the very first time, and the very first message he transmits is "send more peanut butter."
This, sadly, once again confirms that it was actually a good idea to not put squirrels in charge of the messages sent into deep space on the Voyager spacecraft.

Okay, can we talk about the *Voyager* spacecraft for a second? *Voyager 1* is the farthest object humans have ever sent from Earth, and among the many pictures it's carrying into the universe on a golden record is one of a woman eating an ice cream cone, while a man eats a grilled cheese sandwich, while *another* man pours water into his own mouth. *It's amazing.*

I can't point you to the precise comic where Captain America saves the moon, but I'm certain there is one. And if there isn't, guess what: *I am so ready to write it.*

Skyline illustration by Bruno Mangyoku